LAKE CHARLES

ALSO BY ED LYNSKEY

The Blue Cheer
A Clear Path to Cross
The Dirt-Brown Derby
Out of Town a Few Days
Pelham Fell Here
Quiet Anchorage
Troglodytes
The Zinc Zoo

LAKE CHARLES

ED LYNSKEY

WILDSIDE PRESS

LAKE CHARLES

The first chapter previously appeared in a different version in
the *Dead Mule School of Southern Fiction Ezine* (2001). Thanks
are extended to Valerie MacEwan, editor.

Edited by George H. Scithers
Published by Wildside Press LLC.
www.wildsidebooks.com

For Heather, with love always.

CHAPTER ONE

My twin sister Edna seated between Cobb Kuzawa and me snapped her gum. I drove my cab truck, its windows rolled down. The mountain air batting my face was a respite from breathing the ink fumes at Longer-beam Printery in Umpire. Again her gum snapped. Separated since July 4th, they'd yet to exchange a civil word. I'd cajoled her to tag along in hopes they'd bury the hatchet, if only for my peace of mind.

With my elbow jacked out the window, I wished an electric storm had knocked the dragonflies and gnats into Lake Charles, enticing the bass to surface feed and better our luck. Fishing was my all this Saturday morning, so I could forget my arrest for Ashleigh Sizemore's murder. Yeah, right.

His mesh cap worn lopsided, Cobb was half in the bag. His fore-arm tattoo proclaimed, "EAT MORE BASS!" Ogling in his side mirror, he puckered up his fish lips. My eyes darted to the rearview mirror. A St. John of God (the patron saint of printers) medallion on a wax cord dangled from the mirror. The double decker trailer with our bass boats and Edna's jet ski rode steady on my tow hitch. Then a red Cadillac slingshotted into the next lane and, ramping up, overhauled us. I backed off on the gas.

"Christ, did they rob a bank or jewelry store?"

The Cadillac bore out-of-state tags: New York. Tourists in 1979 came, ogled our Smoky Mountains, and spent their greenbacks. These New Yorkers had spent loads on their gas. Their bumper stickers pro-claimed, "HONK, IF YOU LOVE JESUS!" and "POW*MIA: Bring 'Em Home!" Cobb lunged over Edna and cuffed my horn to blare out. The four twenty-something males—the driver sported a Mohawk—paid us no mind.

"Was doing that necessary?" she asked.

Grunting, he shot me a rankled look. "I'd give my left kidney to tear into the mud bog."

"Ha. All pigs like the mud."

"*Oink, oink.* You're the witch who changed me into a hog." He shut his eyes, saying to me, "After we drop anchor, wake me."

"Cobb was born a pig."

"Just give me a straight razor," I said when her tart glance expected my support. "Can't you guys play nice?"

"Apparently we can't."

A cash-and-carry store, the white paint flaking off its clapboard sid-ing, flew by us. I jotted a mental note for our future beer stop. It also had probably the only phone booth for miles around. Yesterday we had gotten a late start. An hour out of Umpire, our hometown not far from Gatlinburg, we'd decided to stop and chip in for a room. It was the motel's last unit. A long workday had left us bushed. I registered us, and we crashed in front of a TV, its touchy vertical hold on Hitchcock's *North by Northwest*. Between his beer swigs, Cobb lectured as Cary Grant scrambled over the presidential mugs on Mount Rushmore.

"That rock sculpture tees off the local Injuns. They hold the Black Hills sacred."

I yawned behind my wrist. "Is that a fact?"

"Now with his G.E.D., Cobb is the world's authority on everything." Her voice was testy. She glared at him sprawled on the foldout cot set up between our single beds. Her hand swatted off his empty PBR beer cans pyramidded on the bed table.

Oblivious to her jibe, he popped a new PBR. "Who can blame them? But they can't do squat."

"Sort of like me."

Now he looked at her. "How is that?"

"I'm stuck between a rock and a sloppy drunk."

Pleased to see his sour reaction, she wiggled over to face the wall. Her pale scalp at her ginger hair's part reflected in the mirror-backed headboard. I noticed her yellow parrot barrettes on the bed table where the PBR cans had blocked them.

"Here's a sobering idea: shut up."

"What a ditz I was to ever marry you. Now quiet, all. I'm going to sleep."

Tossing the empty PBR cans in the wastebasket, he grinned over at me. "What a conjugal bliss it was."

She scoffed through her nose.

I put off the TV and lamp with a plea. "Can you guys cool it?" His saying "sure, mother" was the last thing I heard before I tumbled into a fitful sleep, and the same damn dream unfolded.

Ashleigh Sizemore radiant in the slinky purple gown sauntered from the pillars of smoke. Her smile beamed its come-hither look at me.

"Brendan, why am I dead?"

"I started to call an ambulance, but it was too late. You'd already died. Why does your father blame me?"

"Because you were the last person to see me alive …"

I jolted upright in the bed, my breaths in pants. The sheen of sweat pasted my forehead. I wiped it off. Saving her life had been futile. The M.E. said her PCP overdose was instant, but the damn PCP wasn't ours, and I was no killer as charged. Feeling reassured, what did I do? If I snoozed again, I feared the same creep dream's return would unglue me.

I staggered into the bathroom where its vent fan clanked away. My tingling fingers lay a lit match to a Marlboro. I inhaled, bagged the soothing nicotine, and exhaled smoke. I lived in a nightmare, branded as a killer, but now I was free on bail. The sheriff's deputies could jug me again at any time. My second, deeper puff calmed my jangled nerves. I knew organic causes explained why the dead girl ransacked my dreams.

On the same day of my bail, I began my detox. The literature I'd sent away for said I'd encounter the all-too-vivid dreams the habitual pot users experienced after they went cold turkey. The THC (the kick-ass ingredient in the pot) in my fat cells had to sweat out before I'd be healthy enough to rest in peace. I mused on my present legal quandary.

My arrest for Ashleigh's murder was three months ago in May. Cobb shared some blame for it, too. His dad Jerry Kuzawa and he had left to cut cypress downstate. Adrift without my sidekick, I hoped to inject a pulse into a dead Friday night, so I linked up with this crew.

We'd ridden in their party van over the mountains and heard The Devil's Own, a musical hybrid of Pink Floyd and Foreigner, rock out in Yellow Snake. I flirted with this redhead—"Ashleigh," she'd purred—in a shimmery, purple gown. The side-cut soared to her hips. I didn't get her last name, just more leg than a hot-blooded lad should ever see.

By eight p.m., we filed into the Yellow Snake armory. She and I shared a spliff as The Devil's Own cranked out their spacey music, and we cheered. Then she dug her hand deeper into my pocket. The pocket had a hole in it, and her hot fingers flowed like melted paraffin around my love bone …

Now the vent fan clattered in my ear as I pushed aside her murder and my arrest. I fixed on how I'd find my dad somewhere in the vast state of Alaska. My dilemma struck me as the kernel for a song, but I felt too uptight to scribble down any new lyrics. Instead, my old fears rolled out. I shuddered over my pulling any hard time at Brushy Mountain. Once thrown in prison, I'd glue a shiv to the sole of my foot or stuff the shiv up my bunghole. I'd slice up James Earl Ray leading the scar-faced felons out to trap and bugger me. Caged for the rest of my life behind steel bars, or a worse fate, drowned me in despair. I craved a joint. No, I had to resist my destructive habits. Get stronger.

Daybreak found me all smoked out, and I flushed the butts. I slipped on my boots and headed out to the ice machine. I hesitated since buying more PBR might tee off Edna, but I went ahead and topped off the Igloo cooler with ice. After returning to our room, boots still on, I tumbled into bed. She stirred in hers, and we slept on until the Hispanic housekeeper pecked her passkey on the metal door, murmuring at us.

"Psst, señora y señores, la sirvienta …"

My cab truck jounced off the state road and went down the bumpy lane to the oddly named Lang's Teahouse. It sat on the north cape of Lake Charles, a TVA creation (we'd no natural bodies of water). Edna's elbow jostled Cobb and he grumbled awake. The vista filled us with misgivings. First, the dance pavilion had gone to smash. As breezes rattled the candy-striped tin awnings, the past glories I'd grown up hearing arose in me.

Back in the day, the Chinese lanterns, tiki torches, and mirrored ball had illuminated the dance pavilion. Teenagers jalopied out of the hollows and hills to catch the rockabilly artists like Link Wray and Johnny Horton jam until dawn. The kids parked along the lane and out on the state road. Frisky couples danced on the teak floor, clapped for the encores, and later along the grab rail necked. The more wistful ones skimmed their coins over the water's surface. A fortune in Liberty quarters, Mercury dimes, and buffalo nickels glimmered on the bottom of Lake Charles.

Hands over our noses, he and I slid out of the cab truck. The bilgy odor of decay filled the old marina. Half-sunken wood skiffs rotted in their slips like old dreams run aground. A skuzzy telephone booth near the pavilion tilted. We scared the muskrats to rustle under the loose planks. The T-dock slumped between the pilings and jutted out in the lake shallows.

"It doesn't rate high in looks." His strides moved a bit off-kilter since he'd mowed off a few toes while shod in flip-flops. Alcohol had been a factor.

"You said it." My glance saw a set of horseshoe imprints left in the damp sand. "Does a horse trail run through here, Cobb?"

"I've heard Geronimo trots this way," he replied, untangling his fishing lure.

She monitored the weather forecast on my radio. Scads of heat but little rain—it was August, the peak of the forest blaze season. The fires weren't all bad. The paid firefighter crews bolstered the local economy, and I'd a notion the misguided arsonist lived in Umpire.

"That algae scum is thick enough to walk on." A piece of a 2x4 I hurled into the shoal water and landing with a thunk reinforced my point.

"I'm so-o-o glad we came." She approached us. "'Lots of bass are biting,' he tells us. 'Lake Charles is a gas.'"

"Piss and moan," he said, dismissing her sarcasm.

"Hey, it's all good. Edna, what's the forecast?"

"The next three days are sunny, clear, and hot."

"Excellent. The prime fishing is out in the wide lake."

"Then let's hump it out there. We're already late." His pointed glance landed on her.

"Cobb, we all overslept," I said.

She stuck her tongue out at him.

"Did you come to fish or talk?" he asked me.

"You know I'm psyched to fish. That means we have to get through that." My finger pointed at the gunk. "Cobb, a hatchet is behind my cab seat. Grab it and lop off a couple of saplings, say, eight feet long. We can pole through, and Edna will follow us on her jet ski."

"No, I better go cut them. He'll chop off the rest of his foot." She stamped away to my cab truck.

My eyes lifted to track a jetliner streaking its vapory contrail across the blue dome of sky, and I brooded how the jetliner took the VIPs to important places. Meanwhile an unimportant yokel like me stayed mired in an unimportant spot. Tennessee was too hidebound, and I ached to broaden my horizons. Whose fault was it I hadn't? The inertia was inescapable. After I powered by this bogus homicide rap, I'd shove off one dawn for Alaska. While Edna was gone, I moved the Igloo cooler from my cab truck to my bass boat. She hadn't appreciated my making our beer stop.

Two willow poles landed at our boots. "Here we go." She returned the hatchet and unbungeed the jet ski from the trailer.

"They look made-to-order. Thanks, sis."

My handclaps shooed away the blackbirds squawking on the cattail reeds that choked the concrete ramp. Cobb and I trampled down the reeds and forged a path to the water. Then he directed me backing in the trailer. The jet ski he hoisted off had been on the market long enough to woo its own cult following. She'd borrowed the money from her adoring father-in-law. We offloaded our bass boats, mostly bank-owned, to rest floating in the lake.

He raked his fingers over his black bristle for hair. "Edna, do me a favor. Act as if you have half a brain riding that crotch rocket. Steer away from our fishing grounds, too."

Her thumb hiked up. "Perch and rotate."

"That's the way. Pile on the sarcasm. My shoulders are big."

I rolled my eyes skyward before we got started. He and I plying the willow saplings poled our bass boats through the algae. Inching our way forward worked up a sweat. My arm joints burned while the sun roasted my shoulders, but our engines had no ability to beat this gunk zone. On the jet ski, she followed along in our track.

After free in the clear water, he saw the blobs on his fishfinder radar screen. "Carp." Disgust tinged his outburst.

Loving it, she grinned, set to rib him. A finger at my lips did a preemptive *"s-h-h-h."*

Tapping a fingernail on his radar screen, he shouted. "Nuts on 'em. Head out!"

He blasted off, I tailed him, and we churned up a rooster-tail of water. Within moments, we rocketed at full tilt. Hanging off our left, she rode upright on the jet ski, a bullet-shaped speedster she steered by its handlebars. Her knees flexed to take our punishing turbulence. She smiled and flashed me a victory sign.

Closer to the opposite shore, he signaled me with flat palms to slacken my speed. She streaked by us, her hand waving. At the motel, she'd promised me not to razz him, and I hoped she kept it. The odds didn't look so rosy. We engaged the sedate trolling motors powered off the car batteries and selected Skinny Minnies to cast in the shady pools. A dozen tries later, we hadn't attracted a strike.

"Try the purple gummy worms."

We plied various lures with the same snakebitten luck. Well beyond us, she smoked on the jet ski, cutting nifty figure eights over the water.

He gestured a hand at her. "Behold: our own wild woman of Borneo."

"Aw, she's not afraid to break a nail. Let her have her fun."

He trawled over to me. I knew he'd been smarting since their break up on the Fourth. My two favorite people in the world should stay pals, but my meddling was doomed to fail. I did better at fishing except this afternoon was one anglers preferred to forget. He splashed into the lake, waded ashore, and chased down the grasshoppers. I impaled them as hook bait, but the bad fishing karma dogged us. Our cork bobbers sat inert on the water's surface. Seated again on his bass boat, he lay fire to a crumpled Marlboro, sucked in, and exhaled with a smoky vow.

"I'm not budging from here without a caught bass."

My seat squeaked as I leaned back, appreciative for the mulberry tree shade. We had it made by accessing any point on Lake Charles. Chumps stuck ashore using their bamboo fishing poles rubbernecked at us, but trouble brewed in our paradise. Simon at the bait shop claimed the bass population was on the downswing due to all the silt flushing into Lake Charles. By next spring, we'd lower our sights to catch bluegill, sun perch, or, God spare us, carp. But that was for next spring, not today.

"The bass might be hungrier at the earth dam."

"Too many stumps and logs are snagged there. That dike is also set to uncork." Shirtless, he also wasn't fond of disrupting his sunbathing. "Aren't we in a great spot?"

"This sure beats breathing the ink fumes."

"Is there any future in a 9-to-5?" He mopped his forehead with a bandanna.

"None. Did you stow any vodka in my truck?"

"Vodka is for home sipping. Any more brewskis?"

"Only Rolling Rock but it is cold. Think fast." I lateralled the squatty, green bottle I'd plucked from the Igloo cooler. "Nifty snag, Aparicio."

Cobb cracked the bottle top, guzzled beer, and smacked his lips with zest. He eyed his motionless cork bobber and then me reflected in his mantis green sunshades. "So I put it to you. What's so wrong with drinking a beer now and then?"

CHAPTER TWO

I dodged his question by posing my own. "You guys split up over that?"

"Dumb, huh?" He took off his sunshades and screwed his eyes into slits. "Well, that and a thousand other nits, but they add up fast. Aw hell, what do you know? You're still dating."

"Uh-huh, sort of like you are now."

My snappy comeback made him grin. "Okay, truce?"

"Solid." I floated an idea. "Speak to her again. Do it today."

"Maybe I'll give it another whirl. Maybe we can make a go of it. Maybe I'll go on the wagon." Maybe his voice didn't ring with confidence.

"I figured you guys were in the pink."

"As they say, looks can be deceiving. The honeymoon is definitely kaput. Any hope Salem and you will get back together?"

My headshake came as the risqué tableau of two pairs of naked legs, the bottom pair forked, blazed into my mind. The cab truck seat had cramped us, but where there's a will, there's a way. Afterward, she and I had shared a Marlboro, not the roach I kept in my truck's ashtray.

"She's not a party gal."

"But then you ain't a party guy now either."

"True enough. Sure, I'll buzz her after we get back." Maybe I also didn't sound too confident.

"I saw her banging on a typewriter in Herzog's office."

"I do my best to give it a wide berth."

"You've got your reasons, too."

Edna on the jet ski growled up to stop at a safe distance from us.

Waving her over, I said, "That machine is da' bomb."

Bobbing on the ripples she'd stirred, he grunted. "Miz Fishback is scaring off our bass."

I wound in my fishing rig, the reel whining and the water beads glistening off the monofilament line. "The only bass swim in our heads. Admit it, pal. Today we're skunked."

"Jet skis are still a hazard." He spoke extra loud for her benefit as she shunted up to us. "Doubly so when Miz Fishback is hot-dogging it on hers."

"No more than Mr. Kuzawa does on his souped up bass boat." Her arms, tanned and toned, lifted as she pinned up her wavy, red hair, and the yellow parrot barrettes clipped it into place.

"Brendan, does this stubbornness curse all of your family?" His red-veined eyes blinked at me. Before I could frame a reply, she offered hers.

"I'm proud to say I inherited mine from Mama Jo."

My hand swatted a deer fly gnawing on my elbow. "Maybe emptying bed pans and mopping floors makes her stubborn."

"After she comes home from her shift, I tread on eggshells," said Edna.

"Her people are also religious. They see visions," I said, my own dreams with Ashleigh fresh in my mind.

"But Mama Jo isn't that far-fetched," said Edna.

"I once dated a Gatlinburg honey that was," said Cobb. "One Sunday evening, this fire-snorting evangelist threw out an altar call. Well, Angelina Sue scampered off up front and crashed to the floor, imbued with the Holy Ghost or epilepsy. Then she bounded up and kowtowed at the pot-bellied wood stove. The steel crackled red-hot. Now, dig this part. She bear hugged the stove." He extended his burly arms and closed them to illustrate his point.

"Ouch," I said.

He grinned. "So you'd think, but it didn't faze her. No blisters, no welts, and not a single burn lay on her. It had to be a genuine act of faith. Later I kissed her body cool and white as peppermint all over."

"You did, eh?" Edna's voice took a brittle edge.

I cringed again.

He frowned at her. "Oh, get over yourself. This was ages before we dated. In fact, I never cheated on you, baby cakes. I deserve your thanks."

"Thank you. I wish I could tell you the same."

His manly dignity lost its starch. "What does that mean?"

I spoke up. "I tend to believe his story."

"As a guy, you would."

He threaded a bluc-and-white spoon on the swivel hook and recast his fishing rig out ten yards to splash on the lake. "Why did I let Brendan invite you to be a thorn in my side today?" He reeled in the spoon.

"Me? You're the one who can't say three words without baring your fangs." Her icy glare skirmished with his. "Brendan is trying his best to help us. The least you can do is show him a little gratitude ..."

I left them to bicker and tripped across Lake Charles and up the wooded slopes to savor Will Thomas (he was the only white Cherokee chief) Mountain. A grassy bald capped it, and a dilapidated fire tower perched on the grassy bald. These grass-capped mountains made for a local enigma. Our superstitious cousins in Murfreesboro swore the UFOs, not the Good Lord, had created them.

Mama Jo held that the meteorite bombardment annihilating the dinosaurs had also scorched the permanent grassy balds. I knew the panoramic vista—miles of leafy green—from this one was a picturesque memory to store away. If stranded in an electrical storm, I'd also learned, like *Moby Dick*'s Ahab, you made an ace human lightning rod. Maybe besides suffering the fernlike bruises and my eyebrows singed off the zap had scrambled my brains. It gave me the haunting dreams. I also hated how Uncle Sam declared eminent domain, and the bully took over any desired land. A smattering of the original hill families still eked out their waning years in the parklands …

"Brendan, are you off gathering wool?" It was Edna. "You always drift off into your own little world. I asked you why should I live with Cobb again."

Smiling, I shrugged. "Because you grace the trailer park with your class."

"Ha. But he hasn't changed one iota since I left him."

"Aw, quit busting Brendan's chops." Cobb drained the last slug of the Rolling Rock. "He's trying his best to help us. The least you can do is show him a little gratitude," said Cobb, parroting her words.

Her glare rewarded him.

"Yo, got any more beer?" he asked me.

Now angry, she knew only to attack. "More beer? You never know when enough is enough."

"That's the last bottle," I said, my voice a little weak.

"We'll head back soon," he said. "Get some more."

"What. Honestly. You drink like a fish."

Snarling, he took her bait. "You love to strum that harp, angel face. I'm pretty sick and tired of hearing it, too."

"Your drinking is what worries me, Cobb. Some night driving home drunk as a skunk you'll plow into a Mack truck."

"That'll be the day. I respect my limits, huh, Brendan?"

I did my best ambiguous shrug.

"Drop me a line if you ever grow up." She jerked the jet ski to life and scribed a compact doughnut, her kicked up water droplets spritzing into our faces. Jogging the throttle sent her galloping away toward the earth dam. The foamy water swirled in her wake, and the jet ski's engine dimmed to a buzz.

"She flies off at any time. Hotheaded, Lord yes, she is. Maybe that crotch rocket will cool her off. I sure can't. Getting hitched almost undid me, but I ejected in the nick of time."

I slapped at a cluster of gnats. I saw a kernel of truth in what he said, but she was also my twin sister. I'd read or heard somewhere that brother and sister fraternal twins were unusually close and protective of each other. Staying pinned in the middle of this sniping crossfire sucked. "Buying more beer was a bad idea."

"Why? It was invented to go with fishing." He peered over Lake Charles. "Why we can't make it work stumps me."

His boozing was the flashpoint, but I didn't address it directly. "She's high-strung, and you're laid-back. Your opposites don't attract but repel."

Silence came after he shrugged his beefy shoulders in reply.

The honking Canadian geese flying in a vee beat it south against the leafy backdrop of Will Thomas Mountain. Autumn circled nearer, and its chill seeped into my bones. Further off, I espied a smoke banner pluming skyward. It was another forest blaze, but today was a blessing: for a while, I'd forgotten my homicide arrest.

"This trip is shot to shit. Are you ready to go?"

"I guess." He laughed at his tattoo. "'Eat more bass!' Ain't that a riot?" He reeled in his tackle to stow and stretched back into his T-shirt.

Casting the empties into the dirty lake, I chuckled. "You deserve a rebate on your tattoo."

"Next time we'll do better. Race you."

We dragged up the anchors, revved the engines, and dashed off, zipping neck-and-neck over the water. The gusting wind threatened to peel off our scalps like pot lids. It felt exhilarating. We'd never again share the zest as that last run we made on Lake Charles ending in a dead heat. The late afternoon shadows engulfed the decrepit marina and pavilion. He guided us through the scum zone along the same track we'd cut earlier until our bass boats drew up to the T-dock.

"There's still no sign of her," I said.

"She's goofing by the earth dam. Let her burn off more steam." He lifted his bulk to the rickety T-dock where he swayed a little but then righted his balance. A hand shielding his eyes, he scanned the margins. "Where in the devil did she go?"

"Here, grab this dock line," I said, guiding my bass boat to ease up behind his. "She's been gone for what now, an hour?"

Anxious, he ignored my extended dock line. "At least, I'd say. Her farting around will make us drive home in the dark."

"So we'll grab a couple of motel rooms."

"If we're lucky but they book up fast in the summer."

I tied a mariner's knot to latch my dock line and climbed to the T-dock. "Let's rack up the boats. We'll hear her soon."

"Says who?" He gnawed on a thumbnail.

"Says the percentages." Brave words but the alarm in his voice had caused my heart to stagger a beat. "Let's rack up the boats."

"Screw the boats." He shambled over the dock planks, and he beckoned me with his hand. "C'mon. Your binoculars can glass the banks."

My boots punched through the dock planks as I followed him ashore. I wished the telephone in the crooked booth got 911. My binoculars were on the cab's dashboard, and I rejoined Cobb. He cupped hands to mouth and bellowed out over the expanse of water.

"Edna! Yo, Edna!"

"We'll hear her engine any minute."

He turned his ear to Lake Charles, but only the eerie silence enveloped us. Binoculars up, I scanned the shrubby boundaries, and my head wagged. "There's nothing to see, I'm afraid."

"She wrecked that crotch rocket."

His finger jabbed in the directions I should glass next. A landward breeze hosed the algae's rankness over us. I knew one big reason for his growing anxiety. He'd once told me how much he missed his late mother. A drunk truck driver had T-boned her where her sun visor rod speared her in the temple. He'd been all of eight. Like me, one parent had raised him. My sight fell on our pair of bass boats waiting for us to mount them.

"That algae will be a bitch and a half," he said.

I nodded. "Then I guess we better get on it."

CHAPTER THREE

Two days before Lake Charles on Thursday as I squirmed in the dentist chair, Edna had cleaned my teeth. We talked, or rather she did. I listened.

"Cobb and I might get back together."

With a mouthful of her fingers and a dental polishing tool, my responses were eye rolls and nostril flares. Was she tweaking me? Her arch sense of humor kept you wary, but I saw no trace of her smile. Not reacting, I didn't want her too distracted to slip and gouge my gums. She paused to take a rest. A Nashville hat act twanged a love-gone-to-shit-and-life-is-the-pits song on the audio system, but I preferred listening to the brain-fried dentist office music. She continued speaking as she cleaned my teeth again.

"I haven't talked to him, so don't you breathe a word. I'm not clear on what's what. Huh? Don't speak, Brendan. Anyways, I've been so uptight over it. My muscles get stiff. I stay tense, ready to snap. Huh? Am I bearing down too hard? Sorry."

I slobbered on the paper bib clasped to my neck before I spat. Did she expect me to go in first and soften him up? Neutral like the Swiss, I knew better than to get embroiled in their marital squabbles. Again, I rinsed and spat.

"Didn't you two call it quits on the Fourth? Now you talk out the other side of your mouth. What should I think?"

"Well, excuse me all to hell. Can't I have a change of heart?"

"Like anybody, sure." After hoisting a leg over the side of the dentist chair, I stood.

Giving me her back, she clattered the steel picks and mouth mirrors to fit them into the autoclave. The tobacco smog wafted in from the waiting room despite the posted "No Smoking!" signs. Some bad habits died hard. She was one gasp away from reaming the smoker a new one but turning, she used a more cordial tone.

"Sorry to yap at you. It may sound ditzy, but I could harbor feelings for him. Don't we deserve a second shot?"

"Absolutely. You say he has no idea?" My tongue slicked over the cleaned tooth enamel. The gaps between my teeth were natural Dr. Smith had told me during his dental probe.

"Do you men ever have a clue? If only he didn't drink …"

"Is it that big of a deal?" I asked. "He holds his liquor. He doesn't miss work. No DWIs." I didn't bring up vodka, his new daytime liquor, was an odorless vice.

Thinking, she stared off and then parked her blue-gray eyes on me. She chipped on a smile. "Anyway. Have you sold any songs? Have you heard back yet?"

"A signed letter from Houston Forge Records said professional singers don't record freelance material. Too many legal snafus arise over the copyrights."

The clink of metal on metal was her fussing again at the autoclave. "Are you smoking weed again, bro?"

"Are you writing a book?" I asked the back of her red hair.

"Does that mean no, smart ass?"

"You know I went cold turkey. That's why I'm all jitters." I balled up the paper bib and slung it in the wastebasket. "You really should fill in Cobb."

"When I'm ready, I will. In the interim don't let the cat out of the bag."

"So noted." They were big kids yet for some reason I went ahead and floated the suggestion.

"Tomorrow after work, he and I are off to go bass fishing. We'll stay at the nearby Chewink Motel. Are you busy then?"

She turned, her frank gaze on me, and I caught the touch of a coy smile. "I'm always flexible. Where?"

"Lake Charles."

"So, I'd do what exactly?"

"Bring your new jet ski and let your hair down."

"I'd be too busy untangling his lures or picking off the ticks and chiggers. It's sweet that you asked, but no thanks."

"Just think on it, but don't let it get out. Lake Charles is our private getaway." My scribbled out check covered the damages she gave me.

She stamped the dentist's name—DR. RONALD SMITH, DDS—on the check. I asked her to pencil in my next six-month appointment, but I knew I'd still forget it. My wave acknowledged her farewell nod.

* * *

I left Dr. Smith's office, stepping down to Main Street, all four blocks of it. My glance saw the weather-faded letters, "Umpire", on the century-old brick train depot now refurbished as an upscale restaurant. Our lawyers and doctors dined there, but the menu ran too ritzy for my steak-and-spuds palate and wallet. Grateful Edna hadn't brought up my arrest, I ambled down the baking sidewalk.

The jut-nosed, young woman in faded dungarees and a sleeveless blouse folded up a wheelchair and stuffed it in her yellow Malibu's trunk. An infirmed older passenger (her mother?) sitting in the front seat wilted. Friendly, I smiled. They didn't. Newcomers, I mused as my walk came to a glass-plated shop front.

An air conditioner wheezed in its transom, and the water runoff dribbled down. Pete Rojos waved at me dodging the drips. Inside, I could pick out the old leather from the saddle soap odors blended in the chilled, stale air. He appraised me over a pair of copper-framed glasses smudgy as his windows. His words sounded high-pitched.

"It's hotter than a roasted fart."

"That's one way of putting it."

"Have you got any plans for the weekend?"

"I'm going fishing up at Lake Charles."

"Lake Charles … oh, wow … it's been years."

I fished out the claim ticket to my boots I'd dropped off for reheeling.

"Puma Claws are the toughest heels I sell." His rusty voice mimicked the cicadas trilling in the honey locusts. I slipped off my shoes, and he grinned as my sock feet nestled into the malleable boot leather.

"It feels like I'm walking on cotton," I said.

"You bet your hillbilly ass it does. Puma Claws are the toughest heels I sell," he said again, only prouder. "You can dance all night, and they won't wear thin on you. They're made in the U.S. of A."

Chuckling, I stamped the boots to seat my heels. "How's Salem making it?" I gave him my leather shoes I'd worn in to have him reheel.

His raven-haired, sword-legged, and blue-eyed daughter, Salem shipped off in four days to Vanderbilt University in Nashville. She wore a bronze tan well into January, and I'd dated her. She didn't like pot, but I did, so any serious vibes between us went up in smoke. She lingered as the special girl in my heart.

His eyes hardened into chips of flint. "Why do you give a—"

The cowbells clanked, and my glance followed his to the door. The new cedary Aqua Velva overrode the old leather and saddle soap smells. I took in the tall, big-boned man anywhere between forty and fifty suited in ash gray poplin. My teeth gritted, and I nodded as Herzog slouched beneath the air conditioner spewing down its cool air. His hangdog aura never varied.

"Have you completed my repairs?" he asked Pete. "You stated today at the latest."

"Count on me to deliver the goods, sir." He dug out a brown leather game pouch from under the counter. "I pop riveted the shoulder strap back into place. You're good to go."

"This year I'm being proactive." Herzog removed his wallet and paid. "My hunting lodge is scouting the prime sites. Dr. Smith predicts Lake

Charles offers phenomenal hunting. We like to park near the earth dam and enter the woods from there."

"That's where Brendan is headed this weekend."

Herzog latched his hangdog look on me as Pete went on.

"Brendan, have you picked any hunting spots?"

"I'm too busy earning a paycheck," I replied, protective of our new fishing hole at Lake Charles and no wish to see Herzog—or anybody— poking around there. I settled with Pete now back to his easy-natured self. Next time we met, I'd be wise not to mention Salem to him.

Slotting our money into the register, he winked at me. "Herzog is also a weekend hunter."

"On the contrary. Hunting intrigues me more than practicing law does." Herzog eyed me. "When do we meet? We return to court two Thursdays from now."

"I've got to be off." I sidled halfway through the doorway. "Good hunting and cheers, all."

"Our pre-trial preparation is essential."

"It's under control," I said before the door slapped shut behind me. Walking to my cab truck, I knew Momma Jo had hired Herzog because he quoted her the cheapest rate. But he was a dimwit shyster, and I plain didn't like him. Too pushy, for one thing.

After I got into my cab truck that still didn't burn oil, I cranked it and tooled by the plywood-scabbed shops blighting Main Street. Gentrification hadn't struck yet, but sprawl was a new cancer. Rumbling Caterpillars had busted the sod for a shopping plaza on the old Bishop place across from the trailer park. On principle alone, I'd never even buy a pack of Lifesavers at a chain store.

The twin brick smokestacks to Longerbeam Printery, my employer, spiked into view. The squat adobe building was once the old tannery. Greasy ink fumes now replaced the brackish rankness of the animal hides. Next up was Umpire's small hospital where Mama Jo put in long hours. It was in many ways, the smells included, like the old tannery. Across the street sat Herzog's law office, no place I hated more.

A half-block later after my turn, I slowed into a bungalow neighborhood. Black gums, Kentucky coffee trees, and tulip poplars canopied Mama Jo's chocolate stucco and tidy yard. Trained roses bloomed on the trellis. Her place trumped my furnished flat over Umpire's taxidermy shop. I tolerated the landlord's no smoking and no pets rules, but my neighbor Mrs. Wang owned Oscar, a tabby I fed half the time. I'd also sprung for the repairs on the stove and fridge. After no break on the rent, I'd let this month's slide to pay down on the bass boat.

Watching Mrs. Shaw's son Axel crow-hop off the Special Ed. bus, I chuckled as he raced over and opened the Shaws' mailbox. It was usually empty, and he pulled a long face. On St. Valentine's Day, he plucked out a card. Every so often, I stuck a two-dollar bill in the mailbox to his joyful astonishment. My cab truck nuzzled to the white palisade fence, and I crammed the detox pamphlet under the cab seat before I ranged out. Mama Jo penned up a pair of goats out back to graze on the poison ivy, wisteria, and kudzu. My double decker trailer loaded with the bass boats lulled there, too. Her lawn was a brown carpet laid down by the August drought.

She'd thumbtacked a flypaper strip under the porch's fanlight. I made a mental note to remove the dreamcatcher, a birthday gift from Salem, out of my only window. *Too many dreams leave me too damn buggy.* I saw through the rusty door screen the piano that, all thumbs, I'd never mastered. After that fiasco, she bought me a .410 from Western Auto, and I'd handled it better than trying to ape Ronnie Milsap's riffs. I rapped on the screen door's wood partition.

Her reply trumpeted out. "My hands are sticky! The door's open!"

I stepped inside and let my eyes adjust to fix on Edna's suitcases next to the piano. Her pillows sat on the sleeper-sofa because our old bedrooms were full junk repositories. After she'd left Cobb, she moved back in with Mama Jo on bat extraction day. I smiled. A fluttery noise had kept her awake, so she cajoled me into poking my head through the attic trapdoor. When I did, my jaw sagged. A plague of dirt-brown, furry bats roosted in the rafters. I netted them in an old sheet to evict and puttied their crevice entry I found. Now something sweet displacing the usual barbecued pork smell lured me on. Her china gleamed in the hutch before I skirted the dining room table and puzzled over the Christmas-wrapped gifts on it. Had she hit a red dot sale at the Piggly Wiggly?

The kitchen's steam washed into my sight on the rows of Bell canning jars and colanders of blackberries crowding the drain board. My mouth watered for her jam. Smaller colanders of blackberries gleamed on the countertop. Four gas pilots on low, blue flames heated the four pots. Reddish-purple juices, bubbling and slurping, stewed in them. Locals could hand pick up to a gallon of blackberries without a permit. Fuzzy on regulations, she took all she could tote. Before going to work, I drove her to the grassy balds' trailheads, and we hit the blackberry canes.

Heavyset and tallish, Mama Jo had a bulbous chin, and I'd inherited her yam nose. Her cropped ginger hair shot with gray gleamed from the olive oil she used as a mousse. Some townspeople called her abrasive and blunt, but her tough attitude was necessary for her orderly job. Her steamed up bifocals took dim measure of my inactivity.

"You can grab some cheesecloth and start squeezing. Or else hop on stirring the pots."

Leery of getting her purple-stained hands, I stirred the four pots on the stovetop. The printery's inks smudged enough of my skin. Purple also smeared the wood spoon I used.

"Is work going okay?" I asked her.

"There's no shortage of ill patients. Did you meet with Herzog?"

"It's all good."

"Uh-huh. You'd better get on it. Did Dr. Smith pull your wisdom teeth?"

"That's a bit downstream. Something else bugs me."

"If it's anything to do with Cobb Kuzawa, stuff it."

"Why do you ride Cobb like you do?"

"I don't ride him. What's on your mind?"

"Edna is making noises to patch up her rift with him."

"I already heard it, and he wins my sympathy."

"Hearing you say that is a shock." My wood spoon scraped the pot bottom.

"How'd you like it married to her?"

"True. You've spoiled her rotten."

Mama Jo scoffed. "She's no more spoiled than you are."

"What did you tell her?"

"Nary a peep." Mama Jo's keg chest heaved out a gravelly sigh. "They'll sort it out. Until then I let her crash here. You'd be a smart lad to avoid those shark-infested waters."

My nod agreed. "I've got my own troubles in spades."

"But you've poked in your big nose, haven't you?"

"She might go on our fishing trip to Lake Charles."

"Lake Charles." Mama Jo's face wrinkled in chagrin. "Good grief."

"Cobb's idea, not mine."

"Remember tomorrow is an even number day. You better top off your tank."

"Thanks. I've already gassed up."

"After you kids had nagged me nutty, I ran you up to see the earth dam. That's the last time I laid eyes on Lake Charles."

"Pete Rojos told me Salem is Herzog's secretary."

"Forget Salem. She's out of your league."

"Huh? We dated a little."

Mama Jo's wrist swipe left a reddish-purple daub above her eyebrow. "But then she got a Vanderbilt scholarship, but you were too smart and took up smoking and not just Marlboro Reds either."

"No-no, I quit that bad scene."

Weighing the truth in my statement, she didn't respond. I let my eyes zone out on the dark syrup perking in the four pots as an oracle bubbled. All my life folks had noted a fertile imagination made me different. How could I refute them? Whimsical visions and voices staged a running drama in my thoughts. Spooky stuff for sure, but I wasn't demented. My dreams kept my mental health in the pink.

My memory also had the knack to recount the events clear back to my infanthood. My father, last known to work up north on the Trans-Alaskan Pipeline, had rocked our cradles. He smiled a lot. It was the first smile I remembered seeing. A crescent scar stamped his forehead. Not long afterward, he'd left Mama Jo, Edna, and me high and dry. Edna said she didn't remember him at all.

Three things were certain in my life: death, taxes and Mama Jo's one rule to say nothing of Angus Fishback under her roof. I saw her collect and burn all the Polaroids taken of him. Growing up in a fatherless household, I felt estranged from other kids. Summer afternoons I waited at the front gate, half-expecting Angus to cruise up in a yellow-and-black Barracuda. He didn't. I assembled a miniature Barracuda from a model car kit, a kid's totem I parked on my bureau top. When she wasn't hiding my baseball and glove, Edna kept me company, but she always had her sassy girlfriends to humor her. My best friend was Cobb, but Mr. Kuzawa drummed up chores to keep the rascal busy. So the lots of solitude let me to daydream away my youth.

Uncle Ozzie was our family's champion dreamer. Zany as a box of frogs said the town gossips. I'd one story about him. He'd shriveled to breath and britches. Cancer, said the oncologist. One muggy summer afternoon I prowled down our street on a spine-tingling safari for a five-year-old. I hailed him seated on a plastic milk crate by the grocer. His elfish face in the sun bore a leathery cast. Liberal on the Old Spice failed to mask his dying man's smells of piss and futility. The glossy, blue backstrap to a .44 arched from his baggy trouser pocket. I gawked at it before his tenor quavered as a brisk wind strums the telephone wires.

"A'right boyo, where's Mama Jo?"

"She's fixing the tear the dog ripped in our door screen."

"Uh-huh. Is she done picking berries?"

"Yes sir. Quite a few are for her jam."

His thumbnail itched under his gaunt larynx. "You better scoot back to her, boyo."

"Is it so you can see the haints?" I asked him pointblank.

His lips curved into a wiry smile. "You heard talk, eh? How I'm a lulu. Don't buy it. Ask Jerry Kuzawa. He vouches for me. I see things most others can't."

"If you say it's true, then I believe you."

Uncle Ozzie's face seamed in agony before it ebbed away. The cancer had twisted its dagger blade in his gut. "Don't trust what you see, boyo, with your eyes open or closed."

I nodded. "My scary dreams make me wet the bed."

He tilted his chin, and his eyes showed a burnt orange matte, not the cold, clear blue I'd expected. Then he told me something I'd never forget. "Don't quail. Ever. You're bigger than your dreams. Now scoot on home. You worry Mama Jo ragged, boyo. She tells me that all the time."

"Yes sir."

"That's a good boyo."

Now I watched the blackberry juice slurp in the pots on her stovetop. Edgy to decipher my latest rash of dreams, I'd figured out Ashleigh, the dead girl I'd pushed off me in our motel bed, wished to have her say. How else did the dead speak to us but through our dreams? By my next quickening breath, I heard the supple lilt to her disembodied voice pitching me a new message.

"Brendan, I was murdered. If you'll bear with me, I'll play it back, scene by scene."

"Just as if we're bridge-building with Legos."

"As you wish it, but by pooling our resources we'll unearth the truth, what we both crave to know about the night I died."

"You must know who your killer is. Quit ribbing me. Just name a name."

"But I can't do that without your aid."

"What if I don't want to help you?"

"Then it's welcome to your lifelong rat cage."

"Brendan, I said Cobb will be the death of you." I did a double take at the exasperation furrowing Mama Jo's face. "Did you hear me? What comes over you? You lapse into these trances, grab a blank look, and stare off into limbo. Where does your mind fly? I'd love to know."

"Oh, stop it. You can see I'm standing right here."

"Uh-huh. At least you come by it honestly. I remember when your Uncle Ozzie went to see Edgar Cayce—"

"Oh no, not the Edgar Cayce chestnut again."

"It bears repeating. My brother returned all jazzed how the clairvoyant Cayce had prattled with the angels and saints. He could peer through your ribs and diagnose any ill organs. That's what Ozzie told me. I shiver to admit it, but you've taken his screwball strand of DNA."

"I know. You've told me since I was a kid."

"I do it for your benefit. He conjured all sorts of strange visions before his pistol accident."

Pistol accident? It wasn't likely unless he'd been using the .44's muzzle for a toothpick. "I can look forward to a long and adventurous life."

"Don't sass me. You had better take it seriously. Spiteful souls still gossip on him but never to my face. Thankfully you're not that far gone." She paused, then after a sigh she added, "Yet."

CHAPTER FOUR

No jet ski or Edna showed. She hadn't returned to the old marina. Cobb and I piddled for as long as we could stand it. Barefoot, I slogged into the knee-deep muck and retrieved the cut saplings that we'd used for our push poles. My javelin hurls sent them ashore, and I sloshed back to dry land. He clambered aboard his bass boat, undid his dock line, and skidded off into the green scum. I handed him a push pole, crammed on my boots, and my bass boat trailed his. Our squints merged on an inlet across Lake Charles where we'd last seen Edna steering the jet ski.

Groaning, he planted the push pole on the lake bottom and hoisted his weight to thrust forward. His bass boat slithered over the algae like a sled's runners did over the ice. "What contagion thrives in this witches' brew?"

The pellets of sweat dribbled into my eyes. My fingers gripping the pole were unable to rub off the salt's sting as I grunted. "You don't want to know."

He detached from the scum zone and let his bass boat coast. "One more *oomph*, buddy, and you're home free."

One grunt later, I teamed with him in the clear pool. "If she wrecked, we'd have caught the jet ski's dead man switch cutting off."

"Maybe. If her gas ran out, she's marooned and waiting on us to bring her a can."

"Siphoning gas makes me puke."

He rolled his tense neck. "First we'll go check out what's what."

Our engines cranking loud as a pair of blenders, we aimed at the target inlet, and pushed the throttles to scud over Lake Charles. The wind pasted my hair back into a ducktail, and my eyes canted to the dusk's fireball sun. New fears rattled me. As nightfall swallowed us, Lake Charles grew in size, doubling our search efforts. I, then him, poured it on.

Will Thomas Mountain's burnt purple shadows draped over three young fools who out piddling around had pushed things a little too far. I hated Lake Charles. I hated our trip here. I hated the smoke plumes smudging the twilit horizon. I hated the dozens of fires destroying wilderness. Yeah, I simmered in a hateful mood.

The earth dam's drop-off edge sliced into sight. Tree stumps with gnarled roots, splintered stepladders, and a crimped kayak glutted the concrete spillway. The colder, deeper water close to the earth dam fell to a denser jade, almost opaque color. From the corner of my eye, I saw an arm motion, Cobb indicating to cut it back. I did and we glided closer. His jerky glances inspected the shorelines. Our hopes to spot a disabled jet ski or a stranded Edna were fading with the daylight.

"She may've taken a tumble."

His headshake disagreed. "Can't be. Look again. The water is just a riffle over the spillway."

"But if the jet ski bucked, she'd hurtle over the spillway."

He removed the sunshades and fitted them upside-down on his mesh cap's beak. "Okie-dokie, Brendan. Check the spillway and make a liar out of me. Go ahead. But I'll stick with saying she didn't make it this far."

"Show me your proof."

"I see no sign of her or the crotch rocket. So, what's left?"

"We search on the opposite side of the dam."

"All right, lead us over."

We skirted the rust-pitted overflow pipe sticking a foot above the waterline and pulled the bass boats up on the dam's pebbly embankment. I saw how the water had undercut the earth wall, and I led us up its incline. Anxiety fluted his forehead. On the dry flank, a moonscape of limestone riprap prevented the erosion, but it had failed. I noticed seepage beyond the riprap near the dam's base, a clue to the weakening dam material. He noted it, too.

"Didn't I warn you this dike is set to blow?"

Goldenrod, asters, and jewelweed carpeted the spillover area. We canvassed the length of the dam's crest but found nothing of Edna. Crouching like a pair of cowboys, we talked under an alder tree, him first.

"Other ideas?"

"Patrol the lake's perimeter. She had to put in somewhere between here and Lang's Teahouse."

"It makes sense. We'll split up. You go left, and I'll patrol the right side." He stood. "I can't imagine what became of her."

"She rammed a submerged log, wiped out, and dog-paddled to ground."

He nodded. "At least she'd better sense than we did for not wearing our lifejackets."

"She isn't a big risk taker."

"Only when she took the gamble on marrying yours truly."

His quip fell limp after I said nothing, and we parted company. Perched on the edge of the bass boat's seat, I cruised by the sunny banks not shedding any light on her whereabouts. I hugged the thicketed shore, and my glances darted landward. The shadows blotched out my sightlines, and I despaired.

Our fishing trip had degraded into a gold-plated pain in the ass. I had to mull over why. Then a nicotine fit chafed my nerves, but my cigarette machine sat in the other bass boat. A pang of nausea skewered me.

Kicking this pot habit tested the limits of my resilience. Luckily, simple visual pleasures diverted me.

A blue heron on its spindly, yellow legs scooped silver minnows from the water trickling over a gravel bar under a sycamore tree. I laughed, and the heron took flight. Painted turtles piggyback on a fork of driftwood basked in the dying sunrays. At the next cove, my hand patted back a yawn when a slippery jerk flagged my eye, and my heart was a pogo stick leaping into my throat.

The stumpy moccasin sidewinding over the water charged at starboard. Adrenaline coiled the springs in my legs. My head snapped around. The fiberglass fly rod was a flimsy defense weapon. I saw the thermal sensors pitting the snake's triangular snout detected me. Fear clawed up my spine.

Unable to recall if the moccasins bit their victims underwater, I didn't abandon the bass boat. At the last second, the moccasin—unhinging its needlelike fangs and cottony throat in a defiant hiss—swerved. I blinked but then I saw no serpent. Was my hyperactive imagination duping me? This was too much. I reared upright, balanced my weight, and hollered out.

"Edna! Yo, Edna!"

My ears perked. Cobb's faint shouts also met with no success. I wouldn't put it past her to lay low and let us sweat. He loved messing with his victims on April Fools' Day, and she'd the legitimate right to dish out any payback. The hide-and-seek theory, however, didn't catch fire in me. I half-expected at the next inlet to spot her there snickering at us. Maybe she'd put in at a different landing and already returned to Lang's Teahouse. The mosquitoes ate me raw as I neared my combustion point. The engine swished up water droplets as I took off to go rendezvous with Cobb.

Within ten minutes, I entered the shadows now draping the old pavilion in its golden nostalgia. The Chinese lanterns and boat lamps twinkling along the T-dock reflected off the inky water as I eavesdropped on the lovers' conspiratorial murmurs. *"I could shake it all night. Me, too, honey. More wine? No, I'm already lightheaded. That's the idea. Why you lout, kiss me, again."* By the next moment, I saw Cobb sitting on the T-dock puffing on a Marlboro and listening to the insects hum.

I killed the engine and slid until the push pole ferried me through the algae. My lips quirked in contempt. No simple water hosing could remove the green crud from the bass boat's undersides. A stiff bristle brush, a can of Bon Ami, and elbow grease might work. The drudgery of tackling it depressed me. I'd heard the idea of running a bass boat on its trailer through a car wash.

"No Edna or jet ski?"

I wagged my head. "Nothing of either. You?"

"Ditto. She can't be that far."

"Is this her idea of a joke? Getting payback maybe?"

"A sick joke, I'd say."

"Is the Yellow Snake sheriff on duty?" I hated asking it. Tasting the bile coating my tongue, I closed the final three paces where I leapt to the T-dock. The rotten timber crumbled but didn't collapse under me. I spat out the bile and secured my dock line.

His flicked cigarette butt sizzled at striking the water. "Bonehead move."

"Why? My arrest is separate from this."

"Not from the sheriff's point of view. Report her missing, and he'll throw you some hinky looks. Three guesses where that leads."

My dicey arrest for Ashleigh's murder backed up Cobb's claim. My trust in the Yellow Snake law enforcement ran low.

"Then I'm all ears."

His voice turned earnest. "We can track down Edna."

"By searching where?"

"We haven't covered back in the laurel."

"With just the two of us?"

"All the better reason to get started."

"Do we separate again?"

"No, we stick together. She might be hurt, and we'll need to portage her out."

"I don't like how that sounds."

"Me either."

CHAPTER FIVE

Dank night dimmed the jungled shores of Lake Charles. Cobb's rattles for breath was an attack of nerves, exhaustion, or smoker's lungs. Our shouts ringing out to hail Edna fell hoarser. Soldiering on struck me as asinine, especially given our return trip still left back to Lang's Teahouse.

"Wait up, Cobb. We better turn around."

His grasp dropped from holding a tree branch. "We've barely made a dent."

"What does slopping around in the pitch dark get us?"

"Try your flashlight."

I already knew it was a dud. My flick of the switch sparked no light. "Dead batteries or else the bulb is fried." I pitched the useless flashlight.

"Holy fuck, did she pull a D.B. Cooper on us?"

Kneading the kinks from my corded neck muscles, I appreciated Cobb's sense of humor. "D.B. had some balls parachuting into the toolies, but the Feds will smoke him out. They never back off from a manhunt."

"My money says he's still on the lam."

"My money says he's a pile of bear scat," I said, thinking life on the lam was anything but glamorous despite what the bad asses in the movies showed us.

He grinned. "My aim is to stay out of such a pile."

"Then we better go back before the grizzlies and cougars go on night patrol."

"Damn straight."

After reversing our field, we hacked a portal through the alders enmeshed by clingy vines and prickly briars. A nasty peaches smell lifted off Lake Charles. We broke into the familiar clearing, and Lang's Teahouse bore a malevolent aura before I startled to see the crescent moon's bloody horn tips in the smoky sky, lowered as if to gore us.

He was feeling it, too. "This haunt gives a man the willies."

My nod went to my cab truck. "If we go on, we can reach Yellow Snake inside of a half-hour."

"No, I'm too damn beat. Let's catch our breath a little."

"Then help me start a fire."

The dry chunks of plank came torn off the T-dock while the awning's tin strips clattered in the breeze. He set a lit match to the wad of cedar bark he'd gathered for the tinder. Orange flames strummed up, smoke whiffed into our eyes, and soon Lang's Teahouse stood less ghoulish. The strobes of heat lightning mimicking the paparazzi's camera flashes behind Will Thomas Mountain heralded no promise of rain.

Our bass boats slotted on the trailer's racks, and I drove my cab truck up from the boat ramp and parked. We claimed the fire's upwind side and decked out on my blankets. I saw the bats knuckleball over our fire's flickering radiance. A smattering of pale stars surrounded the crescent moon. His breathing grew heavy.

"Are you awake?" I asked, but I got no reply.

Also falling drowsy, I cast my lot with Hesperus, the dazzling evening star, and it towed me beyond Will Thomas Mountain into a violet haze. Voices spoke in my head, but I didn't go ape shit. Then a wasp-waisted shape materialized—her approach nimble for her elegant tallness. Ashleigh's hand beckoned, but as a reluctant conspirator, I didn't reach for it.

"Brendan, are you there?"

"Yeah, down front."

"Splendid. Time grows short, so listen carefully. I can help you, if you help me. Deal?"

"You see me at Lake Charles, don't you?"

"Indeed."

"I don't like holding our talks like this."

"Oh, do I make you jittery?"

"Right now, yeah, you do. So there."

"Don't be afraid. My voice rings clear and honest. Trust me."

"Why should I trust you?"

"Didn't I let you fuck me? Multiple orgasms rocked that night, in fact."

"That's supposed to inspire trust? We were stoned."

She laughed and then sighed. "So much needs revealing . . ."

Cobb's bark cut in on my rumination. "Are you tripping on me, dude?"

I didn't tell him how often I dreamed of dead folk or he'd freak. "Huh?"

"I said the sheriff won't make Edna a missing person for another twenty-four hours."

"They'll also blow us off by saying she's got a wild hair. Cops are assholes."

"Easy, man. Not all cops are rotten apples. The state cops are pros."

My head wagged. "Man, I don't know what's wrong with me. First it was Ashleigh and now this with Edna."

"Don't think bad things about Edna."

I shifted over to sprawl out lying on a hip, and the fire's heat felt like a balm on my sore back muscles. "Smoking a spliff would level me out."

"True but you've gone straight." He passed me a Marlboro, an inferior substitute. "Speaking of which, I've got a theory. Actually it's based on the rumors I heard from my old dealer."

"What's your theory?"

"I believe local pot growers use Lake Charles."

A bit stunned, I processed it. "Pot? That's a little out there."

"Is it?" He paused. "If I made deals, I'd grow my herbs here. Check out the unbeatable assets. There's access to the state road. Who makes this scene anymore? No narcs, that's for sure. The jungle we just hacked our way through camouflages the plants in the meadows. The lake irrigates the plants because they hoover up the water. All in all, Lake Charles makes for an A-1 set up."

"Why didn't we run across any plots?"

"Because we just got started at looking."

A fear unnerved me. "Did these pot growers capture her?"

"My thought, too," he said. "But they farm the plots in the dryer areas, and I doubt if she'd leave the shore at night."

"Our bass boats will better our luck tomorrow."

"You know it. Like us, she's just hunkered down until first light."

We lounged back on the blankets, the campfire toasting our toes. Under the extreme circumstances, I felt released from my promise to her. "She favors you two getting back together."

"I figured as much, but let's not get into it."

"Cool by me."

The blankets stored in my tool chest had a brake fluid odor. I rolled over to roast my other body half. The ground played our firm mattress, and Mama Jo's quack osteopath would approve of it. The night insects' jazz serenaded us. I hopped up and peeled back my blanket, scraped away the peanut flashbulbs and bottle caps, and then flopped down with a satisfied grunt.

"More comfy now?"

"Since I quit smoking pot, yeah, I am."

"Bravo for you, dude. I know that a few users see the blue devils until the detox finally takes hold."

"Not me," I said, reminded of my Ashleigh dreams. "You remember my Uncle Ozzie, right?"

"Vaguely. He was sort of tetched in the head, wasn't he?"

"Sort of. Mama Jo says he heard and saw things nobody else did. He admitted as much the one time when I asked him."

"Was he a soothsayer who saw into the future?"

"We only talked for a few minutes."

"But you aren't like him, not by a long stretch. Otherwise Moccasin Bend had better hustle out and truss you in a straitjacket."

"Even he never turned that daffy."

"Shit, I'm just messing with you. Pops knew your Uncle Ozzie. They worked in timber and knocked back a few drinks together."

"Yeah, so Uncle Ozzie also told me."

"If you get bounced into the rubber room, we're still cool."

"I appreciate it."

He sprang up and went over to my cab truck. I heard him in his tackle box, rattling lures, rummaging through shit, and just generally aggravating me.

"Where are they?"

"Yo, keep it down." I re-crossed my ankles. This near, the fire blasted my hide, so I backed up a couple feet and stretched out again on the blanket.

He gave a coyote's yip and clomped back to me. His tossed object glanced off my ribs.

"Ouch." I rubbed the sore spot. "What's this?"

"Your own .44 Bulldog. Being a big paranoid psycho, I strap a pair."

Palming the cold steel handgun set off an eerie association in me. David "Son of Sam" Berkowitz had favored a five-shot .44 Bulldog to carry out his sick thrill kills. We pressmen pored over the newspapers, and the Son of Sam was a big story. Well, screw Berkowitz and screw his demon-talking dog Sam. Clutching the .44, I felt safer. After sitting up, I thumb-cocked the knurly hammer and fingered the slick trigger.

"Don't leave home without one," I said.

"Believe it." Cobb hulked into the circle of firelight.

A grim insight struck me. "Cobb, is this fire smart? Your inquisitive pot farmers might spot it and come snooping."

"That's the idea because now we're ready for them."

After notching his balls, he rested in a crouch a few steps from the fire. The flames entranced his gaze. We had Lake Charles at our rear and faced into any oncoming menace. Despite the tension, I felt bored when he began talking shop.

"Big Tiny crowed the pressmen's union is back."

"He doesn't know shit from shinola. The union is done with us in their fold."

"That strike hit ages ago. Time has moved on, and the union wants us. I'd pay to get a union card. It means higher salary, medical insurance, and more vacation. What's there not to like?"

"I agree," I said. "But the union won't risk another go with us."

"We're damaged goods, eh?" He brought over a few broken planks, fed the fire, and flumped down next to me. "Not for nothing, but why is Mama Jo so damn hard on me?"

My shrug came fast. "She's hard on me, too."

"No, this feels personal like I did something bad to her."

"I can't speak for her. She's complicated."

"Why didn't she ever remarry?"

"Maybe for the same reason your old man never did."

"Once is enough, right. Does your old man ever call you?"

"He mails me postcards."

"That's it? Postcards? What does he scribble on them?"

"Just Mama Jo's address," I replied and added, "He's a man of few words."

"It's more like a man of no words." Cobb laughed at his glibness. Self-conscious at how I'd grown up fatherless and he hadn't, I grunted. He gave me a disarming grin. "Pops' history is filled with intrigue."

"Wasn't he a leatherneck kicking ass in Korea?"

"Part of the Frozen Chosin, sure he was, but then later he also spied for Uncle Sam." Cobb deflected my next question by posing his first. "Why did you get Herzog for your lawyer?"

"He's the cheapest in the book. Before you say anything, I've wrestled with my own doubts about him, too." My fleeting thought wondered how he kept his rates down. Incompetence? Laziness? Stupidity?

"He showed he can hold his own in court."

"He did get me bail," I said, with a memory of his projected scouting trip to Lake Charles.

Before I could touch on it, Cobb asked, "Hey, what happened in Yellow Snake? I never did hear it all."

"I'm not up for giving a blow-by-blow account."

More tossed on planks sheeted up the red-orange embers into the dark sky. He stretched out on the blanket. "The gist will do. No hurry either since we're pulling an all-nighter here."

CHAPTER SIX

"That night," I told him, my eyes also enthralled by the crackling red-orange flames. "Mr. Kuzawa and you had blown town, so, I didn't have my sidekick in tow."

"Sorry I didn't call you. Business had beckoned, and you know how Pops is. Work is work. We ran the flatbed truck down to saw up a load of cypress and sold it for a fat profit."

"Anyway. That night. Everywhere I drove, the kids raved about college. Advanced education not in the cards for me, I felt a little left out."

"Brendan, sorry but you're not prime college material."

"Hey, this timber hick nailed a 1250 on his SAT."

"Is that score good? Anyway, the future college pukes . . ."

"Well, I left them in my dust, and I boogied down the old bypass. Kerns's store was lit up, and I swung by and I saw this trick-painted van parked in his lot."

"Driven by the out-of-towners?"

I nodded. "Schlepping inside to buy my smokes, I heard a girl giggle."

"She was just mad keen to get rode hard."

"That part came later, but can I get on with my story? Inside Kerns sat watching TV. His old lady offered me a PBR. 'I'm still a kid,' I told her. 'Yeah, but only the once,' she said. We laughed and I quizzed Kerns about the gang milling around outside.

"'That's my moron nephew who goes by J.D.,' said Kerns. 'His girlfriend is a spoiled, rich brat from Yellow Snake.'" I laughed. He didn't. I took it that Kerns didn't like J.D. or his girlfriend, especially after he had a few belts.

"We chewed the fat a little more. Bored again, I said my good-byes and stepped outside. This time the girl's laugh made me ask, 'Anything doing?' 'Slide on over and find out,' she invited me. So I did. Now, this gal . . ." Here I tapped Cobb on the elbow.

He grinned at me. "She came stacked, eh?"

"Stacked to the rafters," I said. "Ashleigh wore a slinky, purple gown like it was her second skin. They passed me a joint, and who turns down a freebie buzz? I took several hits. They also had an extra The Devil's Own ticket."

"The Devil's Own." He spat into the fire. "Boil me alive in hot tar first."

"Anyway. I hitched aboard the party van. J.D. and Ashleigh commandeered the captain's seats, so I partied with the ass ugly dudes in back."

"Three cheers for the ass ugly dudes."

"Always. 'What's up with this reefer?' I asked this goateed dude sucking on an ice hookah. They called him Goat. 'One toke and you'll talk to the devils.' He bleated through his adenoids. I didn't like him, but I did a hit. 'Go slower on that,' he advised me. 'Or it'll blow off your balls.'"

"Not to rush you, but can you skip over to the motel room?"

Nodding, I saw the stark images inside it replay. Ashleigh's dead eyes didn't glitter. A taut smile barbed her mouth corners. Lying there shocked in the bed, I saw her purple gown she left draped over the mini-fridge. The Devil's Own guitar riffs still reverberated through my skull, and I quaked to howl out my lungs like some rabid, wild beast.

"Well, Brendan …"

"Our motel room felt cramped. Musty. I remember shambling out into the humid night to use the coin phone. I dropped my first dime, lost it in the gravel. Mrs. Cornwell drowsing in her office didn't hear me curse. My call patched through, I sucked in a gulp of air, and I told the sheriff's dispatcher that the girl was stone dead. It was then I realized I was in deep shit."

"Wait a minute," he said. "I thought you said you woke up lying next to a naked corpse."

"Exactly. She'd been dead for hours, and I'd snoozed right through it. Creepy as all get out."

"Hey, I'd have fucked the corpse. Life is about trying new experiences."

"No, you wouldn't."

"Maybe not. Then what happened?"

"Well, dawn was just a shout away. When I pulled up the sheet over her face, the nickel bag slid out and landed on the floor. I knew I had to get rid of her dope. The bath drain sprang to mind. So I went in there, cleared the hairball from the drain, and stuffed in the dope. The running shower was supposed to destroy the evidence."

He spat again into the fire. "Dumb fuck move."

"And how. Busted on a reefer possession was the least of my worries. I was in a hairy jam. She was dead, but I knew I was no killer. The car doors thudded shut, and I flinched in my skin. No sirens had shrieked up, but I knew it was almost finished. My heartbeat pounded like the fist on my door.

"I jerked up from our bed, hurried over to the door, and squinted through the peephole. The two sheriff's deputies had drawn their 9 mils. 'Open up!' one yelled in at me. While grabbing the doorknob, I heard the damn shower gurgling, and I glanced back. The drain clogged with the reefer had backed up, and the water spilled out from the bathroom door. Shit, I'd—"

"*S-h-h-h.*" Cobb rolled up from the blanket into an alert crouch. "A shadow just darted by, there down along the lane."

"Where?" I arose to take a shooter's stance, my .44 thrust forward. Straining my eyes, I also peered out to pierce our dark periphery. "Did you hear it, or see it?"

"Both."

"Cobb, is this a damn leg pull?"

"Fuck no. I stuck an extra box of cartridges under your tool chest. Go get it. But be quick."

My pulse wild as a jackrabbit, I scrabbled over to my cab truck. "How many?"

"Just the one box. Keep your voice down, too."

"No, I mean how many shadows?"

Then my peripheral vision registered the pinkish spurt of muzzle fire, and a slug whined by my ear. More slugs spanged overhead. A low caliber rifle, I recognized. I vaulted over the side of my cab truck and pressed my gut down flat to its bed. My reaching hand groped under the tool chest and tugged out his box of .44 cartridges.

The staccato gunfire was one-sided until he raked out a rapid fire, defensive volley hurling lead shot downrange. In the deafening chaos, I leapt from inside the truck bed and romped back to him now prone behind a rise in the sandy terrain. I also hit the sand. My teeth clenched on the grit. The gun smoke stung my watery eyes. He rolled in a half-turn, and I fed him more ammo. As he reloaded, I eyed down my .44's stubby sight. My finger squeezed the trigger, and my wrist jerked back. Having gained the .44's feel, I kept a tight group of shots centered at where I saw the original muzzle flash.

Another round of rifle shots zinged by us before a lull I didn't trust my punished ears to hear. We had to act, or they'd shove us back to die in the lake scum. I signed a hasty plan to Cobb. He nodded. My Rebel yell whooped out. We charged ahead, aimed low. No return fire punched us. Good, they'd come to just throw a scare in us. He flushed his quarry. Thrashing footfall beat it through the bush and, snapping off shots, he gave hot pursuit.

My foe was huddled in the bushes some twenty paces ahead. I crash-dove to the sand, reloaded, and leaped up to press forward. I deked left and then cut hard right. The man-form reared up like a specter. His muzzle flamed at the spot where I'd just stood. From the hip, I fired. His shriek assured me I was the lucky duck one still upright.

Scared, I stopped—all ears. My heart pinged behind my temples. Boots tromped up from behind, and I swiveled around. My finger hooked on the trigger pulled, and the falling hammer bit a spent cartridge. I heard the dull click, and I felt my gut sink over what I'd almost done.

"Yo, it's me. Drop your aim."

"Shit."

"Shit?" Slicing his hands, he snorted. "You damn near shot my ass."

"Sorry. I nailed one, I think." My voice rang out metallic.

"Mine rabbitted off."

"Did you hear a car start up on the state road?"

"Man, my ears are whistling too loud to hear much."

Both of us waded into the bush until I stepped on a hard arm. My boot flinched back. Cobb lit a matchbook for a hasty look. The shot man lay double-tapped. My .44's slug had penetrated his blood-drenched chest. Cobb toed over the dead man to show his exit wound's gaping savagery. Nausea stitched my sides. The flickering matches singed Cobb's fingertips.

"Zowie," he said, licking at them. "Recognize him?"

"He's Mr. X to me."

"I don't recall Mr. X's name, but I've seen him around my dealer's wikiup."

"Your pot grower theory seems to hold water."

"Yeah, and your voice seems too rough. Are you okay?"

"I'm a little swim-headed." My knees wobbled.

"Jesus, Brendan, I can feel the wet blood on you. Mr. X must've winged you. Does this hurt?" Cobb touched what burned as a white-hot brand pressed just under my short ribs.

"Yeah, man!" I growled through my clenched teeth. "Is it bleeding badly?"

"Bend forward and slip up your shirttail … I'll light another matchbook … good deal, the bullet just grazed you."

"That is a relief."

"You ain't said shit. Just don't black out on me, okay?"

"Help me gimp back to the campfire."

"Here, brace your weight on me." He looked over his shoulder. "Where's my box of cartridges?"

"I left it lying by the blankets. But he's bolted, Cobb, so let it go. He probably left in a car and won't be circling back."

Cobb's brawny shoulder supporting me stiffened. "No way do I let it go, not after tonight. They drew first blood, and now it's game on."

"Lower me to the blankets, Bronson." My blurry gaze tried to negotiate the pitch dark. I knew I had bigger crises to deal with than a bullet nick. "Where in the nine hells is Edna?"

"Don't worry. We'll find her the first thing tomorrow." He slumped down to sit by me on the blankets. "Better grab some shuteye, and I'll stand our first watch."

"Good idea. Did you find the box of cartridges?"

"Right here."

"Lake Charles isn't the sleepy dell everybody figures it is."

"Didn't I tell you the pot growers do business up here?"

Fading off to the black mist, I let him get the last word. The final pang I felt before sleep was a spine-jarring dread for Edna's safety, and now ours.

CHAPTER SEVEN

"Our lab boys found the angel dust in a sandwich baggie." Deputy Wines' smarmy face came too close to my nose. "You duct taped it under the bed table. What a dumb shit stash hole that was."

They'd frog marched me into their interrogation stall after leaving the Chewink Motel in their cruiser. The urine and body odor fumes in the rear seat cage had gagged me.

"Clown, you killed Ashleigh Sizemore," said Deputy Wines.

"I killed her? No, she overdosed."

"Not in our book."

"You think it was mine, and I gave it to her knowing she'd die?"

"That's how the evidence reads."

My pulse spiked to a new frenzy of pounding fright. They kept saying I was a killer. Bullshit. My sidelong glance took in the pair of stocky, cunning, and cold-eyed men in their early thirties. The harsh glare also left them squinting. I squirmed upright in the chair.

"We just smoked a spliff," I said. "I don't know jack on any damn angel dust." Only the shadows on the grimy wall heard me.

"I recovered your contraband wedged in the bath drain." Ramsey sucked between his black meerschaum nubs for teeth. "Mark up another dumb shit move."

"Sure, that was ours, but the angel dust? Uh-uh. A previous guest left it. Or maybe it was left by—"

"Whoa, careful, clown. Accusations that we manufactured evidence light our fuses."

Ramsey rapped his hammy knuckles on the tabletop. "Jot it down on paper. The judges and juries go softer on self-admitted killers. It shows a decent bone still exists in your douche bag of a body. Plus Ashleigh's heartsick dad can close the loop. Your signed confession is win-win."

Uh-huh, I thought.

Wines resumed the tough cop script cribbed off *Kojak* reruns. "Or else Big Al at Riverbend shoves a leather mask over you and straps you into Old Sparky." Wines gripped his chair's armrests to show how tight Big Al cinched the leather wrist straps to Old Sparky. "At the appointed time, he flips the hot switch. Twenty-three hundred volts at seven amps of lightning zap through your skull and scorches down to your toes."

"*Poof*." Ramsey snapped his fingers. "Light bulb city."

Chuckling like a fiend, Wines went on. "When the juice strikes the ticker, I hear the toughest punks shriek out for their mamas. Blood squirts out your mouth and oozes through your ribs. Your shit slops into a bedpan. After all that fun stuff, nobody sheds a tear except for the dyke nuns toting their protest signs outside the gate."

"This is crazy talk," I said, scowling at their incendiary glares. "I'll burn that one phone call and get a lawyer."

Wines' eyes widened in mock surprise. "A lawyer? Why is that? We haven't *formally* charged you, but then we also can't cut you loose. Mr. Sizemore wants your liver on a kebab. You fear for your safety, so we'll book your detention as 'protective custody.'"

"You're also a material witness in a homicide. Both are perfectly legal reasons to hold you," said Ramsey.

"All I ever saw was the inside of my eyelids. I was fast asleep."

"Don't fuck with Mr. Sizemore, clown. He's our next state senator, and his army will plant your punk ass at the bottom of a dark mineshaft."

"Yeah, accidents are so common." The legal pad of paper they'd slapped down on the tabletop nudged my wrist manacled to the O-bolt. "Write it up." Ramsey nodded at me. "A little free advice. Don't underplay how ripped up you feel inside. How you'll lay awake and sweat blood every night, tortured over Ashleigh's senseless death."

"The last I saw that girl, she was alive."

Ramsey ignored me. "How you pulled the stupidest blunder in your short, piece-of-shit life by going to the rock-'n'-roll orgy. With a lifetime of sorrow stretching in front of you, may the merciful judge show you even slight leniency. Juries love hearing remorse spewed from a clean-cut puke, but you gotta take the first step."

My wrist flinched from the legal pad, and I straightened up in the chair. I know I'd done a ton of growing up over the past two hours.

"But I did not kill Ashleigh."

"Tell the truth, clown," said Wines. "Focus on what Deputy Ramsey took the time from his busy tour to explain. We'll go." Wines tapped a fingernail on the legal pad. "You scribble it down. *Capiche*?"

"Hey, can I bum a Marlboro?"

Ramsey held up the pack of cigarettes and flicked the butane lighter to flame. "Write it up, and you get your smoke. But not before then."

Both deputies vacated the Star Chamber, and I sat alone with the cricket fiddling in the corner for company. I didn't waste any time writing a *mea culpa*, but mulled over this latest news. Was the junk PCP—we called it angel dust—the evidence needed to nail shut my coffin lid? They hadn't yet hung a narcotics rap on me. Odd. They probably saw it as a distraction in putting the bite on me for a homicide confession.

My thoughts roared on. Had Ashleigh died of natural causes? That would spare me. Say, she'd suffered a fatal heart attack. Girls got those. Would they check? Hell, no. Any autopsy was a sham, too. When was my phone call? Whom did I get for aid? Mama Jo? Edna? Cobb? Mr. Kuzawa? Jerry Kuzawa was a bad idea. He'd spill a bloodbath in his wake. Once I went free, I had to stay one jump ahead of Ashleigh's lunatic father. I deserved better than rotting at the bottom of any dark mineshaft—

The door squeaked on its hinges and my slitted eyes lifted. Deputy Wines sidled in, Ramsey hot on his heels. They divided at the table and crowded each side of me.

"I see no writing," said Ramsey.

"There's no need for it because I didn't kill Ashleigh Sizemore."

"Deputy Ramsey, I've lost all of my patience." Wines enacted a hand-washing ceremony. "We bend over backwards to let him come clean, and he jerks us off. Mirandize this clown for murder one."

Shaking his head with pity, Ramsey whipped out his dog-eared card. "You have the right to remain silent . . ."

CHAPTER EIGHT

A short while later I sat on a bunk, hugging my knees, before I fell into a trancelike rocking. Echoes clanged off the hard prison walls. Light through the cell's front bars striped me in zebra shadows. The stink of Pine Sol and urine sickened me. A nearby cough surprised me, but my shouted "hey, yo!" got no response, so I went back to my rocking.

Sheriff's Deputies Wines and Ramsey had booted me into this shark cage, and left for the Elks Lodge to tie on a beer buzz. The next duo of sheriff's deputies slated to take a whack at me hadn't yet polished off their drip coffee and Krispy Kremes. Tired, I flumped back on the bunk too hard for sleep and tried to piece together last night. If only I'd planned my strategy at the motel instead of rushing out to call the sheriff. I bolted up from the bunk, paced three steps ahead, pivoted, and took two baby steps to the wall. The white blitz of images hurtled by in me. Okay, channel it, Brendan.

I saw Ashleigh and me in her red Jaguar skidding into the Chewink Motel's parking lot. Right, sure. I remembered "OFFI'E" and "VA'AN'IES" sizzled on the orange neon signboards. What did I smell once out of her Jag? Quince in bloom spread the grapy aroma. Details, my man. Bury these peckerwood sheriff's deputies in an avalanche of the details. What came next?

I skulked into the motel office. Again, what smells? Liver and onions had been sautéed on a hotplate or a Sterno can. Damn, I was getting good at this. I'd looked behind a waist-high beaverboard counter. More details. The signs of habitation included a cigarette butt left smoldering in an empty tuna fish can, a plastic spoon stuck in a cottage cheese tub, and a fizzy, half-empty bottle of Tab diet soda.

I cadged a complimentary green matchbook with a gold bird icon from the Bell canning jar. Later we'd use the matches to light our spliffs. My fingertip tapped the stem to the gizmo that dinged a bell. Nobody came out. Wrong signal, so I did two bell rings. No response prompted me to tap out a series of bell rings.

A chunky woman knotting the belt to her fuzzy bathrobe hulked in the rear doorway. "You ring once. I'm a one-woman crew, and I can't run as fast as most can."

"Sorry, lady. You got a room?" I asked.

"Surely and it's Mrs. Cornwell to you." Her lumbering steps halted at the counter. "I just accept cash. No checks or plastic."

"I've got the money."

"Single or double? Smoking or nonsmoking?"

"Double," I replied. "Smoking will do."

"With tax, that's forty-four dollars," she said without a trace of humor.

"That's kind of steep, isn't it?"

"What say?" She canted an ear at me. Seeing the wires to her hearing aid, I repeated it, only louder. She leaned her pudgy forearms on the counter edge. Slivers of coppery hair framed her meaty face. The five-and-dime store glasses dangled on a bead chain at her neck, and her smile turned mercenary.

"Let me guess. Your hot-to-trot filly sits out in your ragtop, but you've nowhere to race her except in the rear seat. Only your filly won't have any of that. She has some class. Now here you be, your conundrum for me to solve. So, using my racetrack will run you forty-four dollars."

"Fine, you leave me no choice." I culled out two twenties and a ten to stack on the countertop. "I'm in a rush. Keep the change."

Mrs. Cornwell scooped up the three bills to fold and tuck under her watchband. "Unit Seven will get you to heaven," she said, flicking a room key at me. She cackled at her double entendre or my dour frown. I cut out of the lobby back to Ashleigh in her red Jaguar. Too amped, I couldn't fit the key into the door lock. She did it. We reeled inside the sin pit, shucked down, and set the sheets on fire …

Moaning, I sat on the bunk. No, in retrospect, our sex wasn't that memorable. Our mad dash to the finish tape had to be kids' stuff. I ran out of gas, crashed, and we fell asleep, hers a permanent one. When had she died? Scarier even, who'd brought in the angel dust? Who administered it to her? Big gaps broke up my memory. Filling in the big gaps was sure to make my life into a living hell.

* * *

The clack of metal on metal startled me. Keys twisted and doors dragged. Hearing the shoes scuffle heightened my awareness. My heart thudded behind my eyes focusing on a pair of men watching me behind the zebra stripes. One was a uniformed meatball, and the civilian came in woodsy Eddie Bauer.

"Is this the punk ass?" asked the civilian through his Van Dyke beard. Gray eyes alit on me as his fingers combed down the beard. His droopy lower lip quivered as if something mean and nasty gave him a hard on.

"Ready and waiting, Mr. Sizemore," replied the sheriff's deputy, a big fan of the Krispy Kremes Club.

"You got no confession yet, eh?"

"Not yet but we're softening him up for you."

"Much obliged." Sizemore jerked a hand. "Cuff his ass."

Eager to please, the sheriff's deputy tromped into my prison cell and manacled me to the bunk's steel frame before I could react. "Just bang his skull on the wall if you want out."

"If anything is left, I'll do that."

"He's all yours. There's no hurry. His bail hearing isn't until Tuesday." The sheriff's deputy stitched on a sadistic leer before he turned and huffed down the hallway.

Ralph Sizemore, Ashleigh's angry father, poured through my cell door. I coped with the same meltdown of fear as the residents at Three Mile Island must have on that scary day last March.

"You're my little girl's killer." His eyes skittered left to right. We had no eyewitnesses here.

"Look, I only reported her death. It'd be stupid for me to kill her and then tip off the authorities."

"Nice try but I'm a trial attorney." He hulked inches away from me, and I recoiled from the whiskey rancid on his breath. "You phoned the sheriff to make it look good, but I can see through it."

My babbling was uncontrollable. "Some physical evidence is there to prove my innocence. Fingerprints were left on the doorknob maybe."

"You wiped down Room 7."

"I did no such thing. I woke up, and Ashleigh was dead. I made a beeline to the phone outside and notified the sheriff. It even cost me two dimes. I returned and waited until the law showed and pounded on the door."

"Touching. Why didn't you fetch an ambulance?"

"I thought of it, but she'd been a goner for a while."

His lip quivering, he tugged out a palm sap from his hip pocket. "I won this in a stud poker game at Fort Hood." He gave the palm sap a practice swing and grinned like a giant raptor down at me.

I shifted, the handcuffs biting into my wrist.

"Better say your prayers." He stepped into me, his arm slinging the palm sap with his weight hefted behind its swat.

I grunted at the monster pain exploding in a galaxy of pinwheels behind my eyes. The harder blows pummeled me. Maybe I heard a snicker. Then it was lights out. My splashdown into the inky black ocean of unconsciousness didn't resurface to daylight.

No, I weathered a concussion in a Yellow Snake hospital bed. It was some hours before I saw daylight again. At an agonizing turn in the bed, I spotted the two shiny dimes left on the bed table. I'd had a visitor. He'd reimbursed me for the phone call I'd made to report his daughter's death to the sheriff. I didn't appreciate his perverse sense of humor.

CHAPTER NINE

Against all odds, I bonded out of the Yellow Snake prison with Herzog as my counsel. First, the intern doctor discharged me with a whopping bill, and I arrived early at the Yellow Snake courthouse for my bail hearing. A nickel-plated bracelet hogtied my wrists. A bulkier one reduced my ankles to an old man's waddle. A belly chain jangled around me modeling the penal orange. A furtive peek at the courtroom's Peanut Gallery revealed we played to a packed house. Pain ravaged my swollen head, and my lower back muscles felt tied in knots from the tension.

Sheriff's Deputies Ramsey and Wines deposited me to sit at the defense table. A brass desk lamp illuminated it. Herzog wore his customary ashen gray poplin suit and hangdog look. Neither inspired a lot of confidence in me. Waiting, I sized up the oak jury and witness boxes before the elevated bench—they all looked empty as a coffin, me soon to fill it.

"What happened to your head?" asked Herzog, seeing my lumps.

He was my lawyer and didn't know of my concussion and hospital stay? "I tripped on a bar of soap in the shower. That's the official reason. Anyway, did Mama Jo and Edna ride up with you?"

"Yes, they're sitting three rows back. Don't gawk at them. Exercise some restraint." He made a fussy adjustment to his necktie's knot.

"Did Cobb and his dad Jerry come?"

"Yes, I topped off my tank at Kuzawa's A-frame, and we rode together. He shared his ultra-liberal politics with me. He's opinionated."

"He's a warrior," I said, proud to defend Jerry Kuzawa before a fear hit me. "Did the guards screen you with metal detectors?"

Herzog blinked. "Why should they?"

Sweat oozed under my orange jumpsuit. "Cobb and Mr. Kuzawa strap Glocks. I guarantee it. I just hope this deal goes in our favor."

"They brought Glocks into a court of law?" Herzog massaging his temples sighed. "This is bad—very bad."

"Maybe not so much," I lied. "We'll see."

"At any rate, your muster of support is impressive. Your popularity, however, doesn't ensure your freedom. Do everything I tell you."

"I got you. Who is this judge?"

He crooked a finger behind his necktie and loosened it. "Judge Yarrow has the reputation of a maverick. She always speaks her own mind."

That didn't bode well for us. "Did you say you've defended a murder case?" I asked him.

"Um, well, I . . ."

"All rise. Court is in session," said the bailiff.

He prodded me in the ribs, my cue to stand. The punctual judge sashayed through a portal door marked as "Private." She hitched the folds to her black robe, and I saw her red sneakers climb the carpeted steps to the dais. She liked comfort over formality. Judge Yarrow was also a fright. Her face was a peened triangle of tin. My closer look saw her scar tissue came from old second-degree burns. Despite confined by her court's chains, I felt sympathy for her.

"Be seated and quit ogling," he told me. I resented his bossy attitude.

"Just mind your shit, and I'll watch mine."

"Counselor," said Judge Yarrow, cutting our sidebar short. "Is your client prepared to post bail at this time?"

His chair scraped over the floor as he arose. "Good morning, Your Honor. Yes, he is."

Judge Yarrow's stare gravitated from him to me. Fright welled up behind my breastbone. "Have you run afoul of the law before, Mr. Fishback?"

"Nope," I replied.

Her frown stamped the crow's-feet at the corners to her eyes and lips. He leaned to me, his whispering mouth at my ear. "It's 'No, Your Honor.'"

"Now you tell me." I looked back at her. "I mean no, Your Honor."

"That's infinitely better. How do you plead on the count of first degree murder?"

"Not guilty." He elbowed me, a not-so-subtle reminder on courtroom etiquette. "Your Honor," I added.

"Do you deny Ms. Sizemore died in that sleazy motel room?" Judge Yarrow's scars compressed into a truculent glare.

"Ashleigh was still breathing when we fell asleep, Your Honor."

"No doubt she was. Are you mocking the Court?"

"Your Honor, permit me to clarify," said Herzog. "Mr. Fishback means Ms. Sizemore had no reason to fear for her safety. After all, they were friends."

"It seems to me they were more than friends." Judge Yarrow's scowl berated him as I heard a titter circulate through the Peanut Gallery.

Things had already run to shit. Bail was a pipe dream. Judge Yarrow the maverick had all but shipped my ragged ass back to the jug. Resigned to my fate, I listened in on Herzog.

"They both indulged, and it was consensual. He didn't force her to go there."

"How do you know? Were you also in the room?" Judge Yarrow sounded more clipped and impatient.

My yank came at Herzog's dress jacket. "Sit down. We can't beat this stacked deck."

"According to the M.E.'s report, Ms. Sizemore's body exhibited no signs of physical coercion." Herzog took his seat.

"Don't lecture me, Counselor. I've read the M.E.'s report." She leaned back in her throne, intertwined her fingers, and shot her fierce gaze to the next table. "Mr. Prosecutor?"

A short, roly-poly man who was a dead ringer for Ned Beatty, he bellied up to the center podium. "Your Honor," he spoke in a bland monotone. "The medical examiner's report documents lethal amounts of PCP detected in the decedent's system."

"So it does. Do the People oppose Mr. Fishback's bail?"

"Without question, we do."

She trained her attention to a row behind us. "Mr. Sizemore, have you anything to contribute?"

Standing, Herzog objected. "Your Honor, Mr. Sizemore has no business before the Court, and it's improper."

"Objection overruled. This bereaved father deserves to give his input. Be seated, Mr. Herzog. Mr. Sizemore, proceed."

"Good morning and I thank Your Honor." Sizemore's next words would inflict more pain than his palm sap had on me. "Ashleigh was a vivacious, beautiful spirit whom this boy destroyed. He did so without expressing a shred of remorse . . ."

"Perhaps Mr. Fishback comes prepared to do so now." Judge Yarrow shifted to train her facial deformities on me. "Well …?"

Herzog hissed at my ear. "Showtime. Throw yourself on the mercy of the Court and beg like a whipped dog."

"Screw it."

"You don't have to be genuine. Just act sincere and contrite. Only do it now."

"Screw it."

"Brendan, this is no time to go soft in the head. You hear me?"

"Screw it."

"Mr. Fishback, my Court adheres to a tight schedule."

Rattled and sore, I scooted my butt to the front of the hard chair bottom, straightened in the knees, and ascended to my full height. Vertigo left the courtroom spinning around me, but I looked Judge Yarrow square in the eye. I ignored Herzog's finger jabs and spoke with conviction.

"Your Honor, Ashleigh drove us in her sports car to the motel. I freely admit we did what teenagers do there. Then we fell asleep. When I later awoke, she'd been dead for some time. So I hotfooted out and phoned the sheriff. Since then, I've cooperated and told him all that I know. I didn't cut and run. I could've, but I didn't."

As Judge Yarrow zeroed in on one salient detail, she raised her hand. "Wait a minute. Let me get this straight. Ms. Sizemore drove you from her house to the motel in *her* sports car?"

"Yes, it was her idea, Your Honor. Before that night, I'd never been near the motel."

Judge Yarrow's scabrous face lifted over my shoulder to skewer Sizemore. Her displeased voice rang out. "What is this I hear? The kids' van arrives at your residence to discharge your daughter, but before you can say boo, she talks Mr. Fishback into her sports car, and they tool off to her love nest. She strikes me as a tart."

Somebody, most likely Cobb, snickered. The roly-poly prosecutor yawned into his cufflink to fill the edgy silence.

"Your Honor, the boy is obviously a liar—"

Her hand chop cut off Sizemore. "Is he? I've a rap sheet sitting in front of me. Your daughter has a history with the juvenile courts. Arrested and booked on possession of pot and paraphernalia. Now I hear your party girl was also a tart. Frankly sir, I'm appalled."

My fuzzy thinking caught on that Judge Yarrow had a hang up with promiscuous girls.

"Your Honor—"

Her grotesque features shrank into a glower. "Mr. Sizemore, I give you a platform to speak, and this is what I hear? Your round-heeled daughter entices the defendant to a tawdry motel and engages in fornication. Why, this is contemptible. Outrageous."

Flabbergasted as I was by this turnabout of events, Herzog moved to exploit our advantage. "The Defense requests bail be set, Your Honor."

"I quite concur," said Judge Yarrow over Mr. Sizemore's indignant protests.

Applause broke out in the Peanut Gallery with my grin of relief. Throwing my bail had emptied my bank account, but I bought my freedom, at least for now. I vowed to capitalize on it, too. When my glance traveled over the Peanut Gallery's rows of seats, Mr. Kuzawa and Cobb patted the significant bulges made under their jackets and gave me subversive grins. I knew they came armed to fight it out and spring me, if need be.

Mr. Kuzawa came up. "Let's tear ass out of here, son."

CHAPTER TEN

I jolted awake, the bedpan muck from Lake Charles in my nose. I'd writhed on the hard-packed sand before a fitful sleep took me, but no dreams haunted me. Had Ashleigh reneged on our deal to get at the truth? Get real, I thought. She's gone. The dead never speak to mortals. Whom had I been talking to all this time? If not her, then who?

"This is nuts. She lies six feet under," I said aloud.

My wristwatch hovered in front of my eyes. It was six o'clock. My ears still whistled from last night's firefight. My bullet scratch burned my side. I rubbed my eyes to erase the leering image of Mr. X's death rictus. My kicking legs flung off the blankets, and I sat up, leaning on an elbow. After a beat, the vertigo lifted. Spitting didn't expel the dead gerbil—*bleah!*—from my mouth. I wheezed and, after two tries, swayed but gained my feet.

"Crutches might help you."

"Fuck you. Is breakfast fixed?" I turned to Cobb.

"No grub."

"There's more pressing stuff to do."

"First we hide the corpse."

"That dog doesn't hunt, Cobb. I've decided we'll bring in the sheriff."

"Sure, get reamed up the ass. Great idea. You should patent it."

His earthy sarcasm annoyed me. "We'll say last night's turkey shoot was self-defense like it really was."

"Common sense says the sheriff will arrest us, but we can make this right."

"How?"

"Flip a stone here, shake a bush there, and see what crawls out." Heavy jaws set, he swept his hand at the overgrowth beyond us. "Edna out there needs our help."

My hands, fingers spread, went up. "See, ink stains? On yours, too. We're pressmen. Last night we're lucky that we didn't get hurt. But this shit is over our heads. The pros can play the heroes, not us."

He sized up the sunlit boulder field and the craggy knobs. I also saw the distant brush fire's smoke column climbing skyward. "We can make this right," he said as if it was a vigilante's mantra. "If we turn to anybody for help, I'd say we ask the rangers."

My heart lurched for a beat. A sketchy militia contingent self-named the "Smoky Mountain Rangers" roamed the laurel hells, the leafy thickets blanketing our ridges and hollows. Stamped rough at the edges, they'd no hate ideology nor were they your garden-variety gun nuts, or even religious, but you respected them. If you called them ugly slurs like hill scoggins or redneck stump grinders, they'd staple your balls to your ears. A couple of Sheriff Buford "Walking Tall" Pusser's deputies had signed on with them after the big blowout with organized crime downstate. The rangers' leader, a fiery ex-Marine named Cullen, had a long association with Jerry Kuzawa, Cobb's father.

"No rangers are in this. They'll touch off a war."

"Then you and I will go search on foot. A bass boat is too loud."

"We'd also be sitting ducks out on the lake." I scratched my collarbone. "Still I don't know . . ."

"Brendan, this is our best move to make."

I kicked the trailer hitched to my cab truck's bumper. The green algae had dried, and I wondered how I'd make my bass boat shine again. My hands patted down my pockets. "Shit." A Marlboro appeared over my shoulder, and I accepted it along with the matchbook.

"Mull it over, Brendan, but her trail grows colder. A whole night is gone, and we can't just sit on our thumbs. Do something."

Venting out the cigarette smoke, I suspected the sort of creeps with their portraits thumbtacked to the post office walls held her bound and gagged.

"All right, we'll do it your way."

Good thing the jolt of nicotine had sated my hunger pangs. I dropped the Marlboro butt and crushed it under my boot. I found Mr. X under the scrubby bushes. Eyes dull as twin lumps of solder he saw no light. His bowels had voided their shit. Experiencing death this close up left my gut to retch a vile, green crud I spat out on the sand.

"You look rode hard."

"And you look up for digging." I scuffed the ground with my boot tip. "This sand makes it easy."

"We haven't got the time to bury him. Roll him up in your blanket. Add in the rocks for ballast. Ferry out his tied up bundle and chuck it into a channel. The carp will love you for it."

My small shrug said I couldn't top his plan. Although I ignored looking at the blood-splotched bullet wound, Mr. X had a rusty odor mixed with the shit smell. He carried a pouch of Red Man and thirty-seven cents in loose silver but no personal ID. In case his wallet had spilled out, I scanned the area near him but with no luck. I spread out my largest blanket. Then Cobb lifted up Mr. X by his armpits. I latched to the ankles, and we trundled our bulky load to the blanket where Mr. X and his .223 rifle anchored the leading edge.

We selected a dozen or so stones no larger than coconuts for the ballast, and I rolled it all up like a mummy. The lengths of bailer twine I cut up cinched Mr. X's head, waist, shins, and feet. Then we unracked my bass boat, loaded on Mr. X, and launched it from the ramp. I slid beyond the crud zone to where my fishfinder radar measured an eighteen-foot depth. I toed off the mummy, and it plopped into the water. I also ditched the last bottles of our beer.

"Shameful waste," said Cobb. "The beer, I mean."

"Screw the liquor. Now we lock in and get Edna."

"Absolutely."

My bass boat fitted back on the trailer's top rack. I nuzzled my cab truck and trailer over to park them behind a clump of sassafras bushes. I swung my hatchet to lop off some branches to thicken in the leafy screen. A constellation chart and a 1960s astrology text were the plunder from my tool chest. Neither had aided me in deciphering my dreams. The beef jerky sealed in its cellophane wrappers made for our breakfast.

I stood on the T-dock, chewing the beef jerky and studying my dump-site. Bubbles effervesced from there. Did Mr. X still breathe? A scarier question asked would he breathe in my dreams of Lake Charles. The bandana Cobb tied to his forehead was yellow, and I pocketed the red one he gave me. We poured on water and snuffed out the campfire coals.

"How's your bullet wound?"

"Just a scratch," I replied, divvying up his box of .44 cartridges. "We do one junket around. If anything screwy pops up, we'll stop and check it out."

"My idea, too. Saddle up."

The old marina faded to our rear. Stealth wasn't a priority as much as traversing the rocky terrain without blowing out a kneecap or twisting an ankle. We skirted the drying mud flats. Mr. X now in Davy Jones' locker floated up in my thoughts, but I just kept tramping over the stones and sticks. Our effort worked up an appetite, but we didn't slacken our grueling pace until probing a ferny hummock.

"Can you picture what it's like to live at Lake Charles?" I asked.

"After all this, no thanks. I'll stick to the trailer park. Before the TVA built Lake Charles, the ridge runners had the monopoly. Now growing ganja has replaced distilling corn liquor as the main local commerce."

"Two of the growers attacked us last night."

"Exactly. Something else. Lake Charles belongs to Uncle Sam. A high roller—his name slips my mind—deeded it over to score a big tax break."

"How do you know that?"

"The newspapers rolling off the presses interest me."

"Since you're so well read, will a corpse rot fast in the lake water?"

"The carp will eat Mr. X. He can't follow us."

"But his buddy sure can."

Cobb flashed his .44 and a grin. "Bring it on. We're ready."

Doing this felt crazy, but I couldn't think of a better way. Pulling back, we patrolled the higher ground, looking sharp for any cut jungle or terraced slopes, evidence of the pot farming and a clue pointing us to Edna. The sun had burned off the haze often veiling the hills and heated the morning into a Turkish bath.

Sweat patched our shirts as the lactic acid tightened my hamstrings. Completing a circuit of Lake Charles before sunset let us enjoy one of a few rests. An acute need was potable water. I'd brought no canteen and dealing with dehydration or heat exhaustion interrupted our quest to find Edna. First, I brought up last night.

"Cobb, what do you know about these people?"

"Most dealers that I know are mellow, but we're knocking these ya-hoos out of the box. They crossed the line, and I ain't having it."

"Did they really grab Edna?"

"Must be. What else is there?"

"She fell in the lake and drowned."

He jutted his jaw at me. "She always wore her lifejacket, and she didn't drown."

We resumed our trek and crossed several dry washes. Heat and bugs diverted my attention from hunger and thirst. An unexpected stroke of luck was running across a natural spring gurgling from the rock wall. Seeing it first, he pointed, and I nodded. We skated over the loose pebbles, fell on all fours, and scooped up the water in our cupped hands so icy cold it made my teeth ache. It slaked my thirst but not my mounting frustration.

"We couldn't find our asses with a damn flashlight."

His pupils shrank to hot beads. Anger was a rare emotion in him, but I saw plenty of it now. "Your negativity flat out sucks, you know, Brendan?"

"Hey, I'm just being realistic."

"Think positive instead. We'll get her and go home today."

"Did you forget about last night's dust up?"

"No, but give us my wife, and I've got no more gripes. What the dope growers do up is their shit, not mine."

"Your ex-wife," I corrected him.

"Not quite yet because I never signed the divorce papers."

"Actually that's good to hear."

"We'll work it out. You'll see. Everybody will."

"Sure you will."

We saw the natural spring had allowed a homesteader to haul up the water probably in homemade cedar buckets. A dim trail through the grove of ancient black walnuts led us to a sunken rectangle that was lined with dry-fit river stones, the foundation to his house.

Cobb tipped his head at the spillage of stones on the end. "The chimney?"

"Most likely. They could probably erect one inside of a day."

"Doing stonework isn't brain surgery. We could finish it in a day, too."

"Sure we could. Just a stroll in the sun."

The glass shards littering the ground came from the broken flasks of Lydia E. Pinkham's Vegetable Compound and Dr. Kilmer's Female Remedy, the patent medicines women once took for menopause. Mostly alcohol, no wonder it left them feeling perkier. Tiger lilies and summer lilac blooming at the steps were a woman's aesthetic touch. Living in the middle of nowhere, did the homesteader's wife pine for female company? The regrets came up over my break up with Salem, and to be frank, I missed her. Or maybe I just missed the steady thing I thought we'd had going.

The house's square footage looked spacious enough to raise a tribe, and I debated their fate. Uncle Sam had no qualms to grab up more parkland by kicking the families out of their native homes. Or had the TVA's earth dam creating Lake Charles flooded out their place? Then my darker fears returning over Edna's welfare almost crushed me. A sidelong glance at Cobb prompted me to take out my .44.

"Magnums are cool, huh?" he said.

Inspecting the high-power loads seated in my .44, I grunted in disgust.

He reacted. "I'm hearing more negativity. Self-defense is perfectly legal."

"Slice and dice it any way you like, Cobb, but killing is still just killing."

"Get off it. They pushed us into a corner, and it's not our damn fault how it played out."

I grunted again, still in disgust.

CHAPTER ELEVEN

What Cobb and I sought—marijuana shrubs—grew in lush abundance in the homesteader's nearby cow lot. Resembling giant ragweeds, the pot plants with resinous, sticky buds and serrated leaves sucked up the water. That accounted for the sawed-off lengths of the white plastic piper. The pot growers had it in mind to pump the water from Lake Charles to irrigate their cash crop. For now, they toted the water in the 5-gallon buckets we saw. They'd camped in the lot's northernmost corner. Smoking dope made them sick, given the Pepto-Bismol and Vicks Nyquil bottles strewn over the ground. I looked in vain under the laurel bushes for a gasoline-powered irrigation pump, and Cobb jiggled a propane tank used to heat a portable stove.

"Pops said the GIs in Korea heated their C-rations over the Claymore mines."

"That was a ticklish operation," I said, unsure if Mr. Kuzawa's colorful war stories had much grounding in truth.

The charred stones formed an old fire ring. I gauged its cold ashes between my fingers. We arrived too late, but we rounded up more damning evidence. The cheesecloth bundles swaying from the tree limbs just out of reach had air cured the green pot cuttings.

"Come look at this." He jerked a thumb over his shoulder. At every three paces, I saw the holes—ten in a row—dug in the rocky soil. "They yanked out the whole root bulb."

"Sure, roast the roots to grind them up and smoke. How many growers?"

He counted the empty cans in the garbage pile. "Two men for two days cut and cured the bud before they moved on to the next ripe patch."

"That gives us a chance to catch up. Tell you what. I'll give them their props. This is a pretty slick operation."

"It's slicker yet. The pot raised on Uncle Sam's land removes culpability." He saw my blank face. "Uncle Sam as the property owner can't very well arrest himself, can he?"

"No, but I can see one liability: the forest fires."

He nodded. "August is our driest month."

"I believe the fires are the work of a local arsonist."

"Again it's not brain surgery to do. You can tape several matches to a lit Marlboro and leave it smoldering under some dry twigs. They catch fire and you create enough fire to burn down the woods. The Marlboro butt left behind looks inconspicuous enough."

The trick new to me, I wondered where he'd learned it.

An hour later, we rested on our haunches in the meager shadow cast by a pulpit-shaped rock. Our sweaty faces lined in weary frustration gave the score. After locating the first pot plants in the old cow lot, we searched without success near the lake and then further back in the woods.

"So, a local just tends a few illegal herbs," I said.

"You'll never convince me of it." He tweaked his bandanna headband. "See how this logic tracks for you. The grower sows his secret plants back here. He cultivates them and harvests a bumper crop. So he peddles a few nickel bags in town and suddenly finds the buyers are beating a path to his door. He rakes in the profits he never dreamed of and sees a windfall. These boonies are chock full of these sunny meadows, so ramping up his operations is a cinch."

"Why does he spread out planting the pot gardens?"

"Smaller plots lessen the risk the narcs will discover them. Dozens of dinky gardens might be growing in the outback."

"Sounds like you're on the right track."

We resumed our search. Soon intersecting an old bush road and following it, we still looked in the wrong places. The ankle high ruts we tromped in commemorated the sweat equity of the earlier travelers coming this way. My steady plod let me drift off remembering Mr. Kuzawa's tales of his logger days. My father last heard from in Alaska probably toiled for a timbering outfit now that the roughnecks had completed the big pipeline. Whenever I lit out for Valdez to see him, I'd take along a solid idea of what the loggers did for a paycheck.

Mr. Kuzawa recounted with awe the mule-drawn wagons and later the flatbed trucks hauling out the prime oak, hickory, and maple logs. The crosscut saw and broadax were the early loggers' tools. An industrious worker earned a livable wage off timbering to sell the logs for railroad ties. In the late 1950s, chainsaws hit the market, and loggers cut down the trees near the ground. Up until then with their hand crosscut saws, the loggers felled the trees at waist level, leaving behind the dozens of high stomps that I now observed rotting around us.

I'd laid up big plans. The Fishbacks, father and son, would forge an unbeatable team where I envisioned us filing the papers to incorporate our family timber company. Maybe I'd keep the books, and Angus would recruit the logger crew. Later Cobb could fly up after we got the business rolling. He'd make a good supervisor and we'd be our own bosses. I gave us a better than fair shot to make it since the housing construction boom screamed out for wood. The pleasure to think about running such an outfit warmed me with deep satisfaction.

Slogging along as the wagon mules had done, I tramped behind Cobb. My boots rubbed the blisters on the soles of my feet as my adrenaline waned. I saw a cherry tree a black bear had mauled, and my hungry stomach kicked. Cobb stopped to mop his forehead with his bandana. Sweat soaked through the backs of our shirt fabric. I flopped down beside him.

"We can search in a thousand hidey-holes, and a thousand more will pop up. Sorry I took us on a wild goose chase. You had it right. We should've driven to get help in Yellow Snake."

"We'll get to Edna." I paused. "Think positive as a great man once told me."

At an anxious scan of our front, he frowned. "We can't search in near enough real estate today."

"We've gone too far to turn back."

"I'm still game." He pointed a finger. "This bush road must soon hit the state road."

"That's how the loggers' work flow ran," I said. "Flagging a truck on the state road might give us a lift back to my truck."

He agreed and we set off again. One of us in each wheel rut, we moved two abreast. Our rhythmic pace focused my mind. Edna and her captors had to be near us. How did I know? I didn't really, but I didn't want to give up even a skosh of hope. Think positive: I liked that motto. Turning the corner in the bush road, we came upon the wood smoke. I sniffed at it again.

He gave me an excited look. "Is it the growers?"

"Got to be."

The .44 appeared in his fist. "Creep in and overpower the bastards. Pick up Edna. Go on home. Drink PBR. Life is good."

"Sounds like my kind of a plan."

At thirty paces from the bush road, I spotted the bluish tendrils of smoke wafting through the cedar copse. He fanned off just to my right, and we prowled in closer, hunched behind the scraggly cedars, and spied on a campsite. The green-stick tripod held a black steel pot suspended on a chain over the campfire.

The army olive-drab ponchos fastened together created a pup tent. Wicker creel baskets, fishing rods, bait buckets, and hip waders sat by the pup tent. Two sleeping bags and a couple of quilts showed through the pup tent's triangular opening. The sunlight slanting in also fell on a marine band radio.

"It's just the two bubbas. You've got to like those odds."

"Oh yeah." I wiped the sweat from my palm creases and clutched to the .44 tighter.

"I see the new fishing rods, but the bubbas aren't off fishing."

"They're off getting the ganja weed." My gaze joined the deeper woods. "I wonder if Edna is with them."

"Let's see what we have here."

The bright clearing we moved into had a deserted air. No weapons grabbed my notice. I tried to breathe normal and relax my muscles as I ambled over to the trash mound. Our bubbas were no alfresco chefs judging by the pork-and-beans cans, their main staple. It was a skaggy campsite.

"When will they return?" I asked Cobb.

"When they get hungry, and we'll be ready—"

Whish!

From the corner of my eye, I saw the movement of a coppery blur breaking the humid air.

"Ugh!"

Cobb had groaned. Horror riveted my eyes on the four-feather fletching and the sleek carbon shaft to the hunting arrow pierced in the middle of his chest.

CHAPTER TWELVE

His knees buckled as his grin fell flat. Blood dark as iodine stained the entry point of the arrow shaft. His fingers clawed in a feeble effort to grab and yank it from his flatlining heart. I heard the air shushing out of his lungs. He screwed down his eyes as if imploring me to do something. But I felt paralyzed. The last emotion stamped on his graying rictus was complete shock. Rage grabbed my emotions.

My hand was already jerking behind, my fingers digging. The steel lump scraped free from my waistband carry. Swiveling, I chopped up the .44. Only then did I see the killer archer, a tall man. Snapping his eyes down at his crossbow, he fussed with it to notch the next arrow—mine. The bastard cursed at me.

My reflexes were automatic. My arms jacked out, aiming the .44. Its barking muzzle jetted a spurt of flame. The Magnum slug chiseled off a bite of the tree bark. I'd missed the bastard, but I had a better feel for the .44.

His mouth lagging, the archer backpedaled, frantic to raise the cross-bow and plant his next arrow in my heart. I didn't give him the chance. He tripped, and I bulled ahead. Scrambling to his knees, he howled, his eyes stretched in terror. Desperate in his last stand, he hurled the cross-bow at me, and agile as a matador I dodged it.

Again, I fired the .44. Its retort filled my ears. This Magnum slug drilled him in the sternum. I cheered at seeing my bullet hole. He froze stiff, his glassy eyes on me, and then crumbled into a heap. My two insurance slugs gouged two more holes in his chest. His blood frothed at all three holes. The gun smoke burned my eyes, and I coughed. Bitter tears flowing out scalded my cheeks. My nose was running. I spat the snot and tears from my mouth.

"First Edna and now this shit."

My knees gave way as I knelt to the ground. No pulse throbbed in Cobb's jugular. Using the bandana he'd given me, I dried my eyes. It was a shitty way to die. My boy didn't go gentle into any good night. But then who ever does? I was able to wrench out the fatal arrow slick with his blood and wiped off my hands on the bandana.

Sheer willpower curbed the tremors of panic buzzing in me. Break it down, I thought. Use logic. Don't freak as you did after waking in the motel bed next to the corpse Ashleigh. What do I know? I'm alive. That's good. Three men—Mr. X, this archer, and Cobb—lay dead. What comes next? My bruised head was a painful reminder I'd had my fill of dirty sheriffs, so I nixed that idea.

I glanced at the archer. Cobb might've recognized him but I didn't. The archer's pockets yielded a Case knife, but like Mr. X, he carried no wallet or personal ID. The criminals at Lake Charles liked break the law and keep their anonymity. The Case knife sailed into the cedars.

When I flipped him over, I recoiled. Cobb's .44 Magnum load had stamped a hole in the dead archer's chest, tore through his lung, and exited, chewing the flesh into raw mincemeat. I retched before slamming the crossbow into a tree. My inclination was to ditch the dead archer in Lake Charles, but I'd no boat handy. Worse yet, I saw no leads pointing me to Edna. After all this grief, I still had nothing positive to show for it.

Crouched by the campfire, I set a stick's glowing hot end to a Marlboro, inhaled, and did some thinking. My trial rolled up the Thursday after next. What a scream. I'd dropped enough corpses back there to film a Jonestown documentary. I took a final drag before the cigarette butt landed with a hiss in the pot of water. Then I upturned it to extinguish the hissing coals. I saw no gain to spark a fire in the dry woods. Next, I tugged out the bedrolls from the pup tent with mixed results.

The pungent body odor gagged me, but a sealed fifth of a mid-shelf whiskey rolled out. Cool. I fiddled with the knobs on the marine band radio but only raised static. I dropped the radio on a flat rock and disabled it. Inspecting the fishing outfits confused me. Two fishing rods meant two bubbas, and I'd killed the archer, so, that left me with Bubba Two.

My heart drummed as I trudged over to Cobb. The .44 lifted from his beltline was my backup weapon. His Buck knife might be useful, too. It was three o'clock, and I had to find Bubba Two and get to Edna. I used the Buck knife to hack off the sassafras branches and while layering them over both casualties, I sensed Bubba Two was deployed behind a blow-down tree some twenty paces away. Fair was fair. I'd arrange springing my own ambush. Acting casual, I scoped the campsite one last time. My eyes teared at seeing where Cobb lay. I pivoted and left, hustling into the firs.

How far did Bubba Two lag behind me? A hundred yards into the firs, I came to a fallen log. Hatching a plan on the fly, I plunked down on it as if to rest. Had I glimpsed a pants leg dodging behind the boulder a penny toss from me? I didn't light a Marlboro. Nicotine left me too lazy. My hand was a visor at my eyes lifting to gauge how much daylight I had left. As if in a big rush, I bounded off only to fake my trip over a stone and wrenching my ankle. Grabbing it, I grimaced as if I was in crippling pain.

Dragging my bum ankle, I staggered back to the log and waited for Bubba Two. Would he take the bait and ambush a wounded man? I fisted both .44s and tensed to drop behind the log and rip out a heavy barrage of Magnum loads. My slow count hit twenty but nothing happened. A sheepish red then flushed into my face.

"Who's out there?" I hollered.

Still nothing. I'd outfoxed myself because there was no Bubba Two. I returned to the shadows now engulfing the campsite. The two corpses in this heat smelled ripe. My more careful search pulled a green matchbook from the dead archer's pocket. My eyebrows hiked as my thumb pad traced the gold bird embossed on the matchbook. I'd cadged a similar matchbook from the Bell canning jar in the Chewink Motel's office. My curiosity in the dead archer bumped up a few notches.

I grabbed a shock of his greasy hair and wrested his zitty face to the direct sunlight. I still didn't know him from Adam's housecat. My eyes roved to the ganja curing bags lashed to the tree branches. It made sense this pot grower also smoked his product. So then where did he stash his boodle?

The pup tent drew me over. Its poles ripped out of the sand and, enduring the gamey body odor, I peeled away the ground cloth. The prone sleeper had left his foot, hip, and shoulder impressions in the sand. A wet patch of sand in the middle looked recently dug out.

"The fool buried his dope."

I plunged in the Buck knife. Sure enough, its blade struck an object. My hands shoveled out the sand and unearthed a plastic baggie. I sniffed at its opening—oh yeah, badass reefer. I also scared up a packet of Zig-Zag papers, skinned me a fat joint, and struck a match to light it.

I stalled, mumbling. "Getting blitzed is a bad percentage play. I better not do it."

Grinding out the match and joint, I rejected the devil's weed. My kicking the fishing equipment was in frustration. The wicker creel basket rolled off, and the yellow parrot barrette thrown out gleamed in the sunlight. Joy swelled in me. It had to be Edna's barrette. I held the proof in my palm she'd been here. Maybe she dropped the barrette on purpose. After taking the fifth of whiskey, I quit the campsite, moving out again under the firs.

After holding to a dogtrot for I don't know how long, I hit a wall and flamed out. My eyelids grew leaden, and my knees wobbly. A chinaberry tree offered me some shade from the swelter. I flumped down on the soft moss and sobbed a tight gulp before a fitful nap overcame me. From the start, I sensed this dream favored the same motif.

Ashleigh Sizemore, a bundle of curves and sass in a tight lavender gown, was fussing in her matching clutch bag. She lit a rolled joint, puffed it, and offered it to me. "Brendan, let's party."

"Thanks, but I don't need anymore grief."

"J.D. told me in the van you're a wimp." She snapped shut her clutch bag. "Relax some, hey? I won't devour you like Circe did Ulysses' mariners after she cast them into a herd of swine."

"I've never heard of her or them, but don't you owe me a few explanations like on that train wreck you left me at the Chewink?"

"Honestly, this uptight and cranky, you're a regular grinch. Okay, I'll give you one revelation: you didn't kill me."

"I reached that conclusion on my own."

"But you never heard me say it until now. You have a quest to go on."

"What sort of a quest?"

"Simple. Find and catch my killer, and you can save us both."

"Listen you, this is my life. Nothing makes sense in it since I partied with you. Fatal ambushes. Blood-chilling dreams. Pot gardens. Bum arrests. Sadistic sheriff's deputies. I've just about had it with you."

"Your nailing my killer is our way out of this." She began fading to a temporary black.

"You don't leave me much choice."

Then a Eureka moment shook me awake. My heart banged high in my throat because I knew the right person to call and give me a hand. Matter of fact, he'd know how to get to the bottom of things, extra pronto, as he liked to say.

CHAPTER THIRTEEN

"Speak up … you say my boy is dead?"

The man's growl erupted from deep in his chest. My palm capped the handset while my other hand swiped at the welling tears.

"Brendan? Are you there? Okay, that's good. I thought you guys went fishing at Lake Charles."

"We did but then we ran into some flak."

"Where are you, son?"

"I'm still at Lake Charles," I said, staring at the clapboard siding to the cash-and-carry store we'd driven by on Friday.

I heard Mr. Kuzawa snatch an audible breath. "Who the fuck did this to my boy?"

"I better not give out the details over the line. Meet me instead."

"No sweat. Where?"

"Near the spillway at the Lake Charles dam there's an old parking area the hunters and fishermen like to use."

"I know it. When?"

"It's got to be tonight, sir."

"These same shitbirds also shanghaied Edna?"

"It looks that way to me."

"I'll see you there extra pronto."

"You might want to come armed for trouble."

"Ain't no might about it. We've gone to war. This is a dogfight to the finish. Some motherfucker will pay. Big time. Over and out."

I racked the handset and hauled up the phone directory on its chain. My shaky fingers struck another match, riffled through the sticky pages, and tore out the page listing the Tennessee State Police. Cobb had told me the state boys were pros, and I might need the pros on my side since the Yellow Snake law reeked of corruption. My knee nudged the telephone booth door to collapse outward.

As I stepped back into the muggy night, for some odd reason I visualized Angus placing phone calls and mailing me postcards at such a rural store in Valdez. I was at a loss to say why Valdez exerted its psychic tug on me, but it did, and it grew fiercer everyday. Could I drive there in three or four days? I could use a boost from him right now, but as always, he wasn't there for either of us.

Alarm jolted me back to the present. Mr. Kuzawa and I were off to do whatever. 'Gone to war,' he'd said over the phone. 'A dogfight to the finish.' He growled like a junkyard dog, but wasn't he venting? Just then, I heard a car engine drone out on the state road. A pair of headlamps stabbing the dark sent me scurrying around the store's rear corner. I spilled to the dirt before peering out, glad to watch the threatening car chuff by the store, and me.

Simon the bait shop owner had told us their new packing factory ran a graveyard shift, so maybe a local was off to pluck chicken feathers for a paycheck. The car's red taillights dissolved in the dark as I breathed again. I decided to break into the store, get my supplies, and pay for the damages. There was no rear door. So I used Cobb's Buck knife to jimmy a window, crawled feet-first through the portal, and landed on my rump. I shut my eyes and reopened them, adjusting to the interior's womblike darkness. The burlap I rose up from smelled fusty.

My lit match produced a candle stub's glow as I did a 360. The nearest shelves displayed rusty plow points, horseshoes, and hand saws—our region's antiques out for sale. Collectors flocked to the lowland emporiums for the sexy swag like family heirloom furniture. Our ancestors couldn't afford to buy furniture, only plow points to till the rocky soil and raise beans—you know, to eat.

Two-cell flashlights were also out for sale. I used care not to play one's beam over any window and tip off a passerby. A calico resting curled up on the countertop didn't flick a whisker. I thought it stuffed by a taxidermist until I stroked the silky, purring fur. I missed Mrs. Wang's Oscar, but this was a bad time to get sentimental over cats.

"We'll need rations."

I snapped out a brown paper sack from under the checkout counter and smelled the fruity whiff of pot smoke. The damn cannabis was everywhere. I bagged a few canned delicacies like sardines packed in mustard and the less appealing Spam. I stuffed in a fistful of beef jerky, but I skipped the granola bars sold to the leaf peeper tourists. The calico's amber eyes gleamed at me. It did a subpar job as a burglar alarm, a point in my favor.

After I scribbled down my purchases with their estimated prices on a scrap of butcher paper, I computed the sum. I started rechecking my figures but figured nuts on it. An Andy Jackson, our state's most lauded hero, went under the calico's paw. The sleepy storeowner might grouch in the morning, but he earned a tidy profit without having to lift a finger. As an afterthought, I fattened the tip with a fiver, peeled open a sardine tin, and gave the purring calico another affectionate pat.

I polished off the sardines and pitched aside the tin. The same portal was my exit, and I left the store. Carrying both .44s in my pockets, I banged my shins on a rail fence while I moved toward the state road. My footfall slapped in a dogtrot over the asphalt while the dark hush grew deafening. The brutal image of a hostile arrow or bullet piercing my chest hectored me.

There's too much death, I shuddered. All your life you busted your ass, paid your taxes, and bathed daily. Then one day the ax fell, and you scrapped like a shithouse rat just to stay alive. I switched the bulky paper bag to cradle in my other arm, and the cans rattled together. The wood smoke lay acrid and sooty in the air from the fires devouring the treed ridges. I felt nothing but pity for the fire crews knocking down a dollar over minimum because they earned every nickel.

Until the present, I'd nothing against the local pot farmers, but their twisted shit had crossed my family, and thinking about it just PO'd me more. I was damn tempted to carry on Cobb's vendetta against them, but first I'd go find Edna.

***

The mucky stench to Lake Charles grew stronger at my approach to the earth dam. Moving on the pads of my feet, I advanced, halting every four steps, my radar alert for any trouble. At my next pause, I flinched. A hard cylinder had screwed into my ear. My balls rode up as I identified the hard cylinder as a steel gun barrel.

"Pass-phrase?" asked the man with cat paws for feet.

"No pass-phrase. It's just me, Brendan. What did you drive?"

Mr. Kuzawa took the muzzle to the 12-gauge from my ear. It was good to hear again. He abandoned the deeper shadows. Several inches over six feet and built husky like Lee Majors with a bricklayer's shoulders, Mr. Kuzawa used a deceptive shuffle. He liked a flattop buzz cut like seen in the Steve Roper comic strip. His chin, these days beardless, jutted at me.

"A trucker pal dropped me off at the state road, and I took a shortcut through the woods. Spin me up again."

"Cobb, Edna, and I drove to Lang's Teahouse on Saturday. We had Lake Charles all to ourselves, fishing and boating. Then Edna threw a hissy fit and ripped off on the jet ski. That's when the shit started to hit the fan."

"That fucking crotch rocket is an abomination. I kick myself for lending her the money. Did Cobb and she bicker again over his drinking?"

"Naturally. Cobb and I returned to the old marina, but she never showed. So we left and scouted the boonies until sunset. Worried sick, we returned and camped at the old marina. Two hicks sneaked in to bushwhack us, and I greased one of them."

"At night? Do you see with cat eyes?"

"A lucky shot in the dark is all."

"Boy, I'll say. Give me the rest."

"At daybreak, I ditched his weighted corpse in Lake Charles, and we bugged out after Edna. Our hike was rugged going. We bungled across a pot garden, and further on we hit a campsite. As we cased it, a grower armed with a crossbow shafted an arrow through Cobb. I'm sorry. He never saw or knew what struck him."

Mr. Kuzawa groaned and ruffled his brawny shoulders. "Okay, okay. Where's my boy's body now?"

"He's still at the campsite underneath the tree branches I cut." Telling what I'd done sounded pathetic, and my gut muscles clenched.

"Holy Jesus, how can something like this happen to a father?" Mr. Kuzawa shifted in his stance. "My boy can keep. Our first mission is to rescue your sister." He thrust the hard cylinder at me. "I requisitioned this 12-gauge, and it's yours."

"Did you bring any grenades or bazookas?" I said, trying for a joke.

"I can get my hands on any C4 explosives we might need."

"I'll just take your word for it."

We left the earth dam for the gloomy dark woods. My flashlight beam picked up a rabbit trail that we followed. The tangy pitch pine cleared my sinuses. I sensed the proximity of Lake Charles that had attached its psychic tentacles to me. I'd almost broken free, getting as far as the cash-and-carry store where I then teamed with Mr. Kuzawa to return. My best opportunity to reach Edna had to lie along the shores of Lake Charles. The gut-wrenching specter of Cobb's death appalled me. I'd grown too callous over seeing the spilled blood. I'd pray but I hadn't attended Mass, recited a rosary, or made a Confession since my early teens.

"Wait up, Brendan. Your hands are full. If we plow into a shit storm, that's all she wrote. Ditch those damn cans. I hate Spam anyway. Don't get your bowels in an uproar. We'll live off the land."

"Can you be more specific?" I asked, leery to trash any food.

"We'll be scroungers. Save the hooch. I like how it fires my blood."

I rummaged inside the paper bag and pocketed the other sardines. He traded me a clutch of 00-buckshot shells for the beef jerkies but rebuffed my offer to take one of Cobb's .44s.

"Pop guns aren't for me. No, the 12-gauges are boss. In fact, one night before the Chosin Reservoir campaign, I lit a blowtorch to crop off the barrel to a 12-gauge—"

"I'll just go and get rid of these cans," I said, not up for listening to any war stories. I went down to the shore and slung the bag to splat into Lake Charles. By the time of my return, Mr. Kuzawa had cracked open and drained a third of the whiskey bottle, giving his eyes a spooky radioactive glint. I got the bone-chilling impression that he viewed us as a pair of leathernecks back fighting it out on the Chosin Reservoir.

"Did this big bug kidnap Edna?"

"She vanished from the same area, and I found her barrette lying in their campsite."

"Don't let it drive you nuts, son. We'll soon evacuate her." He chambered a 00-buckshot load into his 12-gauge.

As we took off again, I forced a self-deprecating chuckle. "I feel ridiculous marching through the boonies armed like two vigilantes."

"We'll be the rangers."

"No-no, uh-uh. We're nothing like them," I said, knowing their leader Cullen didn't let rational thinking govern his often rash actions. We had to be smarter than he was.

"We're not near the campsite, are we?" asked Mr. Kuzawa.

"Two hours walking. You know, I fixed Cobb's killer. He'd no I.D. on him, but he's dead."

"A commendable action and you've my thanks, but this big bug gave the orders. So now I'll go squash the big bug."

"Kill him?" I arched a hard glance at him.

He gave me a nod. "I'm trembling to explode with rage, and I can't pull out even if I tried. Are you with me or not?"

"All right." I waved at him to press on. "I'm behind you."

"That's all I wanted to hear from you."

Lake Charles was our visible landmark as we crossed a hilly pine forest. Soon the trunks and boulders clarified in the gathering daylight, and a great horned owl, all wings, swooped down at us. Mr. Kuzawa laughed at my cowering. The laurel branches slashed at our pumping thighs, and skirting the boulders slowed our progress. At last, Mr. Kuzawa gave a shout.

"Whoa, Brendan. Take five, son. Going at this clip, I'll keel over from a coronary."

"Blame it on the elevation." I bent over at the waist, bracing my hands on my knees, my lungs also a wheezing bellows. "The oxygen runs thinner up here."

"Uh-huh. Never mind I don't look a day over fifty-five or your pack-a-day habit."

"Don't slam my cigarettes. Their tar counteracts the ink fumes eating away at my lung tissue."

"Sure, you're the Six Million Dollar Man." Mr. Kuzawa shrugged back his bullish shoulders. "Is there less backstabbing at work? Cobb didn't seem to think so."

"Things could always be better. Brothers still don't speak, but the past three years we've done well enough to turn a profit and get our annual bonus. You've got to like that."

"That strike took place—what was it?—twenty-odd years ago. The outside agitators were behind it. Pierre Spartacus split Umpire down the middle. The sides drew up, and it was a local war." Jutting his chin, Mr. Kuzawa scoffed. "What a waste. Why do the stubborn pressmen still fight that battle? Let bygones be bygones, I'd say to them."

My cynical glance saw him nod. Longerbeam Printery wasn't a jewel of a job, but I worked there, and he hadn't for years. What did he know about it? The bitter, deep rancor would never let up. Some men were born to bear grudges. The strike ended before I was born, but I had to work in its ugly aftermath, not much fun on some days.

"Rested up?" I was on my feet.

He motioned with his 12-gauge to usher me off down the swale made a streambed in rainy April. My two-fisted grip to my 12-gauge didn't let up. The .44s in my pockets hit my thighs. Perspiration oiled my palms, and I wiped them on my bandana. My hand sweats were a detox by-product, and I would probably never get over the physical craving to fire up a joint. My tongue felt dry as a stick of chalk. If I ever wanted to detox again, I'd pick a less nerve-wracking time than it was right now. He knew I hadn't slept in twenty-four hours. At the first dry, mossy patch, we bivouacked on his garbage bags spread out for ground cloths, one to each side of a fallen log.

Like a woodchuck, I nestled in a fetal ball position, wishing we'd a tarp to shelter us. The horror of arrows sliced from crossbows replayed behind my closed eyelids, and I feared a fatal arrow had lanced Edna. To calm down, I recited the words to a prayer: "Hail Mary, full of grace, the Lord is with thee, blessed art thou . . ."

* * *

In next to no time, a hand jostled me awake, and I blinked up. My grainy eyesight focused on Mr. Kuzawa crouched low behind the log and murmuring.

"We've got uninvited guests."

I pulled up to my knees, and my fingers shucked out the shells from my pocket. Two shells spilled into the moss where I left them. Swallowing hard, I fed the ammo into the 12-gauge's breech, slotting in a full eight-shot load. "Where are they?"

"Above us. I heard a silhouette slip along the ridge top. They're out of our range, but I can snake my way up and ice them. Easy as pie."

"You *heard* a shadow move on the ridge?"

"When I'm in my foxhole mode, I doze in spurts. It's a handy knack you never forget."

Wishing it was dusk bringing on the dark, and not dawn bringing on the sunlight, I had limited visibility to see much along the patchy ridge. "A bear or a buck is out foraging. Try hollering."

He bawled out. "You there up in the trees! What gives?"

"Ahoy. Who have I the pleasure of addressing?" replied a man's cultured voice from above us.

"Jerry Kuzawa."

"Mr. Kuzawa … is that you, sir?"

"That's what I said. Ain't that you, Herzog?"

My confusion cleared. Herzog my lawyer had told me that he planned to scope out Lake Charles for hunting sites. A memory of our pre-trial meeting I kept avoiding added to my irritation.

"Come down and my 12-gauge won't dust off your balls," said Mr. Kuzawa.

"No cause to perpetrate any violence, Kuzawa."

Mr. Kuzawa's militant eyes darted to mine. "Why is he on the prowl at sunrise?"

"He belongs to the gentlemen's hunt club," I replied. "He takes himself for a mountain man."

"Yeah, and I'm Mary Fucking Poppins."

A lumbering gait marked his course off the ridge and down through the trees. Besides his disturbing my sleep, hunger and frustration also left me in a pissy mood.

"Seeing you here makes me wonder," said Herzog.

"I could say vice versa," said Mr. Kuzawa.

The oafish Herzog halted within spitting distance where his Aqua Velva scent swept over us. "I'm out reconnoitering because my hunting lodge makes it a practice to prepare early. Next week Dr. Smith will race his red ticks and start their field conditioning. He's heard Lake Charles teems with game. Have you spotted any turkey scratchings? Or wing feathers dropped under the pines?" Herzog shifted the strap to the brown leather game pouch that Pete Rojos had fixed.

"We've seen the usual boar hog wallows, but nothing in the way of turkeys," replied Mr. Kuzawa.

"No toms are feeding or roosting in this stinking sump," I said. "Paranoid is my middle name so seeing a hunting license will help to back up your claim."

Unflustered, Herzog produced his wallet and showed me his state hunting license. It was current. Being legal was a lawyer's stock in trade. "If only you were as conscientious in our meeting for your trial prep."

"My sister Edna went missing. Did you see or hear anything?"

"Edna? Lost?" Returning his wallet to his pocket, he wagged his head. "If I'd seen her, I'd have shared it with you."

My gaze appealed to Mr. Kuzawa. "How do I cope with this crap?"

Herzog shrugged. "It's the God's truth, Brendan. But again, when do we sit down and map out our defense strategy? Your trial is right around the corner."

"With you on my team, why should I sweat it?"

He turned to Mr. Kuzawa. "Mr. Fishback's surliness dims his odds to win an acquittal. Can't you reason with him?"

"Brendan is always his own man."

"We still have a little time. How did Edna get lost?"

"Brendan and my boy Cobb walked up on a pot farm and startled the guards." Mr. Kuzawa tossed me the ball.

By now sick of telling it, I chronicled our sordid adventure, summarizing with, "The greedy bastards killed Cobb, and we think kidnapped Edna."

"Good Lord." The shaken Herzog scratched his chin stubble. "Did just a few pot plants provoke that much violence?"

Mr. Kuzawa took that one. "These shitbirds turning a fast buck have no regard for human life."

"Any idea who we're speaking of?"

"A few locals probably peddle grass on the side, but this is much more ambitious. I have to figure a big bug grows beaucoup dope around Lake Charles."

"That's a shock to hear." Herzog widened his stance in a pose he used for delivering his courtroom arguments. The game pouch added the absurd prop. "You've certainly concocted some wild-eyed accusations."

Anger left me snappy. "Nothing about it is concocted."

He took a haughtier tone. "I counsel you already in legal troubles to cease this action."

"Stick your counsel where the monkey puts the whistle."

"Brendan, let Herzog have his say."

"Kuzawa is right. You'd better take this trial more seriously. If you end up executed at Riverbend, my conscious will be clear because I'll know I did my best defending you."

"I don't have time for this tired shit," I said. "Edna needs my help."

"Maybe I can assist in your search. I'm here anyway, and you're my client. Your trial is a week from next Thursday, and I can see firsthand how much this distracts you."

"How much does this extra help cost me?"

"It's all included in the same price, of course."

"Even if it is, buzz off, Herzog. We'll do fine."

Mr. Kuzawa's gnarled knuckles rested on my shoulder. "Not so fast, Brendan. Beefing up our ranks improves our odds of success. Plus you did pay good money for Herzog's help. Why turn away his offer?"

I clammed up, realizing I'd lost the argument. For now.

CHAPTER FOURTEEN

Growing anxious to find Cobb's body where I'd left it, Mr. Kuzawa set our grinding pace. Herzog's gangly strides bringing up the rear sandwiched me between the two larger, older men. I craved smoking a cigarette but now only a quarter-mile from the growers' campsite, we soldiered on. It'd been my suggestion we kick off our search for Edna from there since that's where I'd found her barrette. The sky's pearly overcast, a mix of the wood smoke and haze off the lake, blotted out the morning sun.

Famished, I made an ambulatory breakfast off the tin of sardines. Their rusty taste reminded me of human blood, and I spat out the repugnant mouthful. A log bridge took us to the last cove, and we cut by a bronze plaque left for a firefighter ("Amos O'Doul, 1925-56") who'd perished here in the line of duty. My mood fell into a grimmer pit. Herzog's croak said he wanted a break, and we rested in the next patch of shade.

"Herzog, you're a courthouse regular." A breeze mussed Mr. Kuzawa's wiry, gray hair. "What's the inside slant there on the local pot scene?"

"Nothing really consequential."

"Except we now suspect a big bug grows it here in abundance."

A thumbnail scratched at Herzog's chin stubble. "Are you sure? The news media reports the lion's share of dope is smuggled over the Rio Grande."

"True but smuggling in dope from México or Bogotá attracts unwanted attention, especially at the border checkpoints. The beauty of homegrown pot is removing those risks."

"I still urge you not to pursue this rash action."

"Why not?" I asked Herzog.

"My professional role is to play the voice of reason. Plainly put, I don't approve of what I perceive as your brand of rough frontier justice."

"If your boy got killed, you'd feel different."

"It was inhumane and tragic, I agree. But the rule of law will rectify it, not you both acting as his avengers."

To head off my rising anger, I shouldered my 12-gauge. "We better get a move on."

Mr. Kuzawa emptied the whiskey fifth. "Brendan, walk point." He tossed the bottle, and it smashed on a rock pile. "You have the best feel for this theater of operations."

Hearing his military jargon—"theater of operations"—suggested again that he put us in a different spot than Lake Charles, Tennessee. We'd been teleported to 1950 and deployed in the stark, rocky hills behind the Chosin Reservoir. We held the rat-infested, ice-rimmed fox-holes and fended off the waves of the Communist infantrymen.

I led us up the next promontory into a shifty breeze wicking the sweat off my forehead. The inky vestige to Lake Charles emerged and other familiar landmarks like Will Thomas Mountain grew in clarity. My hope grew to greet Edna huddled by her campfire and squeal in joy to see us. A shallow ravine came before the stand of firs to reach the campsite's rear side.

The rotten meat smell of decay fouled it, and I took short gasps through my mouth. Though death smelled putrid, it tasted even worse. My 12-gauge was a pointer to where beyond the black pot. Head down, Mr. Kuzawa slogged over and crumbled to his knees at Cobb's dead body.

My eyes mashed shut as I cringed at his moan soaring into an anguished, wolf-like howl. My eyes opened. His mouth gaped wider, and he roared out, the agony churning from his mastiff chest. Numb to the core, I retrieved the death arrow, Cobb's blood crusted to its barbed steel point, and I flung it with the busted crossbow into the shrubbery. Jagged angles creasing his face, Herzog paced in wide circles. I wondered if Edna could hear the power to Mr. Kuzawa's keening wail. His final notes trailed off.

"This just ain't right," he said in a hoarse whisper.

Herzog pulled up at his side. "We'll return to my Mercedes and go right on to notify the local authorities."

An old warrior's fury seethed in Mr. Kuzawa's eyes. "Why? For Brendan to get another jailhouse beatdown? Fuck no, we'll bury my dead boy. Make it quick, too. These shitbirds still hold my daughter-in-law."

With smooth deference, Herzog nodded. "I understand, sir. It's always your call to make, of course."

My ink-stained hands felt useless. "We've got no shovels or picks."

Resembling a hoary troglodyte, Mr. Kuzawa brandished a flat stone. His rising shirt cuffs showed the "Semper Fi!" dagger tattooed on his wrist. "We'll just pile on the rocks."

The audacity to his idea freaked me. Appealing for support from Herzog, I saw the attorney—a graduate of the Vanderbilt University Law School, no less—nodding his head in agreement. My wishy-washy counselor switched opinions on a whim, and I distrusted him even more.

"Listen at you." I punched Mr. Kuzawa in the shoulder. "Just listen, will you? You're talking crazy. We have to carry out the body and not build a damn crypt around it. A century ago, that was okay but not in 1979. Am I right, Herzog?"

My turn faced him. His bloodless lips thinned in an exaggerated wince. "The crypt will serve as a temporary container, I'm certain."

"Right. I'll use it as long as I need to keep Cobb on ice," said Mr. Kuzawa.

Cobb kept on ice in a crypt. What shit. Was I alone in my sanity here? I wandered to the tent site and struggled to order my thoughts. Lake Charles' chaos had spiraled into a vortex trapping me at its center. I ached to drive home to my flat. I ached to crack open a cold PBR from the fridge. I ached to erase this weekend. Yeah, I'd go back to work on Monday and breathe the ink fumes, and I'd never bitch about my life again. Scuffing at the loose sand with my boot tip, I unearthed a second plastic baggie stuffed with pot and picked it up.

Mr. Kuzawa's narrow-eyed gaze saw it. "Greed for what you hold in your hand is what killed my boy."

"No, you're wrong." My angry finger pointed at the dead archer under the sassafras branches. "He's the guilty party. So, put the blame on him except he's also dead."

"You're forgetting the big bug's orders to kill trespassers like Cobb and you on sight."

"So what if he did?"

"So now the big bug gets his due."

"Gentlemen please. Your tempers." Then in a surprise move somewhat appeasing me, Herzog posed a compromise. "Our search-and-destroy mission will comb these wilds and eradicate their pot gardens. Socking them in the pocketbook will offer some measure of compensation. At the same time, we can look for Edna, and then we'll reassess where matters stand."

"Then we smash the big bug," said Mr. Kuzawa.

"A distinct possibility, I'm sure."

I glared at the obsequious Herzog nodding like a bobble-head doll. "No, we keep on searching for Edna. But for now, we can build the damn crypt."

We inset the sheets of red slate to forge the liner to Cobb's temporary mausoleum. Mr. Kuzawa swaddled him in the cleanest of the two ponchos used for the pup tent, and I rested his "EAT MORE BASS!" tattooed forearm on his stomach. I waved a blowfly off his bristly black hair. His cadaver's reek burned in my nose, and we hustled to button up the makeshift crypt by stacking and fitting on more slate sheets.

Cobb had one thing right: stonework like erecting a chimney or crypt wasn't brain surgery. We did a passable job. I piled more sassafras branches over the wilted ones to camouflage the dead archer, also a stranger to Herzog and Mr. Kuzawa.

"Leave the shitbird for the wild boars," said Mr. Kuzawa.

Herzog slit his hand on a slate's jagged edge. The klutz used his white linen handkerchief as a crude bandage as he sat down on the overturned black pot. Mr. Kuzawa and I crouched like cowboys. I felt too sick and disgusted to light up a cigarette. Herzog adjusted the game pouch to rest it on his lap.

Anxiety lines furrowed my forehead. Upslope on Will Thomas Mountain was where more cannabis ripened in the other covert glens. Somebody asshole held Edna against her will. I'd little grit left to do more bushwhacking. We left the campsite through the firs left denuded by aphids and adding to Lake Charles' gloom. Herzog pampering his injured hand went first.

CHAPTER FIFTEEN

Our quest for the pot plants paralleled Lake Charles, a dark mirror held up to our souls, and I didn't care to see its reflection. In a quiet part of my mind, I saw us—Edna, Cobb, and me—seated in my cab truck and departing Lang's Teahouse for home in Umpire. But my earnest wish didn't make it happen. Tracking along a flat stretch, we steadied our gait, and my idle thoughts derailed into my habitual reverie.

"Brendan, be a love and lower the blind." Ashleigh tucked in the motel bed sheets pointed her red-tipped finger to direct me.

"I'm on it."

"This motel is so grotty. Our summerhouse is much nicer."

"Your summerhouse?" I lit her Virginia Slim after I made our love nest more private by tugging down the window blind. She inhaled and then vented her smoke into my eyes. What a doll she was.

"It's back on our Gatlinburg estate called Aeaea." She saw my quizzical reaction. "I wondered too and looked up the name. Aeaea is the island where the sorceress Circe held dominion over her male subjects that, if ever disenchanted, she conjured into swine."

I cut in on Ashleigh's mythology lesson. "What about the damn summerhouse?"

"Right, the summerhouse. Well: it's a birch log cabin. A dark lane winds through the trees, making it secluded and ideal for our dissolute purposes."

"Then next time we'll go flop there."

"Brilliant. I can hardly wait." Smiling, her expression turned wistful and enigmatic. "I need a favor."

"What's that?"

"Will you be my bodyguard? I can afford to pay top rates."

"I'd be honored. My friend Cobb can lend me his .44s."

"Hey, I'm not kidding," she said, miffed at hearing my flippancy.

"All right, simmer down and I'll do it. Are you in any immediate danger?"

"No, but what I have in mind is very dangerous."

Wariness served me a dose of caution. "Just how dangerous is it? You see, I charge accordingly."

"Oh, I'm always sure I can meet your price, Brendan."

My eyes refocused, I staggered for a step, my boot almost crushing a corn snake sunning itself on a pancake rock before a grove of beeches shaded our progress. Feces in the wallows made by the wild boars rooting for snails, salamanders, and mushrooms to eat burned out my nose hairs. Something of a grub myself, I knew my porcine lore. Unable to sweat, the boars writhed in the mud's gooey coolness, and the baked on dirt coat also kept off the ticks. The DEET that I smeared on did the same thing.

The boars' upper tusks scraped on the bottom ones to hone them to a razor sharp edge. During the hottest part of the day, they bedded down, and during the cooler night, they foraged. The butchered wild boars offered nutty-tasting pork chops. Their intestines became tripe, and their livers fixed with onions were edible. Shunning food stamps, our religious cousins had starved enough to go shoot and feast on the wild boars. Right now, so could I.

Our wild boars weren't native. One tale I heard as a kid said the pissed off scratch farmers during the Great Depression freed their hogs rather than let the bankers seize them in the foreclosures. Or did Ashleigh's yarn of Circe changing Ulysses' men into swine enjoy credence in Tennessee? After her lovers bored her, Ashleigh also bewitched them into boar hogs driven to root for survival in the Appalachian outback.

We took a sitting break. Mr. Kuzawa wiped a sleeve over his lips. I followed his quiet study of the distant smoke column skirling into the sky. The firefighters struggled to tame the hellish blazes consuming the ridges. My new worry considered if the blazes had trapped and burned Edna to death.

"August is a dry nun's cunt." Mr. Kuzawa flicked his brass Zippo on a Marlboro.

Herzog made a sour face over the earthy metaphor.

"That fire has raged since we got here." I also lit one up.

Herzog tapped out a Marlboro, lit a match to fire it, sucked down, and had a coughing fit.

Mr. Kuzawa laughed. "Lawyer, you better go easy on the cancer sticks."

He made another face.

Mr. Kuzawa looked at me. "Did a lightning bolt hit you on a grassy bald?"

My slight shrug downplayed any amazement. "Yeah and Edna said my heart had quit ticking."

"Did she save your hash?"

"No two ways about it. Lucky for me she knew her CPR."

"While you lay flaked out there dead, by chance, did you spot any white light pulling you to it?"

"Just the opposite. I remember best the sensation of tumbling head over heels through a pitch black abyss."

"The fuck you say. But you're holding up now?"

Again, I shrugged. "The ringing in my ears bugs me the most." My Ashleigh dreams didn't get a mention, at least not until I knew better if I could trust him.

He drew down to the filter and exhaled. "Is the dead girl the one who smoked the dope?"

"It wasn't just her. All of us indulged in her grass."

"Supporting a big dope habit runs some bucks. How did she finance hers?"

"Her father rich as muck gave her a generous allowance." I finished my smoke. Again, the nicotine had blunted my appetite.

Mr. Kuzawa flicked away his butt. Knees crinking, he stretched out his legs. "There's no figuring for the rich."

I stood up with him. Herzog arose and we left, the inept lawyer again put in the lead. As we moved out, I recalled I still owed the Yellow Snake hospital a bushel of money (we'd no medical insurance). Then I thought how Sizemore had issued his violent threats back in May. Here it was August, four months later, and he'd yet to make good on them. I hadn't forgotten his prison cell beatdown, a good reason now to go torch him, but first I had to pull Edna out of her riptide.

* * *

Herzog who first entered a meadow cried out to us. "Brendan, you better see this." On Mr. Kuzawa's heels, I hurried into the meadow bathed in sunlight. "These plants look plenty robust, don't they?"

The cluster of a half-dozen pot shrubs reminded me of the Big Boy tomatoes Mama Jo tended in her vegetable plot.

Flicking his brass Zippo to flame up, Mr. Kuzawa beamed at me. "Burn 'em."

"Not really the best idea," said Herzog. "The smoke might intoxicate us."

"The growers will also smell it and know it's us," I said.

"Then we'll shred the damn contraband," said Mr. Kuzawa.

He and I uprooted the pot shrubs, ripped them apart, and scattered the pieces of stalk, leaf, and stem over the meadow. Our lucky streak extended to the next meadow where we found and demolished more plants. The third meadow had twenty-odd shrubs to trash. Our raid would incense the big bug, and we pulled another step closer to finding Edna. I hurried down and washed off the pot's sticky resin from my hands. Lake Charles' scummy water was hardly any cleaner. I returned, and we rested in the shady verge. Ravenous hunger clawed inside my stomach, and I knew I wasn't alone.

"Kuzawa, I'm on the brink of starvation," said Herzog.

Mr. Kuzawa said nothing, but his stomach also rumbled.

"That Spam I tossed into Lake Charles sounds good right about now."

"We'll make do," said Mr. Kuzawa, unsmiling.

My brow knitted into a frown. "I'm not eating any fish pulled out of Lake Charles if that's what you mean."

"All right, we'll go to Lang's Teahouse, leave in your cab truck, and eat in Yellow Snake," said Mr. Kuzawa.

"Take my keys and go on then," I said. "Bring me a burger and fries because I'm not budging from here as long as Edna is gone or in danger."

Mr. Kuzawa gave my stubborn glare a cool reception. "We can search for her on the way to Lang's Teahouse. Look, we haven't flushed out any shitbirds. I believe Cobb and you mucking around scared them off, and they took Edna with them. Some yahoo in Yellow Snake might give up a lead."

True to character, Herzog nodded in agreement. Feeling outvoted, I felt the cramps grinding my hamstrings since we'd stopped, not to mention the blisters worn on the bottoms of my feet. The bullet wound under my ribs seared with each breath I took. Good thing the rage simmering just under my skin deadened the worst pain.

CHAPTER SIXTEEN

Two hours later, we humped into Lang's Teahouse unscathed, and I un-hitched the double decker trailer. The place had the same odious stench of algae and decay. We took off for Yellow Snake, a carbon copy of Umpire with one notable exception—Yellow Snake fêted its upper crust. Their big money also kept the cancerous sprawl at bay. Piloting my cab truck on the state road, I visualized the wealthy's rarified world where they languished in their chateaus in and around scenic Yellow Snake.

The daughters of the multi-millionaires took their equestrian lessons, attended finishing schools up north in idyllic New England hamlets, and slummed at local The Devil's Own rock concerts. They refined the art of walking with their patrician noses canted in the air without somersault-ing over them. Then I took note of my cynical attitude and hoped it soon cleared up.

"Herzog, are you set for Brendan's trial?" asked Mr. Kuzawa.

Pinned between us, Herzog twisted around. "He'll benefit from my best defense. We only have to meet and prepare."

"Brendan, are you ready to meet with Herzog?"

A jerk of the steering wheel tried to skirt a purple grackle stripping the red, stringy flesh from a road kill opossum. Reacting late, I felt my tires go clunk twice. The heavy-handed symbolism of trampled on the road to Yellow Snake didn't escape me.

"No stress. I've got it covered." I'd had a bellyful of talking about my trial for Ashleigh Sizemore's murder.

Displeasure puckered Herzog's face. "Your priorities are askew, gentlemen. We left two corpses back there, and the authorities are bound to ask of our involvement at Lake Charles."

Mr. Kuzawa clattered his window handle and the wind gusted in to beat our faces. "My boy is one of them." He dredged up something vile from his throat and let it sail out the open window. "Who gives a screw about the dead shitbird?"

Herzog wasn't mollified. "Remember Mr. Sizemore is a heavy swinger. He has political connections, and I know of his law firm by reputation. His attorneys are the best and brightest who play to win, and they usually do."

"Fuck 'em. That's why we've brought you, Herzog."

Flattered, he all but rolled his eyes. "I advise don't trespass on Size-more's estate."

"If we stay on the state road, we can look to our hearts' content, am I not right?"

"From a legal standpoint, you are."

"Then I say legal shaves close enough."

"You'd be foolish to provoke Mr. Sizemore." Herzog braced his hands on the dashboard as we sailed around on a steep curve. "Kuzawa, I don't if you're aware of it or not, but you've got a reputation for raising Cain."

"People like to talk, but some bad shit can't be avoided."

"I disagree. I'm a firm believer it lies within our capacity to turn the other cheek. The choice is ours to make whether to accept or to reject violence as a solution to our conflicts."

Mr. Kuzawa barked out a laugh, and his voice rasped. "Think so? The day my draft notice arrived, what was I supposed to do? Turn the other cheek and not go serve? No sir, I sucked it up and reported for my military service in Mr. Truman's police action."

"You should've appealed it as a conscientious objector."

"Suppose everybody took that ticket out? Uncle Sam issued me an M12 shotgun and said go bag a few renegade gooks in the yo-yo war. So I carried out orders. I lost three toes to frostbite. Korea was cold and it was a bitch to keep your feet warm and dry. The body bags ran up to the ass, but I got back here to the Land of the Big Round Eyes almost intact. A slew of GIs didn't."

"Did Cobb go to Viet Nam?"

"Fuck, did you, lawyer?"

Angry vitriol heated Mr. Kuzawa's words. "We thank you for your service," I told him, then, "Herzog, screw a lid on your views."

He took the bloody handkerchief from his hand cut. "A civil debate on the social issues is always healthy."

"It's healthier to keep your mouth shut," I said. "Piss off the wrong vet, and he'll leave you counting your teeth scattered over the ground. Mr. Kuzawa just has a longer fuse than most of them do."

"Oh. Right. I get your point."

My pinching stomach still demanded fuel. Had Edna eaten since her disappearance on the jet ski? A quarter-mile further, I spotted the sign-board for Gabriel's Diner. Soon after, the parking area I signaled and jounced into was deserted and paved with pea gravel.

"Make it fifteen minutes, tops," I said.

We rolled out. My head throbbed where Sizemore's palm sap had tried to cleave open my skull. The bamboo wind chimes near the diner's entry tinkled as my heartbeat lurched in panic. My hand flew back to pat at the small of my back, and I breathed out in relief. My waistband held the .44 I carried under my untucked shirttail. Our 12-gauges stayed racked along the cab seat.

Mr. Kuzawa's pocket bulge accounted for the other .44 he'd taken from me. His sly wink reassured me.

"Hey, Brendan, quit shaking like a dyke's dildo. Everything is cool, I tell you."

Herzog gave Mr. Kuzawa a disgusted look.

But I couldn't relax. My shaky life was shades of Karl Wallenda's pins losing their balance on the high wire. Just last year he'd taken one false step and splattered to his death in San Juan. The newspaper story I'd read quoted him as saying, "Life is being on the wire, everything else is just waiting." Well, I preferred my life lived not out on the high wire, and the calm waiting was just fine with me, thank you.

The diner's weathered brick-front was snuff-colored. Underfoot the lava rock pathway crunched on our short stroll to the door where I went in first. Gabriel's Diner used a hunting lodge's décor—big on its polished brass, shellacked cedar, and crushed mirror glass. No tables occupied, the "Please Wait to Be Seated!" sign card seemed frivolous.

Straw wrappers, sugar packets, and cigar butts littered the parquet floor while "The Devil Went Down to Georgia" fiddled away on a sputtery radio. The disheveled eatery was a pigsty. My voracious hunger wasn't as picky, and our booth faced the door. My slouch down in the seat relieved the .44's pressure gouging my back. The food slot framed the Oriental fry cook's hard jasper eyes on us. Feeding patrons at this odd hour, I guessed, was unexpected and unwelcome.

"The goddamn sneaky zipperhead," said Mr. Kuzawa.

"Like you said, just be cool," I said. "Let's eat our lunch and go. No muss, no fuss."

"Not if I give the zipperhead something to think about."

Herzog took out the three menus from behind the salt and pepper shakers to distribute. "I like Brendan's idea."

"But who asked you?" said Mr. Kuzawa.

As the server ambled through the batwing doors and to our booth, I already pictured my burger sizzling on the steel grill. Freckled and angular, she brought a wooden smile. The name pin introduced her as Niki.

"What will you'ns have today?" Niki's melodious inflection was sexy.

"Number Two," said Mr. Kuzawa. "Plus grits. I gotta eat my grits."

"You're easy to please."

"I'll grab a burger," I said.

"Sorry. No burgers. All we got is scrapple, ham, or sausage."

I replayed Ashleigh's spooky Circe tale, and I wanted no part of hogs. "Then my friend and I will have the same, Number Two." I didn't give Herzog a chance to speak and say something stupid.

Mr. Kuzawa cocked his head at her. "You look frazzled, honey."

She sighed through her button nose. "I'm about ready to drop off my feet. Good thing tomorrow I'll be off to Shreveport for three days to loaf."

"You deserve it and more," said Mr. Kuzawa. "We drove up to see Mr. Sizemore. Does he live near your diner?"

Her lips pursed into a livid scar. "Are you his friends?"

Mr. Kuzawa shrugged. "I don't know the joker from Adam. We're looking for work and heard he might be hiring."

"You could do better. Mr. Sizemore is mean as a snake."

"Mean as a snake is okay. We need a job, not to scrape up pals."

"Not just mean. I'm saying worse stuff. Illegal stuff, you know, like selling cocaine."

"Selling cocaine?" Mr. Kuzawa looked from her to me. "Did you know that?"

"No, but I'm hardly surprised."

Fear slashed across her face. "Just forget I said that. I'll go and get your orders on."

"Relax," said Mr. Kuzawa. "We heard nothing."

"Have you seen a girl with my looks?" I asked.

"No. Is she your twin sister?" said Niki.

I nodded. "Do you know Sizemore's daughter Ashleigh?"

"Sorry, but I don't move in hoity-toity circles. I'm just a server, and I can't take any more of your questions." She spun on her heels as if I'd asked her to put a rush on our order. Her frame held rigid, she bustled through the batwing doors into the kitchen. Our questions on Sizemore had upset her.

Herzog flipped his menu to the tabletop. "Next time I won't bother looking since you guys do the ordering."

The Oriental fry cook's eyes squinted through the food slot again.

"Goddamn zipperhead."

"Easy," I said. "We came to eat, not to fight."

Mr. Kuzawa scoffed. "What a world. First Uncle Sam pays me to go grease them, and now I'm expected to kowtow and kiss their yellow asses."

"What a world, what a world."

"Herzog, shut the fuck up." Mr. Kuzawa propped up his feet and sat sidewise in the booth.

The fried food aroma wafting from the batwing doors left me salivating. I happened to glance out the front window before my double take saw Mohawk park the red Cadillac on this side of my cab truck. The four scruffy thugs climbed out. Their heads twitched, and eyes speared the diner. Handguns came out. *Hold up*, flashed in me. Gabriel's Diner stood on a remote span of highway, and the dinner stampede was a few hours off. But the morning receipts chocked the register. My lower back muscles tingled.

They grouped by the Cadillac's bumper. A pear-shaped, acne-scarred thug gestured with his free hand, first at my cab truck and then at the diner. He wagged his head as a no. Our presence had spoiled their caper. Shouting, Mohawk flew into a tirade. He seemed to regard the diner as easy pickings, but Acne Scar didn't give in. The other two thugs watched them with hooded eyes, the humor dark on their savage faces. No cars or trucks went by.

"Who's that hollering out there?" Mr. Kuzawa pivoted in his seat, and his eyes stretched to the window. He saw their firearms. "Aw shit, wouldn't you know it? Party crashers."

Herzog, his eyes grafted to the window, startled.

"They passed us in a big hurry on the Lake Charles road," I said.

After reaching behind him, Mr. Kuzawa fisted the .44. "Take cover."

Herzog's chin tipped to behind us. "Can we use another exit? We want nothing to do with this."

"Pussies use back doors, Herzog. We fight," said Mr. Kuzawa.

I watched Acne Scars interrupt Mohawk's talk. Acne Scar's hand urged them to get back in the Cadillac. He'd no grit to duke it out and wanted to leave. But the Cadillac was a gas hog, and they hurt for money, judging by Mohawk's hand chops gesturing at the diner. He lobbied for their pulling the stick up.

"Hold up," I said. "They're making ready to go."

"I tell you what. If they enter upright, they won't exit the same way," said Mr. Kuzawa.

I stretched over the table and snared his sleeve. "We're okay. Just stand down. They'll soon leave."

"They'll first clean out the register," said Mr. Kuzawa.

"No, they prefer soft targets," I said. "Not us. They'll hit another business."

Continuing to look, we saw Mohawk hike up his palms in exasperation, and they remounted the Cadillac. Its doors whapped shut, it revved up, and scorched a pair of rubber stripes scatting down the two-laner.

"We did the zipperhead a good deed," said Mr. Kuzawa. "He should—"

I cut in. "No, he owes us nothing. Wolf down your chow before bigger troubles hit us."

CHAPTER SEVENTEEN

"This Ashleigh Sizemore was a snooty, rich nympho who took you for a ride. Why is that, son?" Mr. Kuzawa's glance was quizzical.

The same thorny question had needled me since our fatal tryst. A road sign welcomed the motorists to Yellow Snake, population 2,503 and "The Mountain Laurel Capital of the World."

I said, "I got lonely."

Mr. Kuzawa scratched his collarbone. "You mean you got the beaver fever, and you didn't play it too smart."

"Our trip taken here isn't too smart," said Herzog, his cadence sounding strained.

"Brendan, where did she die again?"

"The Chewink Motel."

"That motor court has to be the key."

"Mrs. Cornwell was terse in the police report."

"Good point, lawyer. We'll go take a crack at her." Mr. Kuzawa turned to me. "Put us there."

"I'm drawing a blank where it is."

"You were too crap-faced to remember now where it is."

Herzog nodded at an upcoming package store. "We might get some directions."

"Good idea but you stay rooted, lawyer."

"Money?" I asked Mr. Kuzawa. My cab truck branched off, wheeled over the blue stone, and I braked. "I'm cleaned out, and we're riding on fumes."

Mr. Kuzawa slapped a gob of folded twenties into my palm. "Boom times in timber," he said, by way of explanation.

"Boom times—that's where I want to be."

Mr. Kuzawa and I made for the package store. The finicky Herzog, his handkerchief made into a glove, used the gas pump. This late in the day, we didn't have to joust with the queues of motorists rabid to top off their tanks. Would this gas crisis ever lift? The rationing of odd-even license plates on odd-even days was a bitch. The package store's interior walls smelled of fresh paint, and I strolled to the back.

A pregnant blonde clad in a green jumper was stooping to inspect the shelves of refrigerated bottles and cans. She was barefoot. A brat bundled in a cruddy diaper fussed in her one arm. A lit Marlboro smoldered in her other hand. I eyed the six-packs of Falls City and Billy Beer behind the frosty glass doors as the distrustful blonde eyed me.

Feeling self-conscious, I left without the six-pack. It was just as well. My alcohol stupor just gave Sizemore another advantage. A different girl, early twenties with a jeweled navel winking from under her midriff T-shirt and coiffed in the popular Farrah shag, worked the register. She read the total from the meter, and I paid her for the gas Herzog had pumped.

Setting a fifth of whiskey on the checkout counter, Mr. Kuzawa using a handkerchief mopped his perspiring forehead. He smiled at her. "Whew."

"Hot as the hinges of hell, ain't it?" she said, ringing him up. "It hasn't slowed down everybody. Ten minutes ago, a Caddy rocketed into our lot. Just as our sign says, we don't sell unleaded gas. So they cut a sloppy doughnut and bolted off."

Mr. Kuzawa nodded. "We saw the Caddy. Sky blue. A pair of tall, skinny jokers was inside it."

"No, mine was red with four guys, just as I told our sheriff's deputy."

Her saying "sheriff's deputy" clubbed me between the eyes.

But Mr. Kuzawa didn't react. "Are any cheap, good motels in the area?"

"The out-of-towners seem to like the Chewink."

He caught my slight nod. "Sounds good," he told her. "Some directions, please."

She told him as the pregnant blonde in the green jumper padded up and slapped down a six-pack of Falls City on the checkout counter. The cashier dished the blonde taking an unhealthy puff an oblique look and murmured something snarky. The blonde gave the cashier a glowering frown, but we didn't stick around to ogle any catfight.

* * *

"Nope, I don't know this boy." Wrapped in a red muumuu, Mrs. Cornwell inclined her head at me. We'd sardined into the motel office smelling grubby with its liver-and-onion bouquet.

I wanted to stuff her hearing aid down her throat. "I paid you a fifty on a forty-four dollar room."

"Let me think." Her coppery hair upswept in a topknot slanted her eye corners, warping her face into a diabolic cast. Her five-and-dime store glasses dangled on the bead chain. "No, we've never met before."

I heard Mr. Kuzawa crinkling some paper. "Try again, ma'am. Isn't this the same boy?" He pushed a folded Andy Jackson at her.

"Well, he could be." She palmed the bribe to tuck under her watchband, balanced the glasses on her beaky nose, and peered in at me. "In the better light, I can spot a certain likeness."

"Good deal. Now since he is, might Room 7 be open for a look-see?"

The vain Mrs. Cornwell removed her glasses. "I can take you but only for a minute. I'm a one-woman crew, so I can't run as fast as most. Managing an inn alone after Ike passed sorely tests the limits of my endurance."

"As a widower, I can understand your loss." Mr. Kuzawa nudged back his cuff to bare the strap watch he wore on the front of his wrist, a habit of the war vets. "Time also runs short for us."

She fished a passkey from a cigar box she kept under the counter and ushered us into the courtyard. Heat waves shimmied off the blacktop, and we reached Room 7. Its scarred door swept in to let the others enter, and my first glimpse of the familiar wormy chestnut paneling, zinc bed, and green baize curtains triggered the replay of Ashleigh's saucy entry.

That girl glided in on pockets of air. The clingy fabric rustled over her sleek haunches. I thrilled. Pop the bubbly. Brendan is getting his ashes hauled tonight. It took long enough. The purple gown, sheeny as Christmas tinsel, unzipped at the back, but as I tugged at the gown to shuck it off her shoulders, she fussed at me.

"Brendan, whoa there. You pull it over my head. That off-the-shoulder crap is for skanks and strippers. You'll ruin my favorite party dress by stretching it out of shape."

When I did, her hair crackled with static. "My bad. I had better fess up. This is my first time. My first time in a motel, I mean."

"Then it should be special. That's why I wanted clean sheets, not the car seat upholstery. Now be a love and skin us a joint. Grass is a natural aphrodisiac." She doffed her panties like a fig leaf and lounged her tanned curves on the stale blue bed sheet.

"Oh yeah, let's get it on. Where's your nickel bag?"

"Oops, I forgot it. Check in my Jag. Let me dig out the keys. First, look in the glove compartment.

"Good dope, too. What strain is it?"

"Columbian Gold." She arched a sophisticated eyebrow at me. "God's weed."

"Oh yes, damn straight, you Yellow Snake crowd party hearty." The prancing James Brown fired with soul on TV rapped out the bawdy lyrics to "Hot Pants." His horn section blew the tightest arrangements on the rock scene.

"Brendan, I'm frittering away." She drew up the sheet to show a dimple of cleavage. "Just ignore the Luger. I scam shit off Ralph all the time."

"You steal from father?"

She smiled, predatory and cunning enough to throw a fright in me. "Why not? He can afford it."

"But it's not yours to take."

She pitied me as if I was a rube. "Sure it is."

"I'd never steal from my father,"

"You'd be surprised what you're capable of doing if push comes to shove. Are you circumscribed, by the way?"

"I'm a Gemini."

"No, you're hopeless. Go get us my dope, please."

"Yo, Brendan." Mr. Kuzawa was juggling my elbow. "Is Room 7 the right joint?"

"Yeah, we're good," I replied, back with them.

"Don't muss up anything. I just got done all the dusting and vacuuming," said Mrs. Cornwell.

"Just one more moment, please," said Herzog as we bunched at the foot of Ashleigh's deathbed. "What did you observe that morning, Brendan?" he asked in his cross-examination mode. "Take us through it, start to finish."

"Except for the dead gal in the sack, it was no different than waking any other morning."

"Well then, that makes it different," said Mr. Kuzawa.

Herzog prompted me to tease out the details. "Which side of the bed—right, middle, or left—did you sleep on? Was the window blind up or down? Was the deadbolt on or off?"

"She lay on the dark side the closest to the window and bathroom. I slept by the door for a fast getaway. It looked dim so I assume the bed table lamp was off, and the blind was down. No background chatter meant the TV had to be off. Or maybe we put on a movie and used the mute. I forget. The shower ran. See the water stain on the carpet?"

"Right. Where's the phone?"

Herzog's barrage of questions was a pain, but my night here in question came alive.

"I told you the room had no phone."

She sighed. "The phone broke, and I took it out."

Herzog's hand latched to my shoulder. "Recast it in your imagination. Okay, you ducked outside to get her pot. Look around you. Are any other vehicles in sight?"

I reclaimed my shoulder. "The lot was vacant. Wait ... I did spot a sedan in it. I believe it was wine-colored, but at night, it's tough to know the color. It was definitely bigger than Ashleigh's compact Jag. The sedan had a whip radio antenna fixed to its trunk."

"Interesting." A memo pad emerged from Herzog's game pouch, and he scratched down the notes. "Why didn't this item surface before now?"

"Obviously returning to the crime scene has jogged his memory," said Mr. Kuzawa.

"Mrs. Cornwell, do you recall the sedan?" asked Herzog.

"I better go eat, or I'll faint from hunger."

"I'll mark that as a no," said Herzog.

"Can you get us to Ralph Sizemore's estate?" Mr. Kuzawa's next twenty-dollar bribe primed her.

"If it gets rid of you any faster, you bet I will." Gesturing, she described the roads to reach Sizemore's place, and Herzog took it down.

I'd frisked the green matchbook off the dead archer, and I asked our last question. "Do you keep a supply of matchbooks in the office?"

"My niece works in a match factory and gets them in bulk," she replied.

I was tempted to describe the dead archer and Edna and ask if they'd ever been motel guests. I also wanted her read on Ralph Sizemore, the local capo fond of his palm sap and cracking skulls. But she showed an old woman's leaky memory, and I wasn't convinced of her allegiance, so I stuffed my questions, and she guided us back to her smelly office.

CHAPTER EIGHTEEN

My cab truck idled at the entrance as I appraised the ramshackle Chewink Motel in the rearview mirror. A teenage Filipino maid waist-bumped her housekeeping cart out of a unit's doorway onto the concrete apron. Suspicions prickled me.

Did underpaid maids slip passkeys to sheriff's deputies to steal into the motel units and plant key evidence to rig their frame jobs on suckers like me? But no maid would finger a corrupt sheriff's deputy and expect to go on living in Yellow Snake. My chagrin to leave empty-handed was contagious.

"Mrs. Cornwell's evasion perplexes me," said Herzog. "I'd love to know who drove that sedan."

"She's an old lady and gets beaucoup cars," said Mr. Kuzawa. "Sizemore's place is just a few miles away."

"He can wait for the time being," I said as we left the motel. "I believe J.D. driving the party van might know the growers."

"Sharp idea. Phone Kerns," said Mr. Kuzawa.

A mile further brought us to a cash-and-carry store. We stopped in, and I jumped on the coin phone. A gruff Kerns back in Umpire grabbed my ring, and I detailed where we sat, and what we needed.

"J.D. Nelson is nothing but a bum," said Kerns, slurring the end 'm.' The daytime liquor turned him surlier, especially when talking about his nephew. "Got a pencil handy, Jimbo?"

"It's Brendan." I let a tractor-trailer with noisy stacked exhausts rumble by on the state road and then said, "Lay it on me. I have a good head for directions."

Kerns gave me the route and said he'd call his sister as a heads up. I said thanks, reminded him I was Brendan Fishback, and rang off. I returned to the cab truck.

"How did you make out? Did Kerns come through?" asked Mr. Kuzawa.

"J.D. Nelson lives ten minutes away," I replied.

* * *

"Good day, Mrs. Nelson."

"You can believe what you like." A stout though pretty-faced lady, she touched at her brindle-colored hair put up in big, pink rollers. The dirty screen door separated us. "Are you Kuzawa?"

"That's me, ma'am. This is my friend Brendan."

I heard my cab truck's idling grumble behind us and nodded at her.

"Kerns called me. The drunk said I might help you. I rather doubt it."

"Might we step in off your porch? Your neighbors might get the wrong idea about us," said Mr. Kuzawa.

She toed out the screen door. "Hurry. You're letting in the stink bugs and deer flies."

Her foyer hemmed us in as a cozy trio. Surveying her mismatched furniture in the segment that I saw of her living room, I also smelled they'd eaten burned pork chops for last night's dinner. Mr. Kuzawa eyes cutting over cued me to go first.

"Is J.D. at home?"

"Who's J.D.?" She sent me a guarded once over. "If you're smashed like Kerns gets, I don't smell any booze on your breath."

"Brendan means your boy," said Mr. Kuzawa.

"My boy? My son's name is Victor. What's it to you?"

"Murder," replied Mr. Kuzawa.

"Murder? Jesus, what has he stepped in now?" Mrs. Nelson, belching, retightened the belt knot to her sack dress. She lifted her chin and bellowed. "Victor! Out here on the double."

A heavy object in a back room thumped on the floor. A door opened before a blade-featured boy surfaced from the corridor. Victor with his jaw-length blonde hair looked younger than I did. He didn't appear stoned, just drowsy from just waking up.

"What's this J.D. stuff I hear? Named Victor ain't good enough for you?" she asked.

"Aw, get off it, Mom. J.D. was Ashleigh's nickname for me."

"Ah right, Miss Rich Britches. I should've known. Your Uncle Kerns called and said you can lend these guys a hand."

Victor's finger jab accused me. "Why isn't he behind bars? The sheriff busted him for her murder." He kept on pointing at me. I itched to bury my knuckles in his rodent teeth. "I never knew what she saw in him. Goat didn't either. We don't like him."

Goat had been the dude sucking on the ice hookah. "The feeling cuts both ways," I said.

"Her liking Brendan pissed you off, huh?" said Mr. Kuzawa in a leading way.

"I never cared for it, no," replied Victor. "She and I went steady until she dumped me."

"Did it anger you enough to kill her?" asked Mr. Kuzawa.

Victor's tent of hair couldn't veil his shiny eyes. "Don't put that on me. Brendan did that. Why is he free as a bird?"

"He's out on bail," said Mr. Kuzawa. "He also didn't kill her."

Anger at Victor crackled in Mrs. Nelson's face. "We'll take up later why you chauffeured Miss Rich Britches in my van. I guess you won't anymore, but I'll lock it in the garage just the same. For now, finish answering these questions. My patience is ready to snap."

Mr. Kuzawa bore in. "Did Ashleigh supply your dope?"

"Everybody knew she was always solid to cop a score," replied Victor. "Not that I ever did."

"Who was her dope pimp?" I asked. "Paco? Goat?"

"They're just pals. Her dope comes from her rich daddy," replied Victor, eager to shift any blame. "Wasted one night, she told me he grows the ganja by the bushel up at Lake Charles. She crowed how she had all we'd ever want to smoke."

That news juiced my pulse rate, and a sweat not from my detox lined my palms. Mr. Kuzawa shot me a pleased nod. The pieces were starting to fit and lock in together because we'd just identified the big bug.

"Why did you kill her?" asked Victor, back to surly.

"Brendan didn't harm the girl, and we're trying to prove it." Mr. Kuzawa eyed Mrs. Nelson. "That is if we can get a fair shake."

"You can ride easy because we won't fink on you," she said. "I hate Sizemore. This is the thing. You don't come back here again, and you also accept Victor had no role in Ashleigh's death."

"Deal," said Mr. Kuzawa.

"Meanwhile Victor or J.D. or whoever he is now is grounded for two weeks. No, make it a month for smoking dope again."

"Aw, Mom ..."

We left them to jaw over it. Back in the cab truck, we sat with the engine stuttering on the cut-rate gas. We repeated our conversation with Mrs. Nelson to Herzog.

"Do Victor's claims merit any credibility?" he asked.

"Victor tells it straight," said Mr. Kuzawa. "I'm convinced Sizemore is who grows the pot at Lake Charles. Brendan, your take?"

"It's pretty ballsy of him, but I can buy it, yeah."

"We'll assume Sizemore took Edna and killed my boy. You and I *both* want to take him down."

I nodded. "Wrecking his precious plants was a good start."

My cab truck taxied out to the blacktop, and Herzog gave me the correct route numbers to Sizemore's place. I thought I'd keep an eye out for Ashleigh's red Jaguar parked there, but it was still probably in the sheriff's impound yard. That brought up a question. "Did the police report list a Luger recovered from Ashleigh's car?"

Herzog's reply was a negative headshake.

Mr. Kuzawa was surprised. "Did she carry a Luger?"

"She took it from her father and kept it stashed in the glove compartment, but I didn't find the Luger in there."

"Why did she carry it?" asked Mr. Kuzawa.

"She said she felt threatened and wanted to hire me as a bodyguard who could use the Luger."

"Why did she feel threatened?"

I shrugged. "She never got into the specifics. I just wrote it off to her rich girl hysteria."

Mr. Kuzawa zippoed a Marlboro and forwarded the pack to Herzog who in turn fired one up, but I passed. Mr. Kuzawa's hooded eyes acknowledged my refusal then shifted to study Herzog puffing away and striving too hard to fit in as one of the guys. If only I hadn't given in to the easy temptation to see The Devil's Own play live that night. Testy and regretful, I hammered the gas pedal. The engine raced as my thoughts did back to Kerns' store on the eventful night in May. The party van sat in his parking lot just off from the service isle, and the crew invited me aboard.

So I said, "Sure, why the hell not?" and wiggled into the van's rearmost grotto where a black light gave it a surreal tint. Ashleigh lectured on astrology, Ouija boards, and tarot cards. Like my Uncle Ozzie who blew out his brains with a .44 slug, I was a superstitious cuss. She requested my zodiac sign, but I'd no idea and told her. She took my birthday, June 20th, and put me with her sign, Gemini. Her horoscope reading found us to dovetail in a nice fit.

"How about that?" said Goat between the snorts off the ice hookah. "You two are astrally simpatico."

Ashleigh and I smoked some of her mind-bending reefer and soon after I pulled at the hangman's noose snugging at my throat. The wind sailed through my ears. I swayed on the gallows' trapdoor just inches above the spectators clamoring for the news of my fate. Their cheers erupted when my verdict came down—guilty as charged …

She jogged me awake and insisted she play the lead in my dreams. For my "absolutely" reply, we kissed, and she filled my pair of lungs with the joy smoke. Our freewheeling van of happy-go-lucky partygoers crested the fog-shrouded mountains where my head plunged into a tailspin. Ah, so this was a bum trip, a bad go on the grass. But her kiss electrified me.

"Death is but a dream," she said. "Just like the song goes."

"The Devil's Own song?"

"No, silly, our song. You're the songwriter who penned it for us. Soon we'll fly up as the angels to dance on the clouds and sing it."

Then she went down on me there in the back of the party van.

* * *

From inside the cab truck, we directed our sight at the farm lane down the way. It was a calm, even docile scene. Beyond a white plank fence, the sleek, black thoroughbreds grazed in the knee-deep Kentucky bluegrass. I saw six thoroughbreds with others no doubt over the next knoll away from our view. I thought of the horseshoe tracks I'd seen in the sand at Lang's Teahouse. Who'd go riding to Lake Charles? The mounted park rangers went on fire patrols through the rugged wilderness. This record dry month and the wildfires had turned out more horseback patrols.

"Brendan, this is sort of ticky-tack for Sizemore," said Mr. Kuzawa.

"I agree but Ashleigh said her father owns different properties. Maybe this is one of them," I said. "He dupes the ranchers needing legal aid, secures their land for collateral, and then turns around and calls in their debts. They're too strapped to cough up the dough, and he steals the farms out from under them."

Herzog nodded. "Not original but it's an ingenious idea."

"Only another shyster would think so," said Mr. Kuzawa, angry.

"I didn't say he's an admirable individual, but he is clever and treacherous," said Herzog.

"He wouldn't live in that hovel." Mr. Kuzawa nodded his grizzled head at the group of ramshackle buildings.

"Then his tenants will know where they mail the rent check," I said.

I grabbed first gear on the column shift. The newly paved lane smelled of fresh tar, and the sprayed up stones dinged the cab truck fenders. I saw the yellow aluminum siding sheathed the boxy house, and its yard looked threadbare. No push pedal toys or jump ropes dotted the grass. A red tick under the porch crawled out and with curiosity sniffed at us. He judged our scent benign and flopped down to scratch behind an ear.

After my cab truck halted, Mr. Kuzawa scooted down from the cab seat. He craned his head, peering at the farmhouse. Had I also seen a curtain stir in the picture window? He went over and rapped on the door. After no response, he gave us a shrug. I signaled him to go try at any other doors. He loped around the corner. Herzog's game pouch speared me in the hip, and I shifted away. We sat watching, and in a few minutes, Mr. Kuzawa reappeared at an energetic clip.

No sooner had he climbed into his seat than Herzog had to know. "Well …?"

"A pregnant gal named Alicia finally answered my knocks," replied Mr. Kuzawa. "She told me three times Sizemore is a bad man."

My acceleration wheeled us off down the lane. "No big shock there."

"The Arbogasts who lived here pulled up stakes on Memorial Day and moved in with a cousin in Gatlinburg. Alicia stayed behind since she has nowhere else to go. Her father raised hell over her pregnancy.

Anyway, her begging persuaded Sizemore to let her stay on here. But once she has the kid, he told her to hit the bricks."

"Do the Arbogasts own the farm?" I asked.

"They did," replied Mr. Kuzawa. "Through some legal sleight of hand that Alicia couldn't follow, Sizemore assumed possession and then ownership of the ranch and evicted them."

"Does she live alone in the middle of bumfuck nowhere?"

"She told me she has a phone, and the church ladies bring her groceries and stuff."

"Does she know where Sizemore lives?"

"Uh-huh. Tonight is the time to hit before he knows we're after him," replied Mr. Kuzawa.

CHAPTER NINETEEN

Ralph Sizemore merited some thought while we followed Alicia's directions to find him. His posh trappings, starting with the big house, had to enthrall the locals. Deputy Ramsey had bragged how Sizemore was next in line to be a state senator. If deep coffers won victories, he'd buy his way into any desired office. I could see how the red-hot Sizemore had ridden a comet to the top of his politico's game.

After Ashleigh overdosed in our motel room, the local blats (I read them rolling hot off our presses) had pilloried her as a pothead and less complimentary tags. But they let me be because I wasn't the juicy headline to chase. Scandal had chilled Sizemore's meteoric rise. I sensed he'd shelved his lofty plans until the problem—me—disappeared. I knew I had to live on borrowed time. Each breath I drew as a free man was a fluke. That rathole cell in Yellow Snake loomed in my bleak future. For now, Sizemore's drubbing on my head burned in my brain, and my ache for scoring just revenge heated my fight blood. But first, I had to know Edna was out of danger.

* * *

Just off the state road a 5-iron shot down from the entrance to Sizemore's main estate, we cooped in the cab truck. The screen of silver maples hid us rather than our parking at his gate protected by a guardhouse. My pair of colleagues smoked while I nipped off the fifth of whiskey, the liquor brewed by filtering it through maple charcoal. The whiskey filtered through me, and I felt its red-hot mist coloring my eyes. The fiery whiskey dulled my shrieking nerves to a manageable roar. Now Monday at 7 p.m., nightfall drew nearer to set the stage for our smashing third act.

Herzog misread my pensive mood. "Chin up, Brendan. We'll skate through this trial."

Mr. Kuzawa's eyes went flat and hard. "Shit lawyer, what odds do you give Brendan?"

"Better than even."

"Quit blowing sunshine up his ass. My idea is unbeatable. We go in and waste Sizemore."

"Your idea will send Brendan back to the big house for ninety-nine years."

"Ninety-nine years?" Nervous sweat greased my palms and dampened the half-moons at my armpits. I swallowed over a jagged lump. "Behind bars I don't cope so well."

"If we do it slick, the cops will write up our hit as a bloody mugging by unknown assailants."

"Do you have the expertise in disguising assassinations?" asked Herzog.

"Put it this way. I'm clever enough to disguise yours."

As my asshole tightened, Herzog coughed like a goat. "What does that mean?"

"Form your own conclusions, lawyer."

His hands left tremoring, Herzog flicked his Marlboro ash into the dashboard tray. He inhaled a heartier puff. Still uneasy, he talked as if he worked in court. "We better focus our efforts on discovering who harmed Ashleigh Sizemore. For redemption, Brendan solves her homicide. To wit, a lock-tight motive explains the whys and wherefores to her grisly fate."

"Fuck that finesse shit. I'm honing the finer points to my idea." Mr. Kuzawa tossed the Marlboro pack out the cab window.

Herzog turned haughty. "But Kuzawa, you're not Brendan's attorney. I'm the professional paid to advise him, not you."

"He called me when the chips were down. You just popped up at Lake Charles."

"Meaning what?"

"I'm his go-to guy, not you."

"All right, enough already," I said. "We're not—I repeat—not taking out Sizemore." I gave Mr. Kuzawa a meaningful look.

"Hey, I hear that." He nodded. "We go in and rattle his cage and shake out what he knows. He can point us to Edna."

"Fine but I'll do the cage shaking."

Mr. Kuzawa shrugged. "It's your party, Brendan."

Our talk trailed off, and I used the lull to replay Ashleigh and me asleep in the motel bed. The murderous slime had to ooze through the door, or he'd wormed in the bathroom window. Ralph Sizemore put a face on the murderous slime, but proving it was tough. I squirmed in the cab seat and spoke.

"The sheriff's deputies recovered the angel dust taped under our bed table. Angel dust killed her. Mr. Kuzawa is on the right track. Sizemore sneaked in to kill her and plant the fake clue. With us off cruising in the ozone, fixing it was easy. The part I can't figure out is how the angel dust ended up in her system."

"Proven techniques can extract that from Sizemore."

Herzog had a pained sigh. "Did your time in Korea shape you into a total thug, Kuzawa?"

"Back off or I'll show you what Korea did to me. Just call me a ticking time bomb ready to go off when I get pissed enough."

This time Herzog swallowed hard, and I said nothing.

Mr. Kuzawa waved his hand at the state road. "Brendan, go supply for the mission."

Wagging his head, Herzog moaned as I kindled the engine. "What if Sizemore does confess to his daughter's murder? Will you kill him on the spot?"

"I was messing with you, lawyer. We hand over Sizemore to the state cops."

"Their phone number is in my wallet," I said.

"If things get hairy, the rangers stay on standby," said Mr. Kuzawa.

"The Smoky Mountain Rangers? You're not one of them or are you . . ." His face pale as a leper's, Herzog stopped.

Mr. Kuzawa crossed his fingers. "We're like this."

Herzog and I knew if you brought in the rangers, the blood would flow in Yellow Snake's streets.

* * *

The all-purpose store on Yellow Snake's main artery muscled out its neighbors, a payday loan shop, an off-brand electronics store, and a marquee advertising "Apocalypse Now", a box office smash. My cab truck shunted to the curb, and I shepherded us into the store where angular steel shelves walled the aisles. Herzog angled off at one aisle to get a pair of leather gloves for his soft hands. I found the bolt cutters, pry bars, electrical tape, extra ammo, and of course, the cartons of Marlboro Reds.

The soon-to-pop pregnant, short brunette between her indifferent drags off the Newport rang us up. Smitten, Herzog tried to hit on her except bored stupid she spewed a stream of cigarette smoke in his face. His cheeks and ears flushed an ignominious red, and Mr. Kuzawa consoled him.

"Forget her. She's used goods."

Herzog nodded.

From the corner of my eye, I saw Mr. Kuzawa halt and squint up at the transom as if making out something written on it. I stashed our purchases in the truck bed, quit Yellow Snake, and headed back on the state road. Once past Sizemore's gate, I secluded us behind the same grove of silver maples. Time draped heavy on us waiting until nightfall. Examining the indelible ink crusted under my fingernails, I felt chained to the lifetime of a pressman's tedium, but I clung to my plan to go make a fresh start at Valdez.

My alcohol buzz gone left me feeling morose. Mr. Kuzawa and Herzog lit up. In a little bit, Mr. Kuzawa ditched his butt, slumped back his head, and took a catnap. Herzog's eyes never strayed from the state road as if he was expecting a parade to march by us.

I bunched up my fist. "Can I beat out of Sizemore where he has taken Edna?"

Herzog scrunched his face. "Don't bank on using brute force. He's a vicious adversary."

"If he freaks you so much, why did you volunteer?"

"What's the adage? 'Desperate times call for desperate measures.' We're up against it at your trial. I'm an officer of the court, and the legality of what you want to do is highly questionable."

"Tough titty. It's too late to abort."

"That's what I was afraid of."

"Who's in your hunting lodge?"

"We're an eclectic association of professionals."

"English, please."

"Lawyers and doctors, for the most part."

"How many tom turkeys have you bagged?"

"More of a hunting enthusiast, I shun the violence but savor the excitement of the chase."

"Is your lodge in town?"

"We meet at the depot restaurant." He lowered his voice to a sober murmur. "Pay no attention to Kuzawa. His advice is dangerous."

"He's always been solid by me. You can be the getaway driver."

"No, I can keep up and do my part. That's why you paid me."

"I paid you to keep me out of jail."

Twilit licks of crimson and purple inflamed the western sky beyond the bug-spattered windshield. Every so often, a vehicle droned by on the state road, one junker with a muffler dragging the asphalt and kicking up sparks. I glimpsed a red Cadillac whisk by, but it was too dim to make out the driver or passengers. Mr. Kuzawa slept on and I envied his ability to rest at a time like this. By marked contrast, my lawyer fidgeted.

"Herzog, you're a raw nerve, man."

"I don't deny it, but you need me along," he said.

* * *

"How risky is doing this?" asked Herzog.

I'd abandoned the silver maples, turned off the state road, and crawled in reverse down a bush road Mr. Kuzawa had noted earlier. The darkening hardwoods absorbed us, arranging the scene for our nocturnal raid on Castle Sizemore.

"Negligible if we stay sharp," replied Mr. Kuzawa. "By striking due east through the woods, we hit Sizemore's property line. Cross it and then hump over his fields. Be quiet. Don't spook the horses. The high ground near the mansion affords us a vantage point."

Herzog's tongue scraped his lips. "Can you clarify our objective?"

"Make him give up where Edna is," replied Mr. Kuzawa.

"I trust that includes no rough stuff," said Herzog.

"It depends. If he brings heat, we respond in kind." Mr. Kuzawa paused. "Just wait in the truck, Herzog. You'll drag butt and slow us down."

"I'm an outdoorsman," he said. "Your pace won't outstrip me."

"We go in as a group," I said, the final word. "To recap, I'm after Edna and the pot farms. I don't want any fatal accidents." My stare met Mr. Kuzawa's fiery bulletpoints for eyes. My horror replayed the arrow piercing Cobb's chest. "Killing has no place in this."

"Agreed, so back off," said Mr. Kuzawa. "Do you know if Sizemore is weapons savvy?"

"He brought up his poker games at Fort Hood," I replied.

"Probably a rear echelon motherfucker," said Mr. Kuzawa, rich on the scorn.

I let off the gas pedal and notched us in behind a big tree trunk. The humus on the forest floor raised the earthy odor of decaying leaves. My primed 12-gauge fell at my shoulder. The .44 went in my waistband. "Sizemore is no dummy. Our best chance is to catch him off-guard."

Mr. Kuzawa nodded. "If we hit a shit storm, fire at will, and fade back to the woods. We rendezvous here. Don't get lost. Go in a straight line until you hit the bush road."

"Do I go armed?" asked Herzog.

"No way, lawyer. Friendly fire won't shoot up my ass. Stay in back with your head down."

Guided by a faint, red star—Venus, I hoped—there in the sparkly night sky, we rambled between the dark trunks to the hardwoods. The night bugs played a discordant note like jazz fusion. Encountering no undergrowth or brambles, we reached the property line sooner than expected. The knolls separated us from our target thought asleep in his fortress. Mr. Kuzawa's bolt cutters snipped apart the four strands of barbed wire. Herzog curling back the strands pricked his finger.

"Where are your gloves?" asked Mr. Kuzawa.

"I lost them somewhere after the truck," replied Herzog.

Mr. Kuzawa gave a damn-lawyer-could-fuck-up-a-wet-dream headshake. Toting my 12-gauge at port arms, I trotted a few paces behind them. The distant silhouettes were the horses. The tang of wood smoke I smelled touched a distinct memory of Ashleigh's pledge sworn in the van of how one day we'd dance and sing on her clouds. The rise and tumble to these grassy knolls in the starlight assumed the physical aspects of a cloudbank. Consulting her tarot cards, she'd predicted it right. Now with each bounding stride, I aimed my raving outburst at her.

Yo, Ashleigh, I'm dancing on your clouds and belting out our song. It's a bloody fight song. Can you hear it? Can you carol its lyrics with me?

I waited, but I got no response from her.

Ah hey, have another toot off the joint rolled from your father's pot gardens at Lake Charles. Sing on your clouds how he shoved me to the precipice of hell, and how tonight I'm shoving back, baby. I'm shoving back with all my might.

You hear me, Ashleigh? Huh? Can you? Speak up, girl. Don't be shy. Don't be afraid. Don't be aloof. I ride low in the saddle like Jesse and Frank James, the badass brothers who roved these same cursed ridges. Just call me a nightrider, a bushwhacker, and a desperado hell-bent to plug you. Your daddy's barbed wire fences, blowhard threats, and palm sap couldn't keep me at bay. Talk to me, Ashleigh baby. Speak up. I'm all ears for you.

For the first time since her death, she'd no pearls to share with me. Her standoffishness didn't amaze me. She was no real spider woman, just a bad dream. We didn't alarm Sizemore's horses or goon squad. As we crested the last knoll, the mansion's glittery windows vaulted into our eyes. Sweaty and breathless, we knelt at the near slope so our profiles didn't imprint the starlit sky. The half-dozen or more lit windows arrayed below confused us. My fears banded the muscles in my lower back.

"There are too many rooms," said Herzog.

"Just creep in closer," said Mr. Kuzawa. "Keep your voice low, too."

Jets of adrenaline ripped me. I billowed out my chest to snatch in breaths and rein in my flighty heartbeats. I led us scuttling downhill when the rifle fire spattered out. My eyes trained on the nearest bright window saw the orange-yellow spurts to the muzzle flash. Hot rounds stitched the turf inches from me. We lunged flat and hugged the turf where I damn near soiled my pants. Elbows digging, Mr. Kuzawa snaked up to lay even with me, his eyes a pair of live briquettes.

"Ambush," I said.

"But just the one shooter."

"I thought he was asleep. How did he see us this fast?"

"Night vision scope maybe."

"Sounds ugly. Do we pull out?"

"Hell no. Sneak into our range and bring smoke."

A new volley erupted before the lights in the mansion, window by window, fell dark to remove targets for our return fire. My eyes strained to orient us. The lines, corners, and forms gave the shape to the sheds, barns, and mansion, a forbidding bulk within a hardball toss from us. The gunfire slacked off.

Twisting to look behind us, Mr. Kuzawa waved a hand. "Herzog, you're straggling. Catch up."

"Go on. I'll be right behind you."

"First you get with us."

With reluctance, Herzog joined us, and we crabbed to the nearest elevation. From this crow's nest, I saw the orange-yellow tongues of fire pulsate from the high window. The rounds tossed the divots at our cowing faces. We'd two choices: charge in or pull back. Mr. Kuzawa decided, and I sprang up after him. We moved in a zigzag dash toward the porch. Herzog stumbled along somewhere in our path.

I threw up the covering fire, racking my 12-gauge pump eight times. My volleys of lead shot thrashed our attacker off us. Unhurt, we met at the porch. The 12-gauge's recoils left my shoulder twinging. Mr. Kuzawa bapped out the glass pane to the French doors while I reloaded, thumbing in the 00-buckshot shells from my pockets and handling the hot steel barrel. He grappled through the jagged hole in the glass and undid the latch.

"We're in," I said.

"Herzog, stay at the window. At any cop wig-wag lights, you sing out," said Mr. Kuzawa. "We scramble for the pines and link up at Brendan's truck."

Herzog bobbed his head. "Sure, sure. Go on."

After locating the wall switches, I toggled on the light sconces as we hurried forward. The furnishings—Persian rugs, loveseat, and baby grand piano—had a regal but artificial flare. Edna didn't turn up. Neither did Sizemore. My fight blood crackled. I realized the stairs were our fastest way to get at the murderous sniper.

I touched Mr. Kuzawa's forearm. "He wants to guard his escape route."

"Take the stairs. Cut off the bastard at the balls."

Footfall thumped overhead. Hustling, we edged through an archway and found a steel circular staircase. Mr. Kuzawa tilted his 12-gauge: we climbed. I went first, my 00-buckshot load of death chambered. My pulse roared behind my ears. Mr. Kuzawa trailed me by two steps. Our ascent went slow, and no more sounds came. Did Sizemore wait topside to take off my head? Good sense said lay off until sunup still too many hours away.

But my adrenaline was the go juice having the last say. I used an instinctual crouch on the upstairs floor. I froze, my eyes and ears attuned.

The lunar glow from the skylight improved visibility. Mr. Kuzawa emerged at my shoulder.

"No ambush up here," I said.

"Luck favors the ballsy."

We stood, I sensed, in a spacious room. Then ahead of us, I caught a snatch of Sizemore with his Van Dyke beard as he darted through a bright doorway. His thumping tread sent us chasing him to the main stairs we'd missed. We hit the first floor running. His flight shot through the high-ceiling dining room. At a glance, I saw the exterior door flung wide, and I looked out into the dark. He'd streaked over the yard to save his ass. His hillside mansion wasn't so impregnable.

"We scared him off," I said, back in the dining room.

"His goon squad off peddling his dope can't protect him," said Mr. Kuzawa.

"Further pursuit?" I asked.

"Not with him packing a night vision scope on a rifle in the woods." Mr. Kuzawa jerked his head. "Instead we'll go case his set up."

"Find Edna" was my simple directive.

CHAPTER TWENTY

We had to work fast. Herzog split off upstairs and Mr. Kuzawa darted into a hallway. My house tour saw the wine-bar armoire and crystal chandeliers. The half-round Italian marble fireplace used propane gas logs for those too lazy to bust up their own stove wood. I moved on. The sterile white surfaces in the truck-size kitchen didn't impress me. My nose picked out the blue-collar food smells of wasabi and beer.

A pie safe constructed of birch or ash and probably bought at a downstate antique shop squatted in front of a yellow door. I gave the yellow door an extra glance when Mr. Kuzawa barked out to me. I left the kitchen and entered the so-called library. The Reader's Digest Condensed Books and other volumes lined the shelves stacked from floor to ceiling, accessible via a sliding ladder on its rollers.

"Books didn't make the shitbird any smarter," said Mr. Kuzawa.

Before I could speak Herzog huffed in to us. "I saw no weapons, dope, or sign of Edna. Everything looks clean as a whistle."

I was quick to dispute him. "Not quite everything is squeaky clean. Where's Ashleigh's bedroom?"

"I saw the bedrooms on the south wing," said Herzog. "Nothing is in there."

"Show me anyway," I said.

The annoyed Herzog guided us down a maze of hallways, and the south wing had a potpourri and furniture polish smell I put with funeral homes. I poked my head through each door. The four-post canopy bed covered in janky pink and lace but no paisley had to be her boudoir. The citrusy aroma to the pot smoke lingered in her most intimate space.

"I smell the dope," said Mr. Kuzawa.

"Brendan, what are we after?" asked Herzog.

"Look for diaries, snapshots, letters, or notes. The sneaky bitch left something useful behind."

I'd check every nook—under the bed, on the closet shelf, and behind the drapes—where a cockroach took refuge. Her Virginia Slim butts studded the ashtray, and her lipstick rings imprinting the butts matched the red shade of her Jaguar. Her birth control pill compact sat next to the ashtray. I tipped out the bureau drawers and pawed in the straps, elastic, and lace before I got bored. She was partial to sarongs, and I fingered the strands of Mardi Gras beads, but I already knew she was a party girl. Next up was the walk-in closet.

Petite feminine togs crowded the tiered racks. Gypsy skirts and peek-a-boo blouses along with the banana jeans zipping down the ass were her faves. No slinky, purple gown suggested it was her burial apparel.

LPs—Uriah Heep, Black Sabbath, Blue Cheer, but no The Devil's Own—cluttered the closet floor. I toed them into a pile. While frying her brains on pharmaceuticals, I saw she'd grooved to the vintage psychedelic head-bangers.

My frisk under her mattress went unrewarded. Pensive, I stood waiting as I had at Mama Jo's gas range stirring the pots of blackberry juices, but no ghost whispers came. No wraiths bedeviled me. Her poltergeist didn't snipe at my tampering with her belongings. No big shock, I thought. She no longer slept in here but rotted in her clay grave. Dead girls told no tales. Their voices only murmured to unhinged minds like mine.

"Where's her dope?" Mr. Kuzawa slammed shut her desk drawer.

"She was too smart to leave incriminating evidence," said Herzog.

"She wasn't smart enough to stay alive," I said. "Check under her bed again."

Herzog stooped down and looked. "I just see a pair of strappy heels."

His jaws tight as a vise, Mr. Kuzawa scoffed between his teeth. "Tear this room back to the wall studs."

"This is thorough enough for us," I said. "Let's split before Sizemore sics his goons on us."

We exited the mansion for the dark yard and pasture. The weather had altered. An unseasonable cold front marching in had chilled the hills and left us in our shirtsleeves shivering. Mr. Kuzawa clutched my forearm.

"Put yourself in Sizemore's shoes. You're on the lam. Your pursuers carry 12-gauges, but you've almost shot your wad. Where do you streak off?"

"I'd go re-arm myself, say, at the closest store."

"While leaving the store in Yellow Snake, I read Sizemore's name printed on the transom."

"I saw you looking up at it."

* * *

"Brendan, did you find what you came for?" asked Ashleigh with an acidic smile.

"Hardly. Your bedroom yielded no clues."

"My bedroom? You pawed through my stuff. I don't like hearing that from you."

"Then why didn't you say anything to warn me?"

"Sometimes I get too preoccupied."

"Sometimes I think this dialogue between us is bullshit. You're not real, just a figment of my drugged mind."

"You can't pooh-pooh me. You're toast without my aid."

"Oh, go bugger off. I've got my friends."

"Do you really?" She snickered. *"We'll test their loyalty."*

"What do you mean?" My lower back muscles snarled, a spasm almost leaving me paralyzed in my tracks.

More snickers. *"You'll find out all too soon."*

By the next moment, the amber *"Welcome To Yellow Snake"* sign was glimmering in my sleep-crusted eyes. Our trip into town had prodded Ashleigh's wraith to speak and reveal a Judas schemed in our midst. Or maybe not since she took a perverse joy in taunting me. She wasn't trustworthy in life or death. Down a side street, Mr. Kuzawa saw the eight-foot cinderblock walls to an unfinished construction project, the ideal cranny to garage my cab truck, and I ditched it behind the wall. We decamped and following the sidewalks hit the quaint shops flanking the deserted main stem.

The all-purpose store on the next block sat closed. Steel burglar grates guarded the rear windows, forcing us to use the front door. Herzog fretted over the alarm while Mr. Kuzawa used an old skeleton key he carried on his key ring to undo the door's worn lock. I could make out *"~Ralph Sizemore, Owner~"* printed in faded gold script on the semi-bright transom. No alarms screeched, protesting our entry. The motor oil and stronger citronella scents made me sneeze as I eased the door back into its jamb.

"Keep your shit wired tight," said Mr. Kuzawa.

Herzog whined. "Doing this I'll forfeit my law license not to mention my hunting lodge membership."

Mr. Kuzawa's eyes strafed him. "Quit sniveling, lawyer, or I'll stop it for you."

"Let's get back on task," I said to defuse his explosive anger.

"I've had a bellyful of listening to his gripes."

"Herzog, dial it back," I said.

The tall, canyonesque shelves walled the aisles under the grayish, low-lit security lamps. The earlier ambush at Sizemore's mansion left us wary as we divided. He might lurk on any aisle to pop up, draw a bead, and whack us. I prowled right, Mr. Kuzawa moved left, and Herzog entered the shortest route, down the center aisle to the rear counter. We cleared out our sectors and rallied there.

"No Sizemore," said Herzog, sounding relieved. "We can leave."

"The slippery eel is outthinking us," said Mr. Kuzawa. "Herzog, hop up front. At any sight of a cop's wig-wag lights or Sizemore, you holler like a stuck hog."

The long barrel guns on display behind the counter's glass partition suggested how our would-be bandits at the diner had come armed for business. I rummaged below the shelved gun cleaning kits and found the 12-gauge shells in their boxes while Mr. Kuzawa scavenged in the clothing bins.

"Brendan, grab birdshot loads, too, and I'll requisition us clothes. We smell like inside the monkey house wearing ours."

"Can you hurry it any?" said Herzog posted at the door.

"Three Andy Jacksons makes us square. Any surplus can count toward their aggravation," said Mr. Kuzawa.

"It's a hell of a lot less than ours is," I said.

CHAPTER TWENTY-ONE

Herzog's droopy posture said he'd better log in some shuteye but he didn't complain. As we wheeled out of Yellow Snake, Mr. Kuzawa at the helm in my cab truck, the ground mist reflected the white glare off the headlights back into our eyes. As my breath and pulse settled, I cranked the window handle and let in the crisp air. Inhaling the heady fragrance to the honeysuckle robing the roadside fences and mashing my eyes closed were all it took to trip off my dreams.

What did you ask me, Ashleigh? Am I a born psycho? No, I live with a split personality—half-light, half-dark. You said we Geminis are programmed that way. You know, we see the world in black and white. That's what I do.

I said lovers should make love under the stars. No way, you sulked. There'd be no fucking on the dewy grass. The sheets were clean at your lair, so we beelined to the Chewink, Ashleigh girl. We stayed in your decadent crib. Don't you remember us flirting and fucking in Room 7? How you removed this boy's clothes, and his innocence? It was exhilarating and liberating.

After the fireworks, you sighed. "That was awesome, Brendan."

You used a duplicitous tone, but I didn't care. Your huge, luminous eyes hypnotized me. We shared a joint down to the roach you then chewed up like a wafer and swallowed it. Damn that was potent stuff. With your sweaty arm on my bare chest, we plunged into a lavish sleep.

Just after dawn, I awoke and got up. Your coppery nipples peeked above the hem of the sheet at me. I sang out. Ashleigh, time to get cracking. Silence. Ashleigh, where can we go bum a cup of coffee? Silence. Ashleigh, go ahead and grab a shower. Silence. Ashleigh, where did you stow your nickel bag? But you slept on. And on.

Panicky, I grabbed your bare shoulders and jiggled you, gently like a doll at first, and then as the fear unglued me, harder until my own teeth clinked like the dice in a gambling cup.

A tapping came at my elbow, and my eyelids fluttered open. The broken white lines on the two-laner lapsed into my focus, and I felt more of the tapping.

"Wake up, Brendan," said Mr. Kuzawa. "Riding shotgun you can't fall asleep."

"Sorry about that."

"It's not a problem this time, but who knows about the next?"

Then he wrestled the steering wheel and pinned the gas pedal to whip us out into the other lane. He overtook and exploded by a Kenworth hauling a trailerload of doomed hogs off to the packinghouse in Gatlinburg.

Their cold, scared shit blended with mine. You just knew Ashleigh once enslaved the hogs. They'd pet names, but "Brendan Fishback" wasn't one, at least not quite yet.

The Kenworth's high beams soon dwindled to the twin sparks I saw in my dark side mirror. Even if driving like the wind, I'd never outstrip that hog raunch left on me. Never. The hogs' shitty fate clung to me. Their stink was my stink, and their destiny became my destiny. That's how it tracked in my mind because I saw no relief waiting ahead for us in this tunnel of gloom.

Lake Charles was a giant cesspit. Its earth dam created a reservoir to hold all the dark shit running into my life. Two corpses rotted on its shores. Mr. X trussed up in a blanket on the lake bottom might pass for a mobster's hit job. The cab seat grew hard as if I sat strapped in to Old Sparky, the second hand on the death row clock ticking off my final seconds before it was light bulb city.

Mr. Kuzawa addressed my brooding silence. "Don't let the lopsided odds get to you, Brendan. If I drop a dime, we can get a boost in a snap."

"Huh?"

"Cullen."

"Cullen is a psycho."

"Maybe so but he's *our* psycho.

"Skip using the rangers," I said. "Who are those people anyway? Why do you keep saying they'll pitch in with us? It seems like a lot to ask from them or anybody."

"Not really. Cullen and I go way back to Korea."

"Was he a GI?"

"He was a beast."

"So is he your friend?"

"That and I saved his hash more than once. Sizemore's goon squad is nothing with Cullen on our side. We fought and trounced men the twice of Sizemore on his best day."

Further out of Yellow Snake the fog thinned before Mr. Kuzawa pulled into the parking lot to a lit up convenience store. He jostled Herzog awake. "Go in and buy some No Doze pills. Both of you better stay alert. Dozing off is what gets you killed."

The rumpled Herzog shuffled off into the store, and a few minutes later he returned. After hopping out, I let him squeeze into the cab, and my slammed door preceded Mr. Kuzawa's edgy whistle.

"Brendan, you won't believe this shit."

I didn't like his ominous tone. "Not more grief, I hope."

He knuckled his side mirror outward, bettering his sightline. "A red Caddy just nosed up. They docked it on this side of the gas pumps. See it?"

Peering over with him, I nodded.

"A red Cadillac?" Herzog's frame stiffened, his eyes bulging. "Is it the same one that stopped at Gabriel's Diner?"

"Must be. The same four punks rolled out, all armed."

"See the one in a Mohawk?" I said.

"Yeah, he's probably the chief."

"Yep, they're the ones."

"Don't they know when to quit?" said Herzog.

"Brendan, are you up for pissing in their soup?"

"No, but is there any stopping you?" I unlatched my truck door, and Mr. Kuzawa unlimbered our 12-gauges racked along the bottom of the cab seat.

"Have you lost your marbles?"

"Pipe down, Herzog, and keep your eyes peeled." Mr. Kuzawa pumped in the 00-buckshot shells taken from the new box. "If any cop flashes up, you lean on that horn. Make it loud. We'll hustle out and race off like a raped ape."

"I don't like this."

"Herzog, I don't give a flying fuck if you do or not." Mr. Kuzawa prodded the shotgun's muzzle under Herzog's chin whiskers. "I gave you an order, and I expect it carried out. Or else you face grave consequences. Got it?"

Herzog nodded that he did get it.

"Stellar."

An isolated convenience store is always ripe for robbery, but I figured our lads had hatched theirs on the fly. For starters, they'd missed seeing us in the deeper shadows. Then they sauntered into the store, hollering and taking their time. We advanced on the balls of our feet and watched them through the plate glass front. The oldest no more than 25, they hadn't yet graduated to the more lucrative heists like armored trucks and bank vaults. They set their sights on this soft target.

Fear petrified the old lady cashier on the bread aisle. All four showboated, two flourishing their sawed-off shotguns and two with handguns. Some joke I'd have loved to hear left them laughing in stitches. Acne Scars, popping bubblegum, rubbed his sawed-off's muzzle over her pointy breasts and sliding it down there. He whipped up his free wrist and deflected her retaliatory face slap. They demanded the money, but the night's receipts sat in a drop safe she couldn't get into. No longer guffawing, they were finding that out, and it spoiled their fun.

Mr. Kuzawa growled. "They're stuccoed, and she's their hostage."

Standing just short of the glass door's rectangular outspill of light, we could see them but not vice versa.

"They'll just tie her up and be off."

"Not these shitbirds. I'm going in, and I'm greasing them."

His simple blood vow sent a bolt of cold horror through me. "Can't we send them packing?"

"Sure, I'll send them packing to meet their Maker."

"Listen, I can't do this."

"You can and you will, Brendan." I felt his hard eyes on me. "We can't let this kind of shit slide. Just follow my lead."

Acne Scar groping her this time with his hand got Mr. Kuzawa's motor running. Our shuffle went up the concrete steps, and he cracked the door, and I whisked inside it, him behind me. Acne Scars' peripheral vision detected us moving and ducking behind the wire rack displaying the 8-track tapes out for sale.

His New Yorker accent was jerky. "Yo, who was dat?"

"Holmes, you're so stoned. Empty the register." Mohawk pointed his sawed-off behind her.

Acne Scar snapped his bubblegum. "I mean who slid into the bodega?"

"Gimme your cash," Mohawk ordered her. Then I heard the metallic click from his actioning in a live round. "Now. Or I'll blast your old granny cunt all over the bread." Adversarial and strung out, he'd kill her at the least provocation like more arguing over the money in the drop safe. My sphincter retracted in dread.

"A couple fives and silver are in the register," she said. "Take it and be gone."

Mohawk snorted. "There's more. Gimme your purse, granny."

Then Mohawk gestured his chin at Acne Scars. "Grab the fives. We need the gas money. Then do her. No eyewitness."

Acne Gum popped the bubblegum. "Fuck it. Your idea. You do her."

"I'm sick of killing. Take your turn at it."

I paced my short breaths. The adrenaline streamed into my senses, and the moment streamed into its fierce clarity.

"Dial open the fucking drop safe," said Mohawk. "We need the money."

"I already told you only the manager has the combination," she said. "I'm just the night clerk. They don't tell me jack."

"You lying cunt." Mohawk spat. "Gimme your purse. Or I'll kill you."

"Show time, Brendan," Mr. Kuzawa sidemouthed to me. "Give some me some covering fire. Ready, go."

LAKE CHARLES | 113

Jacking upright, he first ejected the ineffective birdshot load from his chamber. I also stood, my 12-gauge frozen in my grip. For me, the events had slowed down. Mr. Kuzawa butted the gunstock into his shoulder pit, cheeked the 12-gauge, and notched the red bead on the would-be lady killer Mohawk. The salvo of lead pellets chopped off Mohawk's hand. His sawed-off slipped and clacked hitting the tile floor.

"Jesus fucking Christ . . ." His stubby amputation appalled him. Each pulse squirted the red spurts of blood. My colon turned queasy. Mr. Kuzawa, cursing his lousy aim, shunted in a new 00-buckshot load. For the space of a breath, Mohawk eyed the 12-gauge muzzle's dark O. "Adios, motherfucker." Mr. Kuzawa's fired volley peeled off Mohawk's skullcap as if opening a can of cat food. The red tufts of bone, blood, and brains spattered everywhere.

Squirming, she wrenched free of Acne Scars' grasp and dove behind the counter. Grunting, Mr. Kuzawa leveled his red dot sight on Acne Scars who jerked a split second before Mr. Kuzawa cut loose and missed again.

"Well, fuck a duck." His eye still riveted on his target, Mr. Kuzawa racked in another shell.

Acne Scars scrabbled by the deep freezers, lunged through the doorway to plow into the back room, and sprinted out the rear door into the night. The last two thugs brandished their handguns.

Their shots flamed wide of us, dashed out the panels of plate glass, and a tsunami of glass shards peppered down on us. The 8-tracks splintered into bits, and their shiny ribbons of tape unspooled like party streamers around us.

Somebody hollered. I heard the Cadillac outside crackle to life. Undeterred and cranking the pump slide, Mr. Kuzawa cycled in new ammo and lined his muzzle on the nearest thug. He didn't cut for cover but as a fool bulled ahead, his gun hand screwed sideways, popping off slugs as in a made-for-TV gangster movie. His aim was poor.

My survival instincts jarred me to take action. Snapping my wrists, I heaved my 12-gauge in the manner of a javelin. Its heavy butt stock clunked the thug in the chest and thrust him back. I pivoted. Mr. Kuzawa's next shot skimmed over the thug scrambling behind the deep freezers.

"Fuck, I need to get me some glasses," he said.

The thug shrieked out to us. "Hey, man! I give up! You hear me? Enough already."

"Deal me in, too," said the last thug now also tucked behind the deep freezers.

"Toss out your weapons," said Mr. Kuzawa.

A chintzy handgun cast from zinc and two sawed-off shotguns scraped over the floor tiles. My boot stopped their slide. By my next hard breath and struggling to cap my own adrenaline gusher, I startled to realize how it all had flared by us in a few seconds.

"Okay now, out, you both. But make it slow-w-w," said Mr. Kuzawa.

Their hands reaching for the ceiling, the two thugs' horror-crazed faces rode up over the top of the deep freezers. They looked my age or a little older and scared shitless.

Mr. Kuzawa motioned his 12-gauge for them to go stand by the counter. "You just be cool over there." He crouched down and collected their discarded weaponry.

The blur of violence, leaving one thug damn near beheaded and sprawled dead at our feet, had a numbing banality on me. It wasn't real.

"Kill the bastards. Do it. Go ahead."

Giddy enough to peal out in hysterical laughter, I glanced over at the old lady cashier. Her eyes, a pair of hot lasers, burned in their vengeful hostility.

Mr. Kuzawa dropped his 12-gauge. "Cover 'em," he said to me with my .44 out. He turned to her. "Ma'am, that's radical, don't you agree? They got it bad coming to them. Now. This is what I saw happen. They slinked in and tried to heist you. But you took out this hidden equalizer." He used his handkerchief to wipe down his 12-gauge and handed it to her. Her gnarled fingers wrapped around its barrel and stock. "That's when all hell busted loose. That one was shot, one escaped, and these two surrendered. Holding them at gunpoint, you took their guns and reported it to your sheriff."

"That's exactly how I saw it," she said, training the 12-gauge on the two thugs.

"Careful with that thing," Mr. Kuzawa told her. "It's loaded."

"Shit happens."

"Just don't end up in the jug with them."

"I owe you two thanks."

"We're only too happy to be of help, ma'am."

Edgy and shaken, I retrieved my thrown 12-gauge from the floor. The pump action was still operable. We stuck around until she finished phoning the sheriff's night desk. Then I tailed Mr. Kuzawa out the door and treaded over the gravel. With the raw carnage boiling in my brain, I doubled up by the cab truck's tailpipe and upchucked. Scraping the strings of saliva and puke away from my lips, I overheard Herzog's high-pitched yammer.

"The Cadillac screeched off, and I then heard shooting in the store. Did anybody get hurt?"

"One casualty." Mr. Kuzawa ignited the truck engine to thunder through its dual exhausts. "The old lady cashier iced him," he lied.

"Good Lord," said Herzog.

I boarded the cab truck and wiped my bitter lips on my sleeve. Mr. Kuzawa floored the accelerator, and we lurched out to the state road, abandoning the war zone at the convenience store for the sheriff's deputies to sort out.

"The cover story you fed her sounds cockeyed," I said.

"Her nametag said Mrs. Simmons. It's her word against the New York punks. Whose tale will rate the most credible?"

"Mrs. Simmons' story will be accepted as gospel," said Herzog. "That's a no brainer."

CHAPTER TWENTY-TWO

Herzog's shoulders sagged. "Can we grab some sleep, guys?"

"Not unless you can convince me that Sizemore has settled in for the night," said Mr. Kuzawa.

"He can't be a machine that never rests."

"Take your No Doze pills."

"The store had sold out of them."

"Shit, you mean after all that."

"Face it: we're stumped." Herzog yawned. "Sizemore was our last best lead, and he slipped through our fingers. Give it a break until the morning. There's little hope to chase him down tonight."

"He must have other holes to crawl down," I said.

Nodding, Mr. Kuzawa worked the gearshift. "We keep riding and smoke him out."

My head nodded and nestled against the rear window as I rested my eyes for a moment. The hypnotic thrum to the truck tires eating up the hardtop enticed me into the realm of dreams, an all too familiar terrain.

"P-s-s-t. Brendan, wake up." Ashleigh's plea startled me to conscious-ness. "You went out like a light on me. Did you enjoy sweet dreams?"

"No, I didn't," I said, feeling the party van's tires under us thrumming on the alpine switchback. "How late is it? Did you bust your curfew?"

She giggled at the idea. "What curfew? Dad is cool, especially since Mom died."

"Sorry, I didn't know she did. How?"

Ashleigh's voice croaked a little. "Last Christmas Eve she cracked up in a paraglider accident out in godforsaken Utah."

"So now you call the shots at home?"

"You'd freak if I told you by how much. Let's discuss something else. Hey, ain't J.D.'s van da' bomb? Can you suspend your disbelief and pre-tend we're Jason and the Argonauts sliding past Aeaea, the island where the enchantress Circe and her pet swine lived?"

"Yeah boy, get a load of the whiffs from the dead lobsters and pig shit. Did you like the show at the armory?"

"It didn't really blow up my skirt. Hey, roll us a jay. Getting straight is a howling bummer. I told J.D. to drop us off at my house. The night is still young, and my Jaguar has a full tank of gas."

"You own a Jag? Hoo boy, I'm in hog heaven tonight. Where are we going?"

"To romp through the mountains and then on to the Chewink Motel. Do you know it? Dad is the owner."

"No, but your dad owns a motel?" Booty call, I thrilled.

"Yeah, ain't that a rip? Wait. Did you bring the right protection?"

"Ribbed for the extra friction." With a magician's hand flourish, I produced the specialty condom.

"Cool. The next stop is ours, and then we're guests at the Chewink. By the way, I'm curious. Do you have any brothers or sisters?"

"One sister."

"Oh—is Edna Fishback your sister? I never made the connection until now. Guess I'm really stoned not to see it. Awesome."

"H'm. Do you know Edna?"

"We've chatted a little, sure. Girlie stuff mostly."

"But Edna is a homebody. She's never gone to Yellow Snake."

Her smile impish, Ashleigh tilted her eyebrows and bangs at my earnest face. "You'd flip out to know where your twin sister has gone and done."

"Bullshit. She's my twin sister, so I ought to know better than you do."

"You're the one who's full of it. I know for a fact Edna has been to the Chewink Motel. Their guest register doesn't lie."

"Why does she go to your dad's motel?"

Ashleigh giggled at my naiveté. "For the same reason her twin brother goes, I imagine."

CHAPTER TWENTY-THREE

The shimmery neon tube letters, including the duds, at the Chewink Motel's entrance spelled out "OFFI'E, VA'AN'IES." My latest communiqué with Ashleigh revealing Edna had used the motel urged me to suggest we return here. After nosing into the gravel lot, Mr. Kuzawa doused the cab truck's headlights as I located the two dark windows to Room 7 where I'd yawned awake next to Ashleigh's corpse. At the office door, Mr. Kuzawa pounded his fist, and the overhead light flaring on blinded us.

"Who is that out there?" asked a querulous Mrs. Cornwell through the shut door.

"Jerry Kuzawa. We came by earlier with questions. Can you spare us a minute?"

"You again? More questions, I suppose. Nope, you better just buzz off."

"We came to search in your rooms."

"You better haul it on down the road, mister."

"Please don't be that way," I said. "A key opens a room door easier than a shoulder does. A key also leaves no costly damage."

"Is that a threat? My sheriff lives fifteen minutes away."

"Always your call, ma'am, but we're fast at bashing in doors and ransacking rooms," said Mr. Kuzawa.

"All right, all right. Just don't go nuts on me. I'll be out directly."

"Thank you, ma'am. We'll be happy to wait."

I stowed the 12-gauges below the cab truck seat, and the office doorknob soon rattled open. Tying off the fuzzy robe, she waddled out to us. The five-and-dime store glasses hung from a bead chain at her neck, and she let out the boiled cabbage odor from her dinner.

"What are you after now?" she asked.

"We're not sure, but we'll know it when we see it," replied Mr. Kuzawa.

She stuck her palm out at Mr. Kuzawa for greasing.

"Show us around again and we'll see."

Her ponderous sighs got us to the nearest unit. She bent at the waist and inserted the door key. The open door allowed for entry. Mr. Kuzawa, his .44 drawn, prowled inside and ran a hasty look-see. No villains hid behind a shower curtain or under the bed.

After our futile search in all thirteen units, Mr. Kuzawa looked at her, his tone gangster sinister. "Did Ralph Sizemore come here tonight?"

"Of course not." She wagged her no-chin head at us. "I can't imagine why he would."

"Doesn't he own the motel?" I asked.

"Own this place?" Her gales of braying laughter echoed over the courtyard. After her derision trailed off to snorts, she responded. "Sizemore isn't the proprietor of this dive."

"Then Ashleigh lied to me," I said. "Her father doesn't own this motel, and Edna isn't here."

"It's just been me for the past twelve-and-a-half years," said Mrs. Cornwell. "No guest named Edna that I know of has ever registered for a room."

Swaying on his feet, Herzog let out a yawn. "So it's yet another dead end."

"Sorry to drag you out of bed," said Mr. Kuzawa. "Just to negate any ill will, why not rent us three rooms?"

Mrs. Cornwell's crabby mood lifted. "That'd do a lot to iron out this misunderstanding."

"I thought as much. Which room, Brendan?" asked Mr. Kuzawa.

"I'm a sentimental softy. Put me in Room 7."

"Ma'am, will Sizemore come crashing in on us?" asked Mr. Kuzawa. "Will you be tipping him off?"

She wrested her robe's flaps tighter. "You're the paying customers, and your dust up with Sizemore isn't my business. Period."

"That's the answer I wanted to hear," said Mr. Kuzawa.

I paid for our room tab from the dwindling wad of twenties, and we left to bunk in our respective berths. Flipping the clean towels and washrag to the bureau top, I postponed a shower and, still dressed, crashed on the mattress. The new ceiling mirror captured my frown. Room 7 at the Chewink Motel in Yellow Snake, Tennessee, sat primed to accommodate cheap rendezvouses and cheaper murders. But I bore Mrs. Cornwell no ill will. She'd her creditors to pay the same as I did.

I rolled over with the recent gunfire still rattling my ears. I squelched the image of the handless, headless thug. Enough ghosts harangued me. A sketchy memory came of the wine-colored sedan staked outside my door that May night. The driver's face remained fuzzy. But then I couldn't sketch in my dad's facial details either. I believed he carried a distinctive crescent scar an inch above his right eye. Did he still weld the seam joints on the Trans-Alaskan Pipeline? The crews had completed it two years before—in 1977—but a lost son had to kick off the quest to find his missing father somewhere.

For me, Valdez marked that spot. The stay behinds might recall Angus Fishback, and I'd learn where his wanderlust had sent him next. He may've rambled on to a logger gig. I smiled at me the lumberjack. I felt I was savvy enough to become a logger. Mr. Kuzawa had taught me to speak their lingo and ape their swagger.

I'd lost a little swagger after Salem Rojos and I parted ways. It still smarted. I sighed. Ah, first love so broke our tender hearts. That night we'd relaxed in the lawn chairs. Their portable TV sat on the rear porch step. What did we tune in? Tony Beretta drove screaming after the villains in his gray muscle car. The citronella candles were a joke because I swatted an army of mosquitoes attacking me. Pete and his wife had gone to bed, and Salem and I sat alone. Squirming in her lawn chair, she parked her bright eyes on me.

Here it comes, I thought. We'd been quarreling all week.

"I won't be at your pot parties, Brendan. Ever."

"So you told me."

"Yet you still go. I can smell the pot on your clothes, hair, and kisses."

With a silent groan, I recrossed my ankles. *She's got to be on the rag*, I thought but said, "I never promised you I'd quit."

"My point precisely, and this is as good a time as any to promise it. Say it. I'm waiting, Brendan."

What a bitchy nag. "Is it a big deal?" I shrugged. "I don't miss any time from work. I've got no DUIs or arrests."

"Well, *I* don't like it. If you respected my feelings, you'd make the promise."

"I tell you what. I'll only come over when I'm straight," I said, sure that my compromise was a generous and fair one. "How's that sound?"

"Sounds like bullshit. You have to decide. It's the dope or it's me. There's no wiggle room left here."

Resentful anger heated my cheeks and ears over her issuing an ultimatum. "Why did you wait until tonight to whip this on me, Salem?"

"It's always bothered me. I like Brendan fine, but the pothead Brendan is a turn off."

The tube picture was jerky. The Rojos watched TV in the backyard to savor any refreshing breezes. Mrs. Rojos had a neurosis that air conditioners bred summer pneumonia. Right now, breezes or no breezes, I sat there stewing. Nobody had called me a "pothead" to my face, and I didn't like the seedy appellation.

"I'm waiting for your answer, Brendan."

"Maybe we should take a break from each other."

"There's no maybe to it." She bolted up from her lawn chair and moved to head indoors. She stopped but didn't look back at me. "Goodbye, Brendan. If you ever grow up, give me a call. I'd love to hear when you've turned it around."

"Hey, I'll do that sometime."

But I'd never updated Salem I was powering through kicking my drug habit, and I had a few major laps to go. That's not to say I liked to live in my hermitage over the taxidermy shop. No nookie was a drag. But hell, I reasoned, I'd meet a galore of other Salems. With its 55,000 rowdy pipeline roughnecks, Valdez was rife with its juke joints, crapshoots, and cat houses all catering to the Good Time Charlies. Sure, I'd take off up north, hunt down Angus, and we'd go set the woods on fire. We Fishback men were babe magnets.

In the final ticks before sleep sandbagged me, I pictured Yellow Snake's gulag, and I prayed to stay free of it. If I could only get the goods on Ashleigh's real killer and erase the bull's-eye from off my back. Despite my best efforts at resisting it, once asleep, I was a failure at staving off the dreams. Yes, the eeriness was back, so I flowed with it rather than battled it.

The pot's smog choked the Jaguar's interior since we hadn't opened the windows. Ashleigh shrieked in orgiastic glee as we squealed around the hairpin curves along the ridges before we descended and docked at the Chewink Motel. After we nested in Room 7 (on this very spot!) she fessed up.

"My dad isn't actually the owner." Her crafty smile was my first glimpse of her deceitfulness.

I stuffed an inhalation and shrugged before expelling the smoke. "So, you fibbed to me. Why?" Her eyelids, I noticed, went liberal on the kohl. Had she always resembled a zombie? Or did the greasy smoke engulfing us distort my sight?

"Brendan, my fair sex lies through our teeth all the time. We can't help it. Tonight you learned a vital lesson on life."

"Meet the sophisticated man of the world," I said, my laugh an ironic one.

"What's it like having a twin sister?"

"Nerve-racking."

"No, I'm serious here. Do you finish each others sentences or can you read each others thoughts?"

"Of course not."

"Did she mature faster than you did?"

"On that I don't have a read at all."

"I wanted a sister. Being an only child has turned me into a self-centered hellion. My nannies told me that while I grew up in their care."

I said nothing because I wasn't going to touch that with a ten-foot pole.

"I've led a melancholy life, Brendan."

Trying to lighten the mood, I laughed. "Who uses a word like 'melancholy'?"

"You're right."

"We need more conversational foreplay. Do you like dirty talk?"
"Skip over that part. Just follow my lead."
"M'm. Keep that up, and I'll follow you to hell—"

I bolted upright in the bed, the sheet falling away. My fingers clutched at my chest. A maniac drummer, my heart banged under my ribs. The air vacuumed in and out of my parched mouth. Even if I was staying straight, I seemed to be coming unraveled at the seams.

"Tighten up," I tried to coach myself, climbing out of the bed. "My detoxed mind is trapped in a whirlpool." My sock feet pattered over the nappy carpet at the foot of the bed. "I did follow her to hell, and now I can't return from there. That's the main rub. Did I jinx myself? I need some air."

I went out the room door. My sock feet stepped from the nappy carpet to the hard concrete apron. The semi-dark courtyard sat tranquil under the streetlights. No traffic flitted by on the state road. Smelling the peat moss used to mulch the azalea beds, I saw the several cars from travelers on their stopover. My cab truck stood undisturbed.

The soft drink and ice machines sat whirring next to the office and coin phone. In my sock feet, I braved wincing over the jagged gravel lot and slotted my coins into the soft drink machine. A bottle thumped down the chute, and I wet my mouth, the soda ice-cold, before I moseyed to the coin phone.

The ratty directory listed the old Arbogast phone number. The phone had a signal. I chinked in my dimes and dialed the number, expecting to get a canned voice telling me I'd hit a disconnected line, but my call patched through. During the rings, I realized I'd used this same phone to call in Ashleigh's fatal overdose. A girl's papery lilt answered. She'd been asleep and I made my hasty self-introduction.

"Sure, I remember Mr. Kuzawa came today. Why didn't you come in, too?"

"Our schedule was tight. Has Ralph Sizemore been there tonight?"

"No, I haven't seen him in several days like I told Mr. Kuzawa."

"That's good. Listen, you better lock all your doors and windows." She yawned on her end. "Uh-huh, but I do that anyway."

"Just make double certain tonight. Don't let him into your house."

"Uh-huh. Brendan, it's way past my bedtime. I'm just registering every other word. Let's do this. Tomorrow you call me again. No, better yet, just stop by. Don't make it too early, please. Say, around nine-ish."

"All right, be looking for us then."

"Thanks for calling. Good night." Her hang up left the analog hum filling my ear.

I racked the phone handset, walked back to the soft drink machine, and discarded my empty bottle in the trashcan.

"Are you doing okay?"

Recoiling as if I'd stepped on a hot 220-wire, I identified the speaker. "Jeez, don't sneak up like that on me." I grabbed a calming breath. "I just buzzed Alicia, and she's battened down for the night."

"Heady thinking. I'll also call her and leave my room's phone number in case she needs help." Mr. Kuzawa plinked in his coins and cuffed the tab for his favorite cola. "You know, I never sleep. Never. I just nap all night. It's a carryover from Mr. Truman's police action." The frosted bottle thudded down the chute. Mr. Kuzawa uncapped the top, knocked back a swallow, and drew down to a cherry ember on his lit Marlboro. He exhaled, then, "But that's just me. Why are you so on needles tonight, son?"

Was he being serious? My look over at him was sharp. "For beginners, that store robbery we pre-empted turned into a bloodbath."

He inhaled and then let the expelled smoke veil his live coals for eyes. His chuckle stirred like an angry hornets' nest. "It did get a little gory, but it's a distraction now."

"All I know is my showdown with Sizemore can't end that messy."

"It shouldn't."

"My murder trial is coming on a fast train."

Mr. Kuzawa's eyes glittered at me. "After this, there might not be a trial. We're all in to see this to the bitter end."

Other burning priorities ravaged my thoughts. Cobb had told me his father knew my Uncle Ozzie, and I decided it was time to let Mr. Kuzawa in on my vivid dream life. "I must be going mental," is how I broached the topic.

"You seem to be doing okay to me. What's up?"

"I'm dreaming in dribs and drabs of the night that Ashleigh Sizemore died."

"Ah, it's coming back to you. Excellent." He drew the Marlboro down to near the butt. Flicking it, he forged a smoke ring. "Bunking in the same barracks has tapped your memory, so let it roll."

I watched the smoke ring break apart. My airway constricted, and a raw voice I didn't recognize as mine quavered. "Men crack up that way. Don't GIs freaked by live combat go loopy and turn into vegetables?"

Modulating to a husky pitch, he rested a bearish hand on my shoulder. "If a vet ever got what we in Korea called 'shook,' the VA hospitals treated him. Isn't your mind trip more akin to déjà vu? It sounds perfectly normal and nothing to lose any sleep over."

"No sir, mine isn't like that." I wasn't clear on how much to reveal, but how could I pull my punches now? "My dreams want to reconstruct the past. I knew Ashleigh the one night, but she talks to me in death as you and I are now. Sometimes she lies about stuff. Other times she taunts me. My Uncle Ozzie was nutty like that, and I've got some gene pool worries, see?"

After a final glug, Mr. Kuzawa flipped the empty soda bottle over his shoulder, and the glass busted on the concrete apron. He belched. "You're not even in the same ballpark."

"My gut level says different. Uncle Ozzie was right bad off. Mama Jo told me he went to visit the psychic Edgar Cayce."

"That he did. Since I chauffeured him in my car to Virginia Beach where Mr. Cayce lived, I can vouch for it. On the trip, Ozzie got all jittery on me. I offered him a snort of booze, but he said he wanted to stay sober and clear-headed."

"Did Mr. Cayce shed any useful light on Uncle Ozzie's gift of dreams?"

"It beats me. I left and met an old sailor pal at a bar. Later Ozzie said Mr. Cayce's eyes had twitched like a shaman's, and he used a squeaky lady's voice. Ozzie sure returned home a quieter man. Look, I don't laugh at the weird shit. My grandma, bless her soul, was a water witch, and my daddy, damn his soul, spoke in the Pentecostal tongues. Hell, on those long, cold winter nights in Korea, I battled my share of seeing hobgoblins."

I returned to this trip. "Today's killing twists my nerves."

"This mission ran gory, but as I already told you, some dark shit can't be avoided. That's life, son."

"I don't like it."

Nodding, he faced across the dark lot out to the state road and without turning said, "Brendan, you've gutted through a lot, but ..."

"But I can only move straight ahead," I said to finish his thought.

He turned to me. "You understand it. But you should also remember I've got your back."

"I can see that. Why are you sticking out your neck for me?"

He shrugged. "That's what friends do. I know Cobb and I left town when you ran into your first troubles, but I'm here now."

"Thanks."

"No thanks are needed." He turned shrewd. "I'll drop a dime, and I can hook up with some fast reinforcements. They fight like tigers, too."

As always, his radical ideas caused my gut muscles to clench. "Later, maybe. We can agree Cullen is our ace in the hole to play if we get in a stiff spot."

"Just give me the high sign when you're set. Cullen takes shit off nobody. He's fearless." Mr. Kuzawa edged toward my cab truck. "Go on in and grab some shuteye. I'll call Alicia and then guard our perimeter."

Locked behind Room 7, I dove into bed with a new spark of a thought. Mr. Kuzawa had commented at Lake Charles that an outside agitator—what was his name? Pierre Spartacus?—had run the pressmen's strike. I made an interesting association. Hadn't there been a Sizemore at the center of the strike? The old-timer pressmen at work used to curse his name. So it might be worthwhile to delve into the strike history.

Sleep came with a few refreshingly dream-free hours. Ralph Sizemore on the attack didn't interrupt our rest. In the predawn's cool, I showered and shaved. My gamey clothes sailed into the wastebasket. The bullet wound I'd taken at Lake Charles grazing my ribs had scabbed over. The new clothes Mr. Kuzawa had bought us at the all-purpose store (was that only last night in Yellow Snake?) felt starchy but fresh and clean to wear. Cobb's old .44 lodged in a side pocket. The sealed bottle of cologne I salvaged from the medicine cabinet patted on with a citrusy sting. I reminded myself we had to pitstop by Alicia's house at nine o'clock.

We shook out of our rooms. Before leaving the Chewink, I stopped by the lobby office, but Mrs. Cornwell was gone. Her Marlboro sat half-smoked in the tuna fish can next to the Tab diet soda bottle. My bell rings failed to summon her, so I tossed our room keys on the countertop, and we left.

***

Mr. Kuzawa dropped a hint that I might update Mama Jo, so we shuttled into a gas station and the phone booths under an awning. Mr. Kuzawa ducked into the exterior restroom. While counting the rings, my other ear tuned in the lyrical genius of the late Jim Croce. His 1973 ballad blaring on a transistor radio inside the open service bay pleaded with a phone operator to put through his call.

"Are you in any hot water?" asked Mama Jo after our greetings.

"It's all good."

"It is, huh? Why did you call then? Quit acting evasive like you do." That famous temper hardened her command.

"I called just to say hi. But the telephone lines have ears."

"So they do. Is Edna okay?"

"The last time I saw her, she was fine." I hadn't lied to Mama Jo, and I spared my soul from hell's eternal roast. "And you?"

"Oh, I'm just peachy keen. Axel let out my goats. I see my osteopath today. The bats are colonizing my attic again. On the plus side, I've finished putting up the blackberry jam. Meantime you're off tearing up the pea patch with Cobb and Edna."

"Actually a little under the weather, Cobb is taking it easy." Again I hadn't actually lied. "Mr. Kuzawa came up with Herzog."

"The fishing at Lake Charles must be unbeatable," said Mama Jo, then, "Decent jobs are hard to come by. Since the strike, the companies don't like it here."

"We stockpiled our vacation, so don't worry." The overdue rent to my flat arose, but I decided not to press my luck and ask her to cover it. I could always pitch a pup tent in the woods.

"Do you have enough gas to do all this catting around?"

"We're not siphoning gas from other tanks."

"Well, I hope not. Another postcard came to the house."

"What's the message?" I asked, my heartbeats on the uptick.

"As always, there are no words. The ice-capped mountains are pictured on the front, and the postmark is still jerkwater Valdez."

"Valdez can't be all bad."

"Uh-huh. Are those weird dreams making you act so reckless?"

"I'm okay. Really I am."

"I want you to see the doctor in Gatlinburg. He can order that EEG test they do at the hospital."

"Why go to all that bother and expense? Nothing will show up. I feel just fine. Save the postcard. Look, I better go on now."

"Bye then."

After hanging up, I kept the phone receiver at my ear, a pretext to stand there and reflect. I needed to be with the web presses, the largest soaring two stories high, at Longerbeam Printery cranking away. The giant rolls of paper fed through the presses, and the newspapers for a half-dozen towns, including Yellow Snake's blat, ejected out at the other end.

My job as the lead pressman was to track the work times on the job tickets. I pulled a sample sheet at every 500 sheets and inspected the color specs. Any hiccups usually came from the second pressman, a boozer named Big Tiny more off than he was on the wagon, forgetting to fill the ink fountains. But I'd forget to jot down the ink fountain settings for later use when we ran the same job ticket, and my oversights also wasted company time and money.

Keeping up the sheet tallies and the maintenance logs were my biggest headaches. Our red jumpsuits made us into orangutans climbing over the machinery to the mammoth web presses. The ink got on my clothes and skin pores. I was a true pressman working hard at my trade under the piercing eyes of our founder, Jeb Longerbeam. His streaky portrait loomed in its gold-frame over the wall above the time clock.

Taking vacation didn't thrill my boss. There was too much strife. My old temptation to chuck it all and hit the road shook me again. Go north, young man for Alaska or bust. I'd get with my dad Angus. That was the right stuff. We'd drink, laugh, and fish. We'd cheer on the Iditarod. We'd do many things.

Then a new image crystallized of Cobb, young and happy, gunning his bass boat over Lake Charles. I liked seeing him that way and not immured inside of King Tut's tomb we left on the mountaintop. More fear gripped me when Edna lost and dazed somewhere beyond Will Thomas Mountain staggered into my imaginings. Where had she gone? Had Sizemore captured her? Had she made it to dry land? Of course she did. No body of water ran deep enough to drown her. She was a tough cookie.

It'd been good to touch home. The trip back to my cab truck was a slow walk. Clay-streaked and dented, it showed its true age in the brassy sun. A silver-armored Airstream clanked by traveling on the two-laner. The Florida snowbirds were getting an early jump on their winter exodus. I yearned to hitch on and leave with them, but all of my reveries never once set me in motion.

I hoisted into the cab truck, and we departed. Tuesday had turned hot and muggy, but the warm air fanned through the open windows over us. Mr. Kuzawa captained the wheel. His wolflike eyes flashed between the mirrors, but I spotted no bogeys lurking in mine.

"Sizemore grows his cash crop and pockets his profits," said Herzog. "He keeps a raft of corrupt officials on his payroll. Do you see the odds you're bucking, Brendan?"

"It's not all bad. Judge Yarrow granted me bail."

"As a maverick judge, she's the rare exception," said Herzog. "She's on a medical leave of absence. Skin treatments, I heard, so we've got our work cut out for us. I'm not being funny either."

"Speaking of funny, here's one for you," said Mr. Kuzawa. "Last night a jangling phone woke me, and it wasn't mine." He angled a hard glance at Herzog.

"There's no phone in Room 7." I joined in with Mr. Kuzawa's glare.

"Guys, I just left a message for my secretary to obtain a status update," said Herzog. "She returned my call, and we talked for six minutes, maybe more. Stuff is perking at the office. For one thing, there's Brendan's case to consider. Her callback must be what disturbed you. My apologies."

My question went to Mr. Kuzawa. "Did you overhear what he really did say?"

"No. Late at night he likes to mutter."

"Oh yeah? Whenever we talk, he speaks right up. What gives, Counselor?"

"Use your heads. I lowered my voice because those walls are paper thin. Disturbing your rest wasn't my intent."

"Who is your office help?" I asked.

"You know Salem Rojos works for me. She'll go into pre-law at my alma matter. Satisfied? Or do we stop at the next coin phone, and ask her to corroborate my claim?"

My curt words beat down his stuffy defensiveness. "Yeah, I know Salem, but Herzog, I don't like you. I never have since the first day Mama Jo hired you to be my lawyer."

"Brendan, you're skating on thin ice. Mighty thin. Insult me again, and I'll drop your case."

I bit my tongue. Lawyers were a necessary evil.

Mr. Kuzawa felt no constraints. "Here on, you stay within eyeshot, lawyer. Another screwy move like last night and I'll slit your throat with my Buck knife. Promise."

"Save your threats, Kuzawa. They don't ruffle me. Working in criminal jurisprudence, I hear them daily. Vulgarity just goes with the territory."

"Hearing vulgarity and experiencing it is like apples and oranges," said Mr. Kuzawa.

The hangdog lawyer said nothing.

* * *

The majestic sycamores cast their pools of shade over our cruise. A part of me wanted to go off and lounge under them, fall asleep, and demand that the dreams reveal everything to me. Then a big "what if" fear raked me. What if my dreams refused to play out to the end? What if they balked at unraveling more threads to Ashleigh's narrative? Where did that leave me? In the lurch, that's where.

Cobb had died for no sensible cause. The shadowy driver parked in the wine-colored sedan at the Chewink Motel hectored me. My manhunt to go after Ashleigh's killer had hit a sand trap. Worst of all, we'd gotten no closer to reaching the wayward Edna. The base of my stomach fell free. I fished out her yellow parrot barrette from my pocket. The talisman offered me the physical proof that she'd been through the pot growers' campsite. Re-establishing that link helped to rekindle my hopes.

We had to be running on the right track. I recalled my thoughts last night before falling asleep at the Chewink Motel to delve into the pressmen's strike and the involvement of a Sizemore. My chin tilt caught Mr.

Kuzawa's eye. He was one historical source to tap, but I also wanted to learn about the bigger picture.

A sly smile prefaced my question. "Is your public library card valid?"

"My library card?" Disgusted, he blew his nose on his handkerchief. "Do you own a damn yacht?"

"I have a library card. What's your interest?" asked Herzog.

"To do some research on local history."

CHAPTER TWENTY-FOUR

It drove me up the wall, but some of Umpire's old families still didn't speak to each other twenty-five years after the strike. Imagine the raft of grudges fed over an entire generation. That's how a nasty labor squabble had left a clannish, quaint Appalachian hamlet. The pressmen's strike sucked out and destroyed our heart and soul. It all started when a few disgruntled pressmen invited Pierre Spartacus, an official with the International Printers Union or IPU, into town. From the get-go, Pierre was a mover and shaker. He went to work.

The autocratic Jeb Longerbeam owned and ran Umpire's printing plant. On the sly, Pierre slipped around and signed up enough membership to give his union some clout. It was a blueprint for catastrophe. Mr. Longerbeam, no champion of organized labor especially when Pierre presented their list of demands, blew a gasket, saying hell no. The IPU declared a work stoppage. No middle, neutral ground existed: you were either pro-union or anti-union.

The loyal pressmen still reported to their jobs, and things turned rough. Crossing the picket lines enraged the strikers. Ugly curses escalated to head knocks. One striker unlimbered a Colt, and a file clerk took a fatal slug in the heart. Urgent calls went to the populist governor Frank G. Clements, and he ordered in the Tennessee State Police. The state troopers pulled double shifts to separate and cool off the unionists and scabs.

The kicker was Mr. Longerbeam's presses continued chugging along, in spite of the smaller work force. The no letdown in the productivity did much to undercut Pierre's bargaining power. After a long, hot summer, both sides agreed to a truce, and the state troopers left Umpire and went home. But Pierre and the IPU had wangled no new concessions, and within days, their membership disintegrated.

Mr. Longerbeam turned vindictive. Few, if any, of the union walkouts took back their old jobs. They went on to eke out a subsistence living on church welfare and joe jobs, or else they left town to stake out a new beginning elsewhere. I know Umpire and the surrounding vicinity including Yellow Snake were never the same again.

After skulking down to the basement of the Yellow Snake Public Library, we learned of this local history. Our eyes glazed over from so much peering in at the old newspaper columns magnified on the fuzzy microfilm reader's screen. Straightening with a grimace, Mr. Kuzawa reminisced.

"Seeing this dredges up a lot. Each morning I ran the gauntlet and got swatted over the head with the picket signs."

"Not a union man, eh, Kuzawa?" said Herzog.

"Don't insult me. If the money got tight, we just took a second or third job." Mr. Kuzawa pronounced each word with care approaching reverence. "Old Pierre swore the IPU would back the strikers no matter how tough it got. He'd have guaranteed them a slice of paradise, if they'd stick it out with him."

"Did he promise this before or after they coughed up their union dues?" I asked.

Mr. Kuzawa's caustic smile didn't waver. "After, natch. The strikers never saw a penny. There at the end the IPU big shots wouldn't give them the freckles off their ass, and I never heard of Pierre's fate. The coward probably slinked out of town late one night with his tail tucked between his legs."

"Why is Sizemore's affiliation with the strike so important?" asked Herzog.

"Because my balls are on the block for a murder I didn't do, and I've run out of ideas on how to get him," I replied. "Look, Victor told us Ashleigh said her father raises huge amounts of pot at Lake Charles, and Edna disappeared from there."

"He's our primary target," said Mr. Kuzawa. "Press on."

We continued poring over the newspaper coverage on the strike. Nearest to the stairwell, I first heard the reedy cadences from the top of the stairs. My heart jolted a beat. I'd a memory of the same ominous voices. Pointing, I mouthed a warning to the others. "Sheriff's deputies are upstairs."

Mr. Kuzawa drew out and thumb-cocked his .44. He leaned and growled at Herzog's ear. "Get rid of 'em. Fast. I'll be watching. *Capiche*, lawyer?"

Bug-eyed, he nodded. "I know the sheriff's deputies from court. Go duck behind those stacks. I've got this covered."

"Make sure of it."

Mr. Kuzawa and I retreated to behind the tall bookshelves. I looked through a portal in the books at Wines and Ramsey trailing a witch-faced, snake-thin lady filing downstairs. The placard upstairs at her unmanned desk had identified her, "Mrs. Ada Zigler, Assistant Librarian."

"Are you taking a nap, Herzog?" asked Wines.

"It's a slow day, and I'm doing a little genealogical research," replied Herzog in a friendly way. "My family is from Yellow Snake, and I'm researching the old newspapers."

His cover story struck me as screwy, but then he had the reputation of a screwball. I hoped the sheriff's deputies didn't check the microfilm reader's screen to see what he had displayed.

Mrs. Zigler's eyes blazed on him. "I saw the light on down here. Can't you read the sign we posted upstairs? This area is restricted to staff only. You lack the proper accreditation. I phoned my sheriff's deputies to explain it to you."

Squinting over the mildewy encyclopedias, I didn't like her snide tone.

"Doesn't your library maintain a reciprocal use agreement with ours?" asked Herzog.

"We do but that's not the point. You're not the staff, and you shouldn't mishandle the microfilm."

"Sorry."

Wines grinned at her. "Aw, dial it back, Ada. Granted Herzog might be a big, clumsy meatball, but he's not hurting anything. He just blundered his way down here. No harm, no foul, eh?"

"Maybe not but we librarians maintain rules for order."

Thinking of something, Wines scowled down at Herzog. "Where's your client, Counselor?"

He blinked innocent-like. "Can you be more specific, Deputy?"

"Don't play dumb. I mean Fishback the killer you got out on bail."

"As far as I know, Mr. Fishback is at home or work."

I shifted to get a better view and brushed against a misshelved encyclopedia. My hand whipped back in time to intercept its tumble to the floor. Just down the aisle from me, Mr. Kuzawa shook his head.

"Fishback has been AWOL since Friday. His cab truck is gone. He didn't call or report for work. His boss is a bit miffed," said Ramsey.

"Now I do recall he went fishing at Lake Charles," said Herzog. "He must be on vacation. Maybe his boss pulled in every direction simply forgot."

"That alleged fishing trip is a crock. Our drive-by saw nobody at Lake Charles, and it reeks to do any serious fishing." Wines shuffled their topics. "What scuttlebutt have you heard down your way on this gory stick up?"

"Sorry, I'm a bookworm, and I don't tune in the TV news," replied Herzog. "What happened?"

"Old Lady Simmons killed one thief before she took two of them prisoner," replied Wines.

"Amazing heroic stuff." Ramsey sucked between his black meerschaum nubs for teeth. "She shoots better than I do."

"Fear and adrenaline," said Herzog.

I watched Wines hook his thumbs in his utility belt, and his taut face turn pugnacious. "I beg your pardon, Counselor."

As I worried if Herzog had overplayed it, I felt something crawling on my elbow and brushed at it. A sting—ouch!—jerked my eyes down to see a yellow-and-black mud dauber. I swatted it to the floor and crushed it under my boot. My jaws clenched as I endured the sting's radiating pain. Tears broke into my eyes as the welt reddened. I brimmed to curse aloud, but I kept my teeth gritted.

Herzog elaborated on his theory. "Fear triggers people's adrenaline to the point where individuals in overwrought states perform superhuman feats."

"Are you bullshitting us, clown?"

"Not at all, Deputy. Well, I know you're busy, and other microfilm waits for me. If I see Mr. Fishback, do I advise him to contact you?"

"Yeah, you do that," said Ramsey.

"If you've jerked us off, clown, I'll kick your nuts up to hang off your ears," said Wines.

The modest Mrs. Zigler made a prim "ahem" noise.

"Herzog, why don't you get out of Ada's hair?" said Ramsey.

"As you wish it. I shouldn't be playing hooky. I should be looking for work."

"A little strapped, are you?" said Ramsey.

"August isn't a terribly busy time. Or profitable."

Wines snorted. "You lawyers are rolling in dough."

"Not this one, I'm sorry to say."

As they re-climbed the steps, Ada lingered at the banister. Herzog thumbed the button to print out a last page. "Just put the reels of archival microfilm in that cardboard box." Her sharp-nailed finger pointed at the top of the reader. "I'll file them at the day's end."

"Certainly," said Herzog after her hurrying up the steps.

My glance over the piles of paper bags overflowing with used books collected for the library's next book fair saw an Exit sign. A smaller one under it read "For Emergency Use Only!"

"Brendan, come read this."

I stepped over and Herzog gave me the page printed off the reader and still warm to the touch.

The obituary of Baxter Sizemore reported that fresh out of law school he'd served as a chief adviser to Jeb Longerbeam, an executive owning the Umpire printery. Baxter had lobbied Governor Clements to order in the state cops, a move that sapped the will of the pressmen's strike. I gave the page to Mr. Kuzawa.

"So Longerbeam got Baxter to lobby for the governor's help to strong-arm the strikers."

"His surviving son Ralph is Ashleigh's dad," I said. "Small world, after all."

Ada Zigler the bulldog guarding the entry upstairs forced us to use the emergency exit. I shoved down on the metal bar to thrust out the door, and no alarms clanged at us. I led our scramble up the exterior steps to the sidewalk, and we pelted down the block to where my cab truck hid behind the same cinderblock wall as earlier.

CHAPTER TWENTY-FIVE

I wheeled us around in the hardpan side yard, and I took measure of the Arbogasts' plain farmhouse before us. What did Sizemore see in it? Nothing actually. He was just a rich bully who got his jollies by throwing around his weight to smash up lives, and my rage heated up by a few more degrees. Just then, a girl's wheat blonde head appeared climbing the cellar outside steps. She toted a wet mop in one hand.

"I thought I heard your truck engine, Mr. Kuzawa." She yawned. "I stayed up last night stuffing comic book orders into their envelopes. Hey, it pays even if it's a pittance and I have to stay busy. Is this Brendan I talked to last night?"

My nod took the credit.

Profiled by the sunlight streaming behind her, Alicia brushed off her baggy dungarees fringed at the cuffs and a peach maternity smock. She approached my age but looked—especially in her soft, pliable face—younger. A girl, actually. She had flawless skin, and her breasts protruded acorn nipples through the fabric. She smiled, oblivious to any danger because her all focused on her portended middle.

"Sorry to barge in like heathens," said Mr. Kuzawa.

She leaned the wet mop against the gutter spout. "Not at all. I'm just a castaway starved for company. Have you had lunch? I fixed a mess of deviled eggs, and I will eat them all unless you help me. Stacking on the pounds, I'll burst apart like a whacked piñata."

"Dandy. Can we eat later?" asked Mr. Kuzawa.

"Well, I'm hungry as a bear," she said.

Mr. Kuzawa gave her the nutshell version of why she was a sitting duck. He concluded with, "Sizemore got away, and no telling what he will do next."

Her girlish face paled. "Brendan told me something about that last night. I haven't seen Mr. Sizemore for several days."

"You're in danger so we'll move you to your grandparents' place," said Mr. Kuzawa.

"I like the idea, but what if I go into labor?"

"We'll go fast. Meantime give your grandparents a phone call to expect us."

"Have you picked up any local scuttlebutt on Sizemore's drug dealing?" I asked her.

"Nothing out here." She wagged her head. "He does that stuff?"

"He's not a very stand up guy."

We hauled her belongings from her bedroom in the farmhouse to load on the bed of my cab truck. I brought out a bassinet, a baby carriage, and milk crates filled with folded cotton diapers. The red tick I'd spotted the last time panted under the porch. She told me Rocko belonged to the neighbors on the next farm. Mr. Kuzawa tossed his last beef jerkies to the grateful Rocko and climbed into the cab seat.

I added the final item, a bevy of teddy bears won at the carnival nickel pitches. When Herzog didn't appear, I went back in the farmhouse and bumped into him. Acting sheepish, he gave me taking a bathroom break as his excuse, and I let it slide.

With no room to spare in the cab, Herzog clambered into the back to ride between the tool chest and our payload. My sore bones and wire-tight muscles nestled into the cushiony seat under the steering wheel. The Arbogast farm receded in the mirrors while Alicia's breasts (more voluptuous than Ashleigh) mashed against my side, a pleasant sensation.

Alicia smiled at us. "My grandparents who just moved in haven't had a chance to drive up and see me. Thanks for your help."

"You're most welcome." I savored the feel good moment since a qualm told me the next one was far away. I saw Mr. Kuzawa cut a hard eye in the rearview mirror. I did, too, but I didn't see Sizemore's goons on our tail. Herzog rode flaked out asleep in the truck bed as if he'd no care in the world. That'd soon change.

***

Soon after, we soon crested the treed mountains and, with my ears popping, swooped down into the next leafy draw. Chatting with Alicia on the drought causing the brush-and-timber fires, Mr. Kuzawa pointed a finger at the cut-off swerving into a deserted, shady wayside.

"Why don't we grab a quick bite?" he said.

"You snatched the words out of my mouth," said Alicia.

Slowing, I signaled my turn. In the rearview mirror, I saw Herzog sit up, a bemused expression on his face. I wanted to find better privacy for us. My cab truck once trolleyed across the parking lot vaulted the concrete curbstone, and my tires crunched over a slate chip footpath that angled into a copse of hollies, their berries already scarlet. The canopy of shade and the musical creek lent us a haven from the road's baking slab.

"Is it legal to picnic down here?" she asked.

"Who cares? We renegades spit on the rules," replied Mr. Kuzawa.

She giggled at his hardboiled patter, but his foxy eyes never let up probing around us. I halted the cab truck, and as I ranged out, I saw the lean body tension making his movements whiplike and stealthy. Something had put him on needles.

"I've got a picnic feeling." He counterfeited a smile. "Alicia, break out your deviled eggs and the fixings."

"May I use your tailgate?" she asked me.

"But of course," I replied, yanking at the latch to flip down my tailgate and create an impromptu table.

All smiles, she broke out a red-checkered tablecloth from her wicker basket. "Give me a few minutes for set up." She waved her hands, shooing us off.

"We'll be off soon, so Herzog pitch in. Brendan and I will scout for unfriendlies."

Herzog's saucer eyes fastened to Mr. Kuzawa fingering his .44's hammer. "Why? I didn't spot anybody."

"That'd have been hard for you to do," said Mr. Kuzawa. "You rode down stretched out taking a damn nap."

"The wind musses my hair."

She laughed at us. "Hey, that's my line, Mr. Herzog."

Mr. Kuzawa and I left the holly bower and tramped up the slate chip footpath. Out of earshot, Mr. Kuzawa diverted me off the footpath to hide from the state road behind the pump house where a corn snake lazed on its hot tin roof.

"Herzog is lying through his stinking teeth," said Mr. Kuzawa. "I saw a sedan shadow us from Yellow Snake. They lagged behind, anticipating our turn, and I saw them whip down a side road to avoid passing us."

Having glimpsed at the mirrors every few minutes, I started to dispute him. "State cops or the sheriff?" I asked instead.

"Neither of them run tail jobs. They'd just haul us off to jail." Mr. Kuzawa's eyes slitted to gauge the copse of hollies. "Somebody knew we'd left Yellow Snake. I'd bet my dog tags that so-called lawyer is Sizemore's stooge, and he phoned Sizemore from Alicia's farmhouse before we left."

I didn't want to admit what by now was more than apparent. My bullet scratch inflicted during Mr. X's raid at Lake Charles burned my side. "Herzog is my lawyer and I paid him."

"Brutus was also thought to be an honorable man."

I nodded as my acceptance sharpened. "A few other things look fishy. Herzog's late night phone calls from the Chewink Motel leave him on shaky ground. His claim to be out scouting wears thin, too, doesn't it?"

"Paper thin."

"We didn't just bump into him at Lake Charles. Wasn't it a cinch locating the pot gardens? He had an uncanny sense of where to steer us. Why didn't we tangle with the badass growers?

"Cobb and you sure did."

"Fucking A we did. At the store while off finding his gloves, Herzog probably clued in Sizemore. How else did he lay armed in wait with a night vision scope to cream us at his mansion? Herzog also said he lost his gloves in the woods, but probably he left them as a marker pointing the way to us."

"Your making bail got Sizemore jumpy, and he needed a spy. Herzog grabbed the bribe."

Resentful blood heated by the new rage blasted into my face as I nodded.

"We'll deal with Herzog in a bit. Right now Alicia is our main concern."

"No guarantee I can keep a lid on my temper."

"You gave her your promise, so we should get her moved."

My headshake was forced. "Fine, let's get to it."

Back underneath the shady hollies, she'd laid out a tailgate feast of pickles, ham sandwiches, potato salad, and, of course, the deviled eggs, but I didn't bring much of an appetite. Murder and deceit churned those glass shards together, tearing an open slash in my gut.

* * *

Smiling like the butcher's dog, Mr. Kuzawa smacked his stomach. "Man, I'm full as a stuffed tick. Brendan eats so little. That's how he stays bayonet-lean."

Her laugh was nice. While she and Herzog cleaned up, I palmed Cobb's .44, what I'd trade for a Zebco reel, an ice chest of Pabst Blue Ribbon beer, and a long, sunny afternoon of bass fishing on a pristine natural lake, not the gummy, man-built Lake Charles. Or I'd opt for a weekend at sloshing through a clear-as-vodka mountain stream, casting my home-tied flies to snag and release the rainbow trout. When had I last taken a break to trout fish? Eons ago, it seemed.

Sad to say any trout fishing was a farce. That musical creek behind us had dulled to a plodding note. Rehashing my talk with Mr. Kuzawa at the pump house relit my flame-tipped nerves. The betrayal I felt stoked my fury. Something better give and fast, or else I'd explode.

From the get-go, Herzog had played me for a chump. He was Sizemore's boy, no denying it. The crushed glass grinding in my stomach gave me cramps. I stalked to the passenger side where the cab truck doors sat ajar. For a picnicker, Herzog sitting there looked glum and haggard. This unexpected side trip to move Alicia to Umpire had fouled up their big plans to nail me. My heartbeats galloped, and I almost went out of my head.

"Something rotten has loused under my skin," I said.

"Is the trial stressing you out?" He placed his fleshy hand on my shoulder. "Don't worry. I have it in the bag and sewn up tight."

I shook off Herzog offensive hand.

"I just bet you do." The hulking Mr. Kuzawa had sealed off the driver side door, pincering Herzog between us.

"Kuzawa, do you mind?"

"Matter of fact, I do mind. A lot."

Herzog sighed. "We're holding a privileged attorney-client discussion."

"No, I fired you." The snarl coarsened my voice.

"Uh, Brendan. Will this turn nasty?"

Her simple question startled me. I swiveled my head to her. I'd never seen a person turn so ashen. "You better go wait behind the pump house because our picnic is almost finished."

Mr. Kuzawa added his instructions. "Watch for the corn snake and stick your fingers in your ears."

"Snakes don't scare me," said Alicia, doddering off down the slate chip footpath. "But hearing loud noises do."

"Say, what is this?" Herzog heeled up his doughy palms at me. "You can't just dismiss me as your attorney. Your trial is too soon for a different one to get up to speed on your case."

"My trial is a sham. How many jurors have Sizemore bought off like he did you?"

"What? Do you think I'd accept a bribe to throw your case? That's an outrageous insult."

I let the cold silence stretching out speak for me.

After a bit, Mr. Kuzawa, his eyes on the footpath, said, "Alicia has made it to behind the pump house."

"What's gotten into you, Brendan?" said Herzog.

"You're Sizemore's boy," I replied.

"That's why he laid the lumber on us at the mansion," said Mr. Kuzawa. "He knew we were en route since you tipped him off at the store while getting your gloves."

"Untrue." Herzog grabbed at a straw. "The shots were fired at me, too."

"Really? You were a straggler," said Mr. Kuzawa.

"You told me to stay behind you."

"You've never been behind us," said Mr. Kuzawa.

"How much? What is nailing my ass worth?" I asked.

"Thirty ducats of silver, eh, Judas?" said Mr. Kuzawa.

"Judas? Me? You're off base. I've never took one dime."

Mr. Kuzawa snorted in bitter derision. "Business is bad. You're hard up to take anybody's dime, dirty or not."

"Some cash flow difficulties have hit my office."

How had he clued in Sizemore from the store? Snap. The way occurred to me. "Give me that damn thing." I stripped the game pouch off Herzog's shoulder and his grabby fingers. I dug under the flap, and an expensive handheld radio came out from it. The pilot lights behind my eyes whiffed out as my temper ran ice-cold. "Who did you blab to on this?"

"Dr. Smith now knows when to run his red ticks at Lake Charles."

"Lame," said Mr. Kuzawa.

"This explains the tail job on us." I rattled the handheld radio inches from Herzog's nose. "Secret phone calls placed in motel rooms. Gloves fumbled in the woods. Snipers perched in mansions. The guilt wafts off you like stink off a skunk."

"You'd better come clean with us, lawyer."

"I deny it all," said Herzog in a huff. "Ridiculous."

I didn't think twice. The .44 blammed. Its recoil snapped my wrist. Herzog squawked, and his hands clutched his uninjured knee. I'd missed him on purpose—a scare tactic. My slug lay embedded in the cab seat, just nicking him like the round had grazed my ribs. The acrid gun smoke replaced his Aqua Velva smell. I hoped he didn't go into shock—I still had to ask my harder questions.

"Spill your guts." Mr. Kuzawa's .44 lifted like a chalice. "Or I'll do it for you."

The horror to our violence trumped any loyalty in Herzog left for Sizemore. Herzog gargled out his half-intelligible words. "What do you want to know?"

"You're a spy. Sizemore bribed you after I made bail."

"Okay, yeah … sort of."

"Sizemore framed me for Ashleigh's murder."

"I don't know … really, I don't."

"Plausible enough, Brendan." The bore to Mr. Kuzawa's .44 speared Herzog's stubbly chin. "You better press on."

"Sizemore grows the pot at Lake Charles."

"Yeah, okay, he does that."

"Edna saw it, and Sizemore grabbed her."

"He told me as much."

"Where is Edna? She better be okay."

"Now that I don't know."

The growers' campsite emerged from my dervish of thoughts, and I made a link. After Cobb died from the shot arrow, I hadn't outfoxed myself. The spy I thought was hiding from me hadn't been a phantom conjured by my grief-stricken mind. The spy was real, and I was looking at him.

"I get it now. You were the second man. I got a glimpse of you at the growers' campsite spying on me. You bunked there when you arrived at Lake Charles, waiting for us to show at Lang's Teahouse. You knew we were coming because I told you at Pete's shop."

"No, I never did that."

Mr. Kuzawa gave Herzog a shove. "Can you turn any slimier?"

"You bet he can. He watched the archer kill Cobb, I said.

Herzog wagged his head in emphatic denial. "No-no. I was never there."

Mr. Kuzawa's face contorted. "It's curtains for the crooked lawyer."

"Where is Edna?" I asked.

A hapless shrug was all Herzog could muster.

Anxiety over Edna's strife diverted me as my sore gaze traveled out to the state road. Cat-quick, Mr. Kuzawa seized the screeching Herzog. When my eyes sliced back, Mr. Kuzawa had spilled Herzog on the turf, manhandled him to his knees, and stoved the .44's stubby muzzle between his teeth clinking on the steel like fragile china.

"See you in the fires below, Judas."

Herzog squawked, begging for mercy. "Don't, don't. Please—"

"Wasted breath, lawyer."

Hollering, I lunged into the cab and clawed to grapple over the seat. "Wait! Quit!"

Too late. Mr. Kuzawa's .44 thundered—*blam!*—and the expiring Herzog flumped over, sprawled like a sack of rice. Stepping away, Mr. Kuzawa chuckled as an escapee sprung from the lobotomy ward.

"Suicide. Damn. We lose more lawyers that way."

"Are you fucking nuts?" The gunshot had left my ears ringing.

"Get a grip, Brendan. What's done is done."

I swallowed. Twice. "Christ … I guess it is then. Doctor it like it was a suicide. We'll pick up Alicia and go on."

"I'd deal him another slug, Cobb, but it'd jeopardize the fake suicide."

Doubled over by the tailpipe, a supporting hand on the cab truck, I vomited the deviled eggs and rest. The taste of death—bitter as quinine pills—fouled my tongue and mouth. I hocked to spit but it was an indelible taste. Mr. Kuzawa strode around the cab truck's front, and pawed my shoulder in a parental way.

"This isn't so bad. Keep the faith."

"Yeah, sure," I said. "Keep the faith."

The experienced assassin marched back and staged the corpse just so, and we loaded into my cab truck. The horror tingled to the roots of my teeth. After hammering the gears into first, I edged out from the holly trees, stopped to collect Alicia quivering by the pump house, and we hit our stride again.

CHAPTER TWENTY-SIX

The cars stood stranded along the two-laner taking us to Umpire. The flaps to their empty gas tanks wedged out. There was a gas shortage on. I passed the bedraggled hitchhikers, but with no spare time, I couldn't play the Good Samaritan and pick them up to fetch their gas.

Our conversation ran thin. The stoic Mr. Kuzawa showed no compunction or contriteness over his mobster-style execution of Herzog in the holly grove. I still heard the fatal gunshot and couldn't believe what'd happened. My hands ached. Dirt track racers said they gripped the steering wheel hard enough to leave their palms bleeding. I didn't want to see what the oily dampness was on mine. My eyes kept grazing the rearview mirror, but no demons hounded us, and Alicia's cargo held fast. The risible irony of our safeguarding her new life while strewing the corpses throughout the Tennessee hill country wasn't lost on me. Any end to this dementedness lay nowhere ahead in my view.

I put on the radio for background noise. A man with a cheesy British accent advertised his proven system to make you a real estate mogul. After all, his system had enriched him. I mulled over why then he had to plug his book if he already lived as a king. Mr. Kuzawa reached over and killed the radio. Alicia shifted between us. Every mile registered on my odometer was a tenser and closer one to Umpire.

* * *

On the outskirts of Umpire, the rumbling earthmovers and scurrying hardhats rushed to build our new shopping plaza across from the trailer park. Edna's disappearance and Cobb's murder cast a sullen pall over my homecoming. My stomach wall lurched, but I swallowed the upsurges of bile. By the next curve, I drew in a lungful of the greasy smoke—the fires now ravaged our wind-scoured ridges. Every eastern Tennessee hamlet, it seemed, was burning. Was Armageddon's promised havoc at hand? If so, it suited my dark mood.

Alicia strained to clear her throat. "My grandparents just retired and moved to Umpire."

Mr. Kuzawa kept his surly quiet, and I nodded at her. "Did they now?"

"They just rave at how soul-stirring these mountains can be."

Mr. Kuzawa cared nothing of the local scenery. "Who's the daddy of your kid, Alicia?"

"Oh. Him. The last I heard, Kyle sold tires in Talladega," she replied in a bleak monotone. "I haven't seen him in months. It's just as well. He and I weren't in love."

Mr. Kuzawa grunted his disapproval and hearing that irritated me. Before I could say anything, she went on.

"Dad threw me out, and the Arbogasts took me in. Strict Catholics, they don't hold with abortion and help girls like me. Dad is still livid. I told him mistakes happen, but I sure won't make a second one. My baby girl will go up for adoption."

I felt Alicia's shudder as she went on.

"Mr. Herzog said he was worried about me."

"Uh-huh." Mr. Kuzawa glared out the windshield. "That Judas sold us out. He'd stab anybody in the back if it made him an extra nickel."

"Is Mr. Sizemore really that dangerous?"

Her avid eyes spurred me to nod. "He's bad news. Stick near home until this thing can blow over. I'd give it a week or more."

"Something else. Expunge us from your memory. If the cops ask, just play dumb with them," said Mr. Kuzawa.

"Got it. I never saw Mr. Herzog. My grandparents moved me in with them. They'll go along with the story, I'm sure."

"Dandy. Here's something else. How you decide to lead your life is your business, but I'd ponder your unborn's future. Then put yourself not in it. You'll never get to enjoy any Kodak moments together like first communion, proms, and graduations. Do you follow what I'm saying? Over the long haul, you might come to regret and resent your decision if you make it without due thought."

My clenched teeth pained my jaws. Here the hypocrite preached to her after we'd asked her to ignore Herzog's brutish death at the wayside. I made a throat sound.

"Alicia isn't a kid. She knows what's best for her."

"Just my two cents," said Mr. Kuzawa.

"Yeah and mine, too," I said, testier.

"Hey, you both have given me good things to mull over."

"Alicia, isn't our turn just up ahead?" I asked.

It was. Her grandparent's scaled-down cedar cabin with a slate roof anchored the end of a windy, gravel lane. As soon as I keyed off the engine, a tall, spare man still energetic in his late sixties, bounded out the front door. Mr. Kuzawa lifted her down, and she ran into the man's embrace. Her grandfather, whose name I missed, lugged away the bassinet, and we made short order of unpacking her stuff. Her grandfather tried to reimburse me for the gas, a thoughtful gesture but I refused his money. He asked me if I was sure.

"Please don't ruin our good deed."

"Thanks for everything. Drive safe in all this smoke."

"Did Alicia tell you about our situation?"

"I got the gist of it, yeah."

"Ralph Sizemore is an evil man. Stay sharp."

"I survived Iwo Jima, so I'll know what to do if he comes looking to make trouble." Her grandfather's chisel points for eyes told me that he could protect his own.

"So you're the one who moved Alicia, and you never saw us tonight."

He didn't probe my motives. "Wilco, roger."

They traipsed into the cedar cabin with no glance back at us. I took over at the wheel, and we coasted on gas vapors to the state road, but within minutes, we shambled down Mr. Kuzawa's hemlock-lined driveway. I moored us twenty paces from his A-frame. He slid out of the cab truck and sluiced the gas from an antique bubblehead pump into my tank.

The tang to the evergreen sap tingled in my nostrils. I saw his flatbed truck laden with jack pine logs, his next load ready for transporting to the sawmill. Taking care of my dilemma was costing him money. I saw he'd draped the Rebel flag over the flatbed truck's rear window. When his hand pressed to my shoulder, I saw the two middle fingers were missing. Chainsaw mishap, I guessed.

"Are you holding up okay?"

He asked a damn good question. Was I? A low wind moaned through the stand of hemlocks, and I heard a boozy whippoorwill chime from under the shrubbery, and its obedient mate flew out of my narrowing range of sight.

"Look, we just can't go on acting like the judge and jury—"

His shoulder punch interrupted me. "Keep it real. Sizemore's goons had us in their crosshairs because Herzog had sicced them on us."

"Right, he was setting us up. We had to stop him." The whippoorwills had taken aloft. Any clarity of thought crashed in my tired mind. "Can we chill out and then go on? Edna is still hurting."

"I know she is. New dreams?"

The frustrations piling up tipped over in me. My tone came out harsher than I intended. "I've had no new dreams. Just forget what I told you. They're unreliable. Why I get them is quirky. Stoned, Ashleigh and I went to the motel to screw our asses off. Later I woke up and bumped her naked stiff off me. I panicked and sprinted out to use the phone. The sheriff's deputies arrived on the scene, and you know the rest of the sorry ass story."

"Don't lose hope, Brendan, and toss in the towel. A hunch tells me we're on the homestretch."

A spark jumped up in my dull brain. "Do you put our shadow car this afternoon with the sedan I spotted that night in the motel parking lot?"

"Sure, I'm with you. Sizemore staked out your motel, then sneaked into your room after you fell asleep, and slipped Ashleigh the fatal Mickey Finn."

I nodded. "Did they follow us after we left the wayside?"

"I saw nothing in the mirrors from the second we left it. Sizemore's goons had peeled off us."

"So they didn't see us let off Alicia."

Mr. Kuzawa nodded. "Are you phoning Mama Jo?"

"I think it's better not to rile that quiet tiger."

"She's worried sick about you, I'm sure."

Why did he always hassle me to call her? Why did he even care? "We talked at the gas station. What's new to tell her? Herzog tried to double-cross me. Edna is still missing. We're trying to manhunt a faceless killer?"

"All right, we'll recharge and then go find Edna. Maybe you can keep something down this time."

"It's worth a try." The crushed glass mangling my stomach again gave me reason to wince.

"Cullen will drive Herzog's Mercedes at Lake Charles down to the wayside, and help stage his suicide."

"Make it convincing," I said. "Or we get a hot squat on Old Sparky at Riverbend."

"Snap out of your funk. The rules of war say spies take a death slug."

His line of reasoning didn't gel in me, but I was too bushed to point out this was no damn war, and he'd no right to play the executioner's role. "Forget it then," I said to placate him.

Pleased, Mr. Kuzawa nodded. "Some dark shit is better left buried."

*　*　*

Minutes later scrubbing in the shower, I couldn't wash Lake Charles' filth off me. Instead, I drew a mental map of my pilgrimage departing Umpire and pushing north to my new haven in Valdez. Would I require a passport to get through the Canadian checkpoints? I'd buy a down-filled parka after I hit Valdez. Next Cobb settled into my thoughts as a deep-seated guilt.

My Valdez trip was a solo one because he'd died in large part by my recklessness. I visualized the jetliner I'd watched streaking its vapory contrail in the blue dome above Lake Charles. The steep gas prices made it cheaper to fly to Valdez, but then I'd miss the stop-off to tour Mount Rushmore in the Black Hills. Cobb had said it upset the local Native Americans as Uncle Sam did us by erecting the dams and altering our Smoky Mountains.

When the shower's hot water ran out to spew down in icy cold torrents, I jumped out from the stall and toweled off. On my trip down the hallway, I paused at the ajar door to Cobb's old bedroom and peeked inside. He'd taped Edna's high school graduation portrait to his bureau mirror. They'd never get the second shot to make their marriage work. I clamped off my wistful memories. Right now, my all was to bring Edna home and restore my normal life.

Mr. Kuzawa said we'd better return to Yellow Snake under the cover of night, and I might rack out on the sofa. Meanwhile he'd keep an eye out for any unfriendlies.

***

Feeling almost human again, I drove us off in my cab truck, the now dark two-laner tracking north to Yellow Snake. Mr. Kuzawa drained one brown pint of straight corn whiskey and cracked the seal on the second pint. His eyes glowed hotter than radioactive lumps. He rarely slept.

The speedometer needle kissed 80 m.p.h. as we careened by the dark wayside and its starlit cadaver of Herzog. My darkest thoughts dredged up Edna imprisoned in a similar hellhole. Later, we switched off our driving duties, and now riding shotgun I tried to relax. The tires' rhythmic drone shortening the miles to Yellow Snake lulled me into a fitful sleep.

The anxiety and dread teeming in my subconscious produced a montage of images, and at first, no recognizable people or coherent places took shape. Soon the colors grew in clarity to set up my next dream. At first, I fidgeted to shake it off, but the film reels clanked behind my eyes as my rumination spun out on its own volition.

I was sitting propped up against a doubled-over pillow in the motel bed. The TV showed the late night news—turmoil had reigned in Iran since the Shah dying from non-Hodgkin's lymphoma had booked. An IRA bomb had killed Lord Mountbatten aboard his posh sailboat in Ireland. Violence bred violence and not just in Tennessee, but violence gorged on a global span.

On the local news, the camera panned across the tongues of fire encroaching from the wooded ridges and threatening to scorch a home. The newscaster said the homeowner hadn't insured it. I heard Ashleigh singing in the shower stall (The Devil's Own had no fret of any competition). I fired up a new Marlboro from my last one smoldering in the ashtray. The dope I'd fetched from her Jaguar lay on the bed table by her pack of Virginia Slims.

Her shower cut off, and I heard a car engine bark to life. Before I could get up to peep out the window, she flounced out of the bathroom, a towel sheathing her. She walked pigeon-toed, and I noted her calves bulged too thick. She plunked down on the edge of the bed, and her baby shampoo fragrance titillated me.

"Did you just hear a car pull off?" she asked. "It's late for the motel guests to be going out."

"You just heard an ad on the TV."

"I guess so. Can you dig it? I sit polluted and can hold a conversation." She winked at me from under her wet bangs.

"Mortifying, isn't it?" I pointed my finger. "Are those puppies real? I've got to know." I lunged, my fingers hooked claws to unknot the bath towel. Her breasts bobbled out like a couple of coconuts. They were real, sure enough. She sprang sideways to elude my grope and, snickering, tied the bath towel back in place.

"Don't. Let my hair dry." Brushing the longer bangs into her eyes, she smiled. "Why did you go stag tonight? Don't you date a girlfriend?"

Angry Salem Rojos giving me the heave-ho still smarted. "She doesn't party. I do. Ergo, any romance between us was doomed to fail."

"I see. She's a tight-ass ice princess." Ashleigh saw my withering look over her snarky characterization of Salem. "Anyway. Your friend Cobb intrigues me. Tell me more."

"What else can I say? His dad fought in the Chosin campaign."

She crinkled her nose as the bath towel dislodged again. "Did he kill anybody over there?"

"Put it this way. Mr. Kuzawa kicked some major butt in the Land of the Morning Calm. Cobb said his dad later did some undercover work for Uncle Sam."

"You guys and your guns, yech." A shiver made her rose-tipped breasts jiggle. "I feel grungy enough to hop into the shower again."

"You want a back scrub to go with that?"

"Need you ask me? First though, skin us a joint."

"Ashleigh, your bud is primo."

"My dope pimp calls it 'sinsemilla,' Spanish for 'without seeds.' The female bud is tenfold more potent than the male bud, but then we girls are always that way."

"I'll say. Who's your dope pimp? Paco? I may need a new source. Stems and seeds chock the homegrown pot I get. It tastes like I'm smoking a shredded croaker sack."

"Paco is just a pal like you I met at a show. If I told you my real dealer, I'd have to kill you." We laughed, mine high-pitched. "It's safer if I keep that under wraps, at least for now. I'm sure you can dig why I have to protect my source's confidentiality."

"Sure and I adore you girls harboring your dark secrets. The mystery only adds to your allure." I paused. "Say, what's your dad's line of work?"

"Greed. Ralph is independently wealthy. He inherited our main estate from my grandfather Baxter Sizemore. But Ralph craves dominion over as much as possible, me included if he could swing it. What he fails to grasp is that everything in life comes with a price tag, and my price tag is the steepest of all."

"But he sets down no house rules." My exhaled pot smoke dispersed its fruity, soothing aroma. "That's pretty cool. Mama Jo can be tough on Edna and me."

"For now it's bearable. You never bring up your father, Brendan. Is he lenient enough to let you get away with murder, so to speak?"

"I wouldn't know. Angus made tracks early. From time to time, his postcards arrive postmarked from Valdez."

"What's in Valdez, pray tell?"

"He worked as a roughneck on the pipeline."

"Now Ralph wouldn't last a day performing manual labor."

A punch on the shoulder jarred me alert. It was dark, and it was cold, and the heater circulated cool air. My teeth chattered. We were moving. I saw out the windshield the wisps of ashes from the wood fires curling like snowflakes in the conical beams of our headlights.

"Update," said Mr. Kuzawa.

"I told you to forget my dreams."

"Update," he repeated.

"I had one dream, but nothing was new in it."

"Well, I've got some news." Mr. Kuzawa adjusted the rearview mirror by an inch. "A ways back, I leaned over to goose the heater switch. My glance skimmed the rearview mirror, and guess what I saw?"

The goose bumps prickled down my back. "That sedan is tailing us again?"

"You got it. I can't make out the model or color in the dark, but I executed a series of turns, and I couldn't shake them."

"They mean business."

"Uh-huh, but then we do, too."

"What comes after we hit Yellow Snake?"

He shrugged. "Maybe we'll lose them, or else they'll slip up."

Slip up ignited an insight. *Motive, dummy.* "Did we slip up? Why did Herzog shoot himself? We left no note. A lawyer would lay out why he did it."

"My agency used to tell us only a third of suicides write a letter. We know Herzog was pinched for cash. He admitted it to the sheriff's deputies at the library. The locals called him a loon on top of a loner. Loons get stupid, and loners get depressed. The authorities will think that life's pressures got to him, he cracked up, and he ate his own bullet."

"If any witness saw him with us, we're toast," I said.

"Who saw us together? Mrs. Cornwell not wearing her bifocals is blind as a bat. Alicia will stay mum, and she really saw nothing. Niki our server skipped off to Shreveport to hang out. All of us whites look alike to the zipperhead fry cook. The store clerk just blew her cigarette smoke into his face. He stayed in the cab while you and I talked to Mrs. Nelson and Victor."

Nodding, I said nothing and felt tapped out. I'd gone over my limit of spies, jails, overdoses, kidnappings, beatings, double crosses, bullets, and, all the furtive glances I'd taken over my shoulder day and night.

CHAPTER TWENTY-SEVEN

They were back. Mr. Kuzawa told me to watch the cab truck mirrors. Our wary tail job gave us an extra cushion, but their persistent high beams never snuffed out. Within the next mile, we galloped up on dogleg curve in the two-laner and a sunken dirt road tracking straight ahead into the deep woods.

"Give them a taste of their own medicine," said Mr. Kuzawa.

The cab truck barreled off the two-laner onto the sunken dirt road, coasted a short distance, and halted in a dirt track skid. After extinguishing the headlights, Mr. Kuzawa worked the column shift into reverse, dumped the clutch, and the cab truck—its rear tires digging—hurtled us backward. At the last second, he cut the wheel and swerved in behind a craggy rock formation. A dust cloud sifted by us. Only when he downshifted to first gear did I catch on. Our pursuers would come up and wonder just which road we'd used.

Meanwhile the rock formation, one of many, was our concealment, and he nestled us behind it. We hopped out and scaled some twenty feet to reach the rock's cap. The chilly air smacked my face. My foot balanced on the narrow ledge gave me a commanding vista of the crossroads. My cold fingers clinging to the fissure in the rock ached. The bands of muscles across my lower back tightened.

After a few minutes, our tail job traipsed along the two-laner, and observing the divergent roads seemed to baffle them. The sedan sledded off the two-laner, came to a crunching halt, and its doors flailed out. Two stickman shadows moved by the front fenders and into the headlights' triangles of brightness. They left the engine idling. The binoculars I'd had the quick wits to bring up with us magnified the agitation in their postures. I also saw them clicking their flashlights on and off.

"I told you they'd stop." Mr. Kuzawa below me was helping to buttress my perch on the rock wall. He whispered up more. "Who are they?"

"The dark makes it hard to see them."

I focused my binocular lenses on the headlights. The shadows cloaked the pair of men until they advanced into the tunnels of brightness. I was able to make out their dark suits over narrow ties and white dress shirts. One man's coal black pigment contrasted to his partner's onion white skin.

"They're a salt-and-pepper team," I murmured down to Mr. Kuzawa. "They're in dark suits, and their boxy car has a whip radio antenna screwed to the trunk. No weapons are in sight."

"Dark suits and a boxy car, you say? A whip radio antenna is on the trunk. Aw man, shit."

Processing that, I wet my lips. "What do you mean?"

"Our salt-and-pepper partners ain't with Sizemore. They're G-men."

His revelation unnerved me. "Feds?"

"Probably DEA or maybe FBI."

"*Sh-h-h.* They're heading this way."

The white man headed down the hard surface of the two-laner, craning his head as if for a clearer sight angle. His flashlight beam crisscrossed the pavement. Then I panned the binoculars wide right. The black agent, shorter and stockier, halted ten or so paces on the sunken dirt lane we'd taken. His flashlight beam spraying back and forth inspected his front, and I could see our stirred up dust eddying in the shaft to its brightness.

"Earl, what's your read?" asked the white man, his abrasive bass amplifying over the dark. "Did they go your way? Or did they stick to the hardtop?"

"Well, Gil," said Earl, speaking with a drawl. "I can observe a bit of dust and a fresh skid mark. Their taillights didn't seem to follow the hardtop's arc. I say that indicates they forked off this way, but we've lost their signal, so that's no aid."

"That's par for the course in these toolies. Playing the percentages, we'll stick to the hardtop. There's no good reason why they'd use the dirt road."

"With these squirrely mothers, logic doesn't seem to fly," Leaning in to peer, Earl hosed his beam to probe between the shaggy tree trunks. "They'd have their nutty reasons. The dirt road is a local shortcut, maybe."

"No sir, we'll continue on the hardtop."

"I don't know . . ."

Gil's voice was a bark. "I'm pulling rank on you, Earl. I say we follow the hardtop."

"Sure, Gil, whatever. I'm easy about it."

Flashlights off, they did an about-face, and their shadows stalked into the headlight's bright streams again.

Gil's sharp look included Earl. "These hillbillies are gun crazies. Take that convenience store robbery."

I saw Earl's curt nod. "Yeah, Christ. The glass and blood splattered all over. The crime scene photos look as if an abortion took place in there."

I replayed the store robbery we'd thwarted: taunts, gunshots, and corpses.

"Tell me why four New York punks are even in Tennessee," said Gil.

"Just off on a long joyride," replied Earl. "That's the song they sang at their police grilling. The state boys collared the last punk in the hot Caddy. He'd run out of money, gas, and luck."

Gil's face buckled in its anger. "The shotgun-toting granny is a liar. She thinks she's so clever. Somebody sure as shit gave her a hand."

"Boss, don't let it pop a blood vessel. Who gives two farts? The local yokels can handle that part of investigation."

I watched Gil jerk his shoulders. "True enough. We just work the federal side. All right, let's bag it for the night."

"Holiday Inn, tally ho and none too soon."

The car's doors thudded shut, and the V-8 engine growled to life. The sharp-dressed agents skidded broadside, squealing to grip the two-laner and then lit out in the direction of Yellow Snake. Spidering down from the rock wall allowed us to sit down and rest at its base. The pellets of sweat dribbled off my forehead. The feeling returned and eased my finger cramps. Mr. Kuzawa got my capsule summary of what I'd overheard, finishing with, "Now the DEA narcs are in our pants."

"No, we're just a useful conduit. Their tentacles are out for the local pot growers. Just the major operations get them juiced up."

"Major operations?"

"It stands to reason. We learned Sizemore raises tons of pot at Lake Charles, and now the Feds have caught wind of it."

An inspiration excited me. "That's how we get rid of this hot potato. See?"

"Not really, Brendan."

"We tie up what we have on Sizemore and dump it on the DEA."

"But no solid evidence pins the dope on Sizemore. Besides our goosing the DEA might jeopardize Edna's safety if he feels the heat and decides to end it all in a messy hurry."

That made sense. We needed to drum up the proof. Mr. Kuzawa drew out a flashlight from his pocket and knelt down at my cab truck. He aimed the beam's oval on the front bumper and, leaning, groped his hand underneath it to get at something.

"I verified this electronic tracking gizmo belongs to our pals."

Taken aback, I studied the James Bondian transmitter—no larger than a pack of Marlboros though weighing a bit heavier—Mr. Kuzawa had given me. "That's the signal they just mentioned. Why didn't they dog us from the wayside down to Umpire?"

"Because while we chowed down at the wayside I deactivated the tracking gizmo. Then I flipped its beeper on before we left my place. That's why I waited until dark to return to Yellow Snake, and how they keyed on us again. But I had to be double sure. They lost the signal after we deployed behind this big rock." Mr. Kuzawa flipped off the tracking gizmo. "We'll sign on again, but we'll do it when it suits us the best."

"When did they plant it on my bumper?"

"Probably while we were inside the library."

"What tipped you off?"

"Their surveillance was too slick for Sizemore's crew. Once a Fed myself, I played a hunch and found it."

"How long were you a Fed?" I asked.

He grew curt. "We'll just leave it at a few years."

I quit my nosy questions. Mr. Kuzawa told me he thought Sizemore had returned to the mansion and making another nighttime raid was too risky. So we elected to bivouac in my truck cab parked behind the rock column. Our seats were comfortable enough. Soon I heard his heavy breaths, but having rested earlier, I didn't feel sleepy and stayed vigilant. Herzog's game pouch jabbed me in the hip. I disabled the handheld radio and tossed it from the window. Bored, I let my imagination tune in to Valdez's pulsing nightlife. The soft neon to the ad signs glowed as a beacon to the lost sons. I'd better look hard and fast, or else I'd miss seeing it.

I tagged along with a gang of pipeline roughnecks out barhopping. With the long necks in their grasps, they took swigs between belting out cheers. They were a happy-go-lucky bunch, and you couldn't help but want to join their off-hours revelry. Shivering in the dark, cold cab, I started to feel bereft and hollow on the inside. The high times in Valdez stood a world away from Lake Charles, and I'd never get there by sitting on my thumbs as I was now.

Mr. Kuzawa moaned in his sleep. He garbled something about "Chosin," "blood," and "death."

I just let him be.

* * *

At daybreak, my cab truck accelerated back to Sizemore's main estate. My leg and arm muscles were sore from our rock climbing the night before, but my sidelong glance took in a visual treat. Out Mr. Kuzawa's window, the cerise red streaks painted Wednesday's breathtaking sunrise on the indigo horizon.

We traversed Yellow Snake through its residential streets and parking lot cut throughs. My radar didn't key on any sheriff's deputy or government sedans. A geezer pushed a power mower trimming between the geometric-shaped hollies in his bonsai garden. A lady who resembled a youthful Dinah Shore plucked her newspaper bundle from its toss into an azalea bed. Beyond the town limits was the driveway entrance to the Arbogast farmhouse where Alicia had cooped.

Mr. Kuzawa tipped his chin at it. "Set a Zippo to it."

I nodded. "Sounds good to me."

"The last time we searched in Sizemore's house, so now we'll check in the outbuildings."

Soon we rode up on Ralph Sizemore's main gate. But instead of driving by it and turning on the nearby bush road that we'd used before, Mr. Kuzawa tamped our brakes, and we slowed.

"Rub out any rent-a-cop guard," he said.

"You're kidding, I hope."

"I'm not ready to get my ass shot up, are you?"

I retrieved the 12-gauge stored under the cab seat. A rustic guard hut constructed of fieldstone with a red slate roof sat at the base of the serpentine driveway. No guard waved a gun at us turning at the gate into Sizemore's driveway. It snaked us uphill between the fenced pastures. The fields of jade green grass I saw rising and falling to the tree-clad foothills was worthy of a tourist postcard.

Sizemore's mansion on its own knoll supported a steep-pitched roof, and the gutters were patinated copper. Steel bars girded the angular windows, and the building had the grim charm of a prison cellblock. A bungalow sat tucked behind it under the maples, and a blue Javelin parked under their shade. No fancy car driven by Sizemore was in sight. Further on, I took in a tennis court and a below ground swimming pool, neither looking in recent use. Ashleigh had excelled more as a doper than as an athlete. Just the pothead calling the kettle black, I scoffed.

My truck bumped off the driveway pavers and traveled over the mowed grass. More eye candy awaited us. Svelte thoroughbreds raced in the next pasture. We rolled by an outdoor ring, paddock, and stable complex, all well kept. Ashleigh Sizemore had blossomed into a nubile girl on this fairytale set where I played her venomous troll. One kiss from me and her graces went all to smash. My sight turned hazy as I dipped into a brief reverie.

"Sorry about that, Ashleigh. It's a knack I have."

"I can see you're closing in on my actual killer."

"Our odds are improving all the time."

"Excellent. You've one more small matter to do in my service. It will test your courage more than anything else has so far."

I shook my head. *"Can't. I'm almost out of this. Did you know all along Herzog was double crossing us?"*

She laughed, no teeth. *"Brendan, you're so gullible. Friends will always fail you."*

"Then I don't believe I want to talk to you anymore."

The bite of anger jolted me back to real time. "We'll case that first building," I said, pointing.

The newer sheet metal building was a machinery shed or tack room. Its dented sliding garage door faced us. As we approached it, I saw where our wheels mashed down the grass over an old set of tire tracks. There were also the imprints of horseshoes, and I keyed on a memory of spotting those left in the sand at Lake Charles. Once out of the cab truck, Mr. Kuzawa stalked over and kicked the sliding door, making a clanging racket.

"Locked."

"Can you jimmy it with a pry bar?"

An inside doorknob clattered, and we saw a young lady, olive-skinned and possibly from India, sidle into our area of sunlight. A few years older than me, she filled out her khaki shirt and denim trousers, every bit as striking as Salem but a few inches taller. The lady moved in athletic, take-charge strides, and I enjoyed seeing the vigor in it. An ash blonde ponytail spilled from the rear of her mesh cap. Her hazel eyes harbored glints of humor despite her stern game face.

"Mr. Bates and Mr. Henderson?" she said in a crisp tone, and I couldn't place her clipped accent. Kennedy's Boston, maybe. She tipped up her clipboard and examined an invoice held on it. "Are you the wrecking crew from Yellow Snake?"

Instant fear stalled my breathing.

"Sure, that's us, but you're not Mr. Sizemore," said Mr. Kuzawa, his smile cunning.

She'd no return smile. "Obviously. I'm Ms. Sutwala, the estate manager. Mr. Sizemore left for a jaunt on his bridle trail; however, I'm authorized to represent him."

"A pleasure to meet you, Ms. Sutwala," I said. That was bullshit because neither of us offered a hand to shake. She also didn't wear a wedding ring. I'd gnawing doubts just how far we could take this mistaken identity ruse. "Do you expect Mr. Sizemore to return soon?"

Ms. Sutwala's demeanor turned frostier. Her hazel eyes, now without humor, pierced me. "He'll return in a few hours, but I'm in charge of this teardown project."

"I didn't doubt your authority," I said.

She tapped the clipboard against her thigh, her impatience sign.

"Just outline the teardown for us," said Mr. Kuzawa.

"I'm gathering estimates to demolish this building." Ms. Sutwala pointed the clipboard behind us. "Mr. Sizemore claims it's been an eyesore."

"Is that right?" The thoughtful Mr. Kuzawa scratched his brambly neck. "Any preference on how to do it?"

"You should know the best method."

I nodded when her hazel eyes flashed on me.

"Poor Mr. Sizemore has had a tough time, I guess, since Ashleigh died," said Mr. Kuzawa, anything but sympathetic.

"He's been a little upset, yes."

"Of course she was a little hellion," said Mr. Kuzawa in a leading way.

Ms. Sutwala's angry lips compressed. "So what? She didn't deserve to die as she did. Nobody does."

"Oh, don't get me wrong. I recently lost my own boy."

"My condolences then."

I sought out any credible pretext for entering the building Sizemore was in a big sweat to get rid of.

"We'll duck in to check the structural part," said Mr. Kuzawa.

Ms. Sutwala spaced her chukkas apart and knitted her brows into an expressive hash. "Why? It's just your basic wooden beams."

"Okay but what's got you so damn sore?" asked Mr. Kuzawa.

"Just go do your estimate and turn it in."

"Cool by us." My elbow nudged Mr. Kuzawa, our exit cue. We returned to the cab truck and glided over the pasture to the driveway.

"Christ, what pissed her off?" asked Mr. Kuzawa.

"She didn't appreciate your hellion crack."

"Did I say anything not true of Ashleigh Sizemore?"

"No, but you came on too blunt."

"Is Ms. Sutwala covering for Sizemore's pot farm?"

"My gut says no."

"Then what's hiding inside that damn shed?"

"My hope is it's what leads us to Edna."

"The right time has come to stir the pot and meet our DEA pals."

My cab truck wended down Sizemore's driveway and shot out the main gate. As we improved speed on the state road, a silver-and-white panel truck slowed crawling by us. My glance over saw *"HENDERSON & BATES, INC., PRO DEMOLITION ACES"* painted on its flank.

"Uh, you might want to step on it," I told Mr. Kuzawa.

CHAPTER TWENTY-EIGHT

They'd corralled us after Mr. Kuzawa juiced their electronic tracking gizmo planted on my truck bumper. The four of us conspired at the rear booth in the pancake diner on Yellow Snake's main stem. The white guy actually was Gil, and as he talked, the darker-skinned, shorter Earl kept his bladed eyes on us. Our coffee mugs sat empty, but the DEA's menacing scowls had frightened off our server. Mr. Kuzawa looked cool. He was the pro, not me, at handling this. I just sat back, trying not to look too scared or clueless.

"Mr. Kuzawa, we've assembled quite the dossier on you," said Gil. "Even if a loose cannon, you became a legend in the foreign intelligence arena. Assignments completed in the Prague, Bogotá, Paris, México City . . ."

"You didn't get the latest dope." Mr. Kuzawa folded his arms on his chest. "Nowadays I cut timber. Period."

"Why did you go to Sizemore's estate?" asked Earl.

Armpit sweat eked a slime trail down my ribcage. My pulse went a little haywire as my lower back muscles balled up. I had to chip in something intelligent. "We heard he's hiring, and our bank account is in the red."

"Uh-huh," said Gil, his manner skeptical. "Checking bank accounts is easy enough."

"Not without the appropriate warrant." Mr. Kuzawa unfolded his arms. "Are we finished here?"

I knew our fishing expedition was anything but finished.

"Not by a long shot, Kuzawa, so just cool your heels," said Earl. "Henderson and Bates in town have the same commercial name you gave the farm manager."

"Do they? Son of a bitch. Well, she insisted on calling us that."

"You didn't correct her misrepresentation."

Mr. Kuzawa jutted out his lower lip. "So what? How hard is it to flatten a large shed? We're strapped for cash and can use the work."

I chewed over how they knew we'd talked to Ms. Sutwala until they lobbed a hot potato into my lap.

"Mr. Fishback, your trial is bearing down fast." Gil used an officious smile. How many men had he killed in his line of work? Had he anguished over it? Since back in May, I had. He went on. "What's the criminal charge? Murder one, if I recall it correctly. That's a big hurdle to clear."

"A mighty big hurdle," said Earl.

"You'd be a bright lad to tell us the whole truth." Gil paused. "We'll highlight your cooperation in our official report. That'd be a real feather in your cap."

I imagined a drop of ice-cold sweat beading on the tip of my nose. The DEA knew too damn much about us. Gil hadn't brought up Herzog's stiff or the others dead at Lake Charles. Maybe that zinger was coming next. Faking my nonchalance, I lifted my shoulders with boyish charm. "What's on your mind?"

"Your attorney has gone AWOL. Mr. Herzog's secretary, a Ms. Salem Rojos, hasn't seen him since Friday afternoon." Gil's hard eyes speared me. "Care to comment?"

"I haven't seen Herzog in a few days," I replied, my airway shrinking to the size of a drinking straw.

"That's it. We've got no more comments," said Mr. Kuzawa.

Now angry, Gil tapped an index finger on the laminated tabletop. "You're two cool cats sitting there, aren't you? Well, listen up, cool cats. We have your cat nuts in a pair of vise grips. We sure do. Fraud and trespassing charges are possible, not to mention Fishback's flagrant violation of his bail bond. Be more forthcoming, or we'll clamp down."

Leaning forward, Earl grimaced at me for effect. "Ouch, man, ouch."

Yawning, Mr. Kuzawa wasn't daunted. He'd been entrenched on the outpost line at the Chosin Reservoir the nights when the bugles gave the signal. Seven divisions of the Chinese Nationals assailed their foxholes. The Reds assaulted in wave after wave like a tsunami pounded away at the beach. I doubted if Gil or Earl had ever fended off such lopsided odds. Taking confidence in that, I let Mr. Kuzawa do the talking.

His languid eyes drifted over to our DEA interrogators, then narrowed into beady lasers. "You tailed us down from Yellow Snake."

My heart rate juiced up. Had they seen Herzog riding in the bed of my cab truck before we turned at the wayside? Then did they see us leave *without* Herzog?

"Affirmative. You were moving the pregnant gal," said Earl.

"We've got better things to do, so we pulled off," said Gil.

"Bullshit. I muted your electronic gizmo before we left the wayside, and you lost us," said Mr. Kuzawa.

"You're mistaken. We never use those," said Gil.

Earl nodded behind his banner of blue cigarette smoke. "Right. That's strictly TV fare."

"You've run your surveillance on Sizemore since May," said Mr. Kuzawa.

The 10-watt light bulb flickered on in my head. The wine-colored sedan I'd seen parked in the Chewink Motel's lot when I called the sheriff from the pay phone hadn't been Sizemore. No, Gil and Earl had been spying on Ashleigh and me. We'd heard their engine crank up and leave as we sprawled on the bed watching TV. They must've returned later to check on us again. After I returned to our room from using the phone, they deduced that only teenage lust kept us entertained and left for good.

"You followed our Jaguar to the motel and then you left. I heard your car engine start. Later you returned to give us another look. When I went out to use the pay phone, I saw you in the lot. You got bored and split again."

"How about it, Gil?" said Mr. Kuzawa. "Does the boy tell it straight? Were you playing cat-and-mouse with them that night?"

"I'll only admit our investigation reached an impasse."

"Too bad. You should've stuck around. The boy was reporting a murder. Ashleigh Sizemore had OD'd in their bed."

"I'll only admit our investigation reached an impasse."

"Of course murder doesn't fall in your bailiwick. Narcotics are your all, and Sizemore is your big fish, huh?"

"I'll only admit our investigation reached an impasse."

"So you keep saying. Maybe we can help you out on that," said Mr. Kuzawa as his opening gambit. "But one hand washes the other, you understand. You Feds specialize in cutting deals. So, tell us what you need, and then let's make a deal."

Gil bared his rodent teeth. "Fine. A major drug player has operated in this sector, and we've had Sizemore under our scrutiny. He wields a big stick in the local politics, so we tread lightly and don't want to make waves unnecessarily. But we've learned big dollars funnel through his criminal organization."

"His criminal organization sells beaucoup pot?"

"That's just for starters. Sizemore has grander ambitions to grow fatter profits. His plans are to fly in the cocaine shipments from down south. The prop planes just track up the Appalachian mountain chain to avoid any radar detection. So it's expedient to shut down his enterprise."

"How are you privy to all this?" I asked.

"Our people infiltrated his workings," replied Gil.

Narc, I thought. "Is Paco your inside man?"

Gil tapped an unlit cigarette on its end. "Yeah. Since Ashleigh's arrest for pot, our suspicions have increased. Now we're taking down her father."

"Good luck with that," said Mr. Kuzawa.

"Yeah, well maybe I'll create some luck by starting with two arrests here." He dropped the cigarette on the tabletop, brought out two pairs of handcuffs, and dropped them beside the cigarette. "Now, what's your involvement?"

"Our involvement?" I swallowed but I'd no spit left in my cork-dry mouth.

"Quit your bluffing. You don't have dick on us," said Mr. Kuzawa.

"Don't be so smug and sure." Gil smirked as his hands screwed down their imaginary vise grips crushing our nuts. "The bottom line is we lack the hard evidence to make our arrest of Sizemore stick. Foremost, *where* does he raise his narcotics? Not even ditch weed grows wild on his estate."

"Yeah, we know that, but the name of the game is *quid pro quo*." Mr. Kuzawa sipped his coffee and all but smacked his lips at them.

"Why do we trust you?" asked Earl.

"Why not? You compiled my dossier. My credibility must still carry some weight."

Gil cranked forward bearing down on his bent elbows. "You've got our ear. What do you want?"

I fastened my rapt eyes on the handcuffs. Then I glanced at Mr. Kuzawa who was in control of pulling the right levers. I wished I'd half the confidence he did. He gave each of the Feds a calculated stare.

"Complete immunity. That's my price. You wipe the slate clean on us both. Any headlines go to you glory hounds. We just want back our lives. That's it, gents."

Eye blinks telegraphed between the two DEA operatives. "This is separate from his homicide rap." Gil used his cigarette as a pointer at me.

"No soap. I'll repeat it. The *entire* slate gets wiped clean for us both."

"Why? Are there more deaths?" asked Gil, sounding wary.

"What we've got didn't come so cheap. Dope dealers are dog-eat-dog."

"How many are dead?"

"Two drug mules bought it at Lake Charles," replied Mr. Kuzawa.

Earl zippoed another cigarette. He exhaled through a grimace. "Two are dead, you say?"

"That's it. Don't forget collaring Sizemore is a big coup," said Mr. Kuzawa.

Gil smiled, all lip. "We know that. Now, we'll bury these two dead drug mules in our official reports. Nobody refers to them again. Understand me?"

I nodded. Gil acted sanguine, as if this tidying up process went on every day in their shop. Dead bodies disappeared in the gnat shit print of their official reports. Lives amounted to statistics and numbers.

"What two drug mules?" Mr. Kuzawa was cagey.

"Precisely. Now, our superiors will have to approve your proposal," said Gil.

C-Y-A, I thought.

"Make it snappy. Don't leave us twisting." Mr. Kuzawa, rising, scraped his chair over the floor. "Brendan, we'll go on now."

Elated not to do the perp walk out in handcuffs, I didn't grin in relief but trailed close to Mr. Kuzawa's strides from the pancake diner. Gil snapped out a warning to stay reachable, but my pace didn't slow down or break.

* * *

After collapsing on the seat in my cab truck, I rotated the ignition key, cuffed the column shift into first, and we tailed a middle-aged counter-culture type in her psychedelic VW microbus weaving down the block.

"I sweated like a boar hog," was how I summed up my face time with the DEA.

Mr. Kuzawa's scoff downplayed my fears. "We'll hear back fast. Striking deals is their strong suit, and they'll snap up ours."

"How did they know we talked to Ms. Sutwala?"

"Obviously she's their undercover agent there."

"She might have an idea where Edna is."

"She knows a lot more than Gil or Earl does."

"We'll pave the way for Sizemore's arrest, and get me off the hook for Ashleigh's murder but …"

"Even with all that, you're still not happy?"

"I've counted on nailing Sizemore as her killer while clearing my name."

"He'll do big slammer time on the narcotics rap. Your getting any hotheaded revenge will score you the same deal. You want no part of a federal pen, believe it."

"But he's getting off too easy."

"He had Cobb killed, and it chaps my ass, but I'm realistic enough to take what I can get."

"Suppose the DEA votes us down? They might decide to keep watching Sizemore until he trips up enough for them to arrest. Where does that leave us?"

"They'll play poker, all right. It's fast and expedient." Mr. Kuzawa clanked down his window. "If you feel shorthanded, I'll get us fast reinforcements."

I envisioned a throng of action figures armored in bulletproof vests and equipped with automatic rifles swarming Lake Charles. I shook off the specter. "Leave Cullen and the rangers out of this. Okay?"

"Whatever you say."

My thoughts wrapped around a detail Cobb had told me about the land ownership at Lake Charles. He'd told me a deep pockets donor had ceded the Lake Charles property to the federal government, and I put my blue chips on Sizemore as the benefactor. Cobb had caught the property transfer notice in the newspapers apparently not read by the Feds who also didn't talk to each other. Clarifying the detail would nail down our evidence against Sizemore and pry the DEA off our backs.

CHAPTER TWENTY-NINE

After traversing Yellow Snake's main street, we doubled back, and juddered down an alley behind a Lebonanese restaurant, staying sharp-eyed all the way. No furtive sedans dogged us. Mr. Kuzawa liked my idea, so we moored opposite the Yellow Snake Courthouse where I'd last frog marched into while tricked out in irons for my bail hearing.

Four beige Corinthian columns hoisted the courthouse's elegant portico. A titanic revolving door had once admitted the citizens through the circular alcove, but we grabbed the exterior brass knobs to pass through the double oak doors. The mustiness to old books and lemon furniture polish hosed over us. The corridor we took was narrow and ill lit. The middle-aged clerk, still slender with prim breasts, seated at a walnut desk was dabbing a piece of sticky Scotch tape to pick the lint off her uniform blazer. At hearing our tread, she hid the piece of tape under her desk. Petula read the name pin above her left breast pocket. She smiled, and her eyes shone blue like her blazer.

"You gentlemen appear lost. May I help you?"

"We need information on Ralph Sizemore," said Mr. Kuzawa.

Dark emotions clouded her face. "Is he a friend?"

"Anything but," said Mr. Kuzawa with a disarming chuckle. "He gave us a hard time over the fishing rights at Lang's Teahouse, and we'd like to know if he really owns Lake Charles like he claims he does."

My nod reinforced the lie.

"Oh, I despise the arrogant way he runs roughshod over people."

"Ain't it the awful truth," said Mr. Kuzawa.

Reassured we were also just folk, she left her post and shepherded us downstairs to the sub-ground level where it felt even mustier. She lit the overhead fluorescents, wrested down several heavy as a brick property transfer record books, and talked all the while.

"Lang's Teahouse. There's a blast from the past. The old marina has a colorful history. The first owner—I can't recall his name, but he was Irish, I think—built the dance and roller skate pavilion to entertain the young people. Later the marina and ramp went in for the local boaters to use."

"Lang's Teahouse in its heyday was a swinging hot spot."

Somehow, I couldn't picture Mr. Kuzawa bringing a date to the dances at Lake Charles. I could see him camped out on Will Thomas Mountain to get an early morning jump for a bear hunt.

"Didn't Baxter Sizemore buy that property?" she continued. "That was the summer I had my first girl, Shirley Lou. What a scorcher it was, and no rain fell in months. The forest fires blazed away and spread to every ridge and the smoke—oh dear God—that wretched smoke. We'd bloodshot eyes and runny noses everyday for—"

"How did Baxter Sizemore get the property?" I said to correct her topic drift.

She selected the likely record book and riffled through its crinkly pages with expert ease. "This should tell us. Let's see. Right. Okay. Mr. Jeb Longerbeam sold the property to Baxter Sizemore for the princely sum of one dollar. Nine hundred and ninety-nine acres. No hold on, the adjoining tract was one thousand and one acres, upping the total to two thousand acres."

"Mr. Longerbeam rewarded Baxter for busting the pressmen's strike. Then his son Ralph inherited the land," I said, recognizing how Lake Charles was a vast acreage to conceal and raise bushels of illegal pot.

"You know, my memory is Ralph Sizemore donated the sizeable tract to the federal government," she said.

"Then he set up the land gift with an ulterior purpose in mind," I said.

"His ulterior purpose was greed," said Mr. Kuzawa. "The kind sending crooks to prison for a long time."

Petula nodded at us. "If that's true, it couldn't happen to a better person, now could it?"

CHAPTER THIRTY

Mr. Kuzawa thought we should have another go at Ms. Sutwala before Ralph Sizemore returned from his horseback ride. Unfollowed, we motored out to his estate, through his front gate, and up his curvy driveway. I didn't slacken our speed where the pavers gave way to the pasture. Our objective was the same sheet metal building.

My cab truck's loud glass pack mufflers alerted Ms. Sutwala who was shutting a gate at the stone barn. She lit out at a frantic run to intercept us. Arriving first, she blocked our entry into the sheet metal building.

"You're trespassing," she said, out of breath. "You're also not Henderson and Bates. Gullible me."

"We never made that claim. You did," said Mr. Kuzawa.

"Cute. Never mind. Who are you? Let's see some ID. Dig out your badges but just so you know, I maintain DEA jurisdiction here."

I glanced at Mr. Kuzawa who'd been dead on about DEA Agent Sutwala.

"Gil and Earl know us," said Mr. Kuzawa, flashing her some official-looking but long-expired government ID in his wallet. His willingness to play off her second mistaken identity of us left me uneasy but not enough to object. She didn't like us invading her turf.

"Shut up," she said in a contentious whisper. Her hazel eyes blazed with indignant fury as she regained her breath. "Your barging in like this busts my cover. I've spent weeks at busting my hump setting up this sting, and you botch it within minutes. Just turn around and clear out now."

Mr. Kuzawa tipped his head. "What's inside there?"

"Nothing that's important. Look, making enemies at the DEA is a bad career move."

"We're already in this up to our necks," said Mr. Kuzawa.

Adopting a civil tone, I elaborated. "We're not here to jam your spokes. We talked to Gil and Earl, and they gave us the lowdown on your Ralph Sizemore probe."

"We just went through all this with them over coffee," said Mr. Kuzawa. "Call Gil if you want to verify it. We'll wait."

She broke off her outrage, and the exasperation left her dispirited. "As usual, I'm kept in the dark. I didn't know Gil and Earl had briefed you. Why? The DEA is still a boys' club. Okay, Sizemore put his car in here. A recent home invasion frightened him, and he moved it to a more secure spot."

"So why did you want to keep us out earlier?" asked Mr. Kuzawa.

"Simple. I don't like you."

"This won't help out but I'll fess up anyway. We're the guilty party breaking into Sizemore's place searching for evidence."

She grew more distressed. "That's highly illegal. You should've cleared it through me first. We shouldn't be working at cross-purposes."

"Sorry. The next time, for sure. Where did you go then?"

"I was away grocery shopping in Yellow Snake. When I drove up, Sizemore looked a wreck, all cruddy and wet. He said he'd had to chase an escaped horse from out of the woods. I didn't believe him. While he was gone, somebody—apparently now you two—had broken into his residence. Nothing appeared stolen. I reported the incident to my field office, and Gil and Earl rushed down again."

"We know. They've been tailing us."

"They have?" Her eyes clouded with dismay.

"Gil must be your agent-in-charge." Mr. Kuzawa shook his head. "Some things on the job never change. When a case starts to gain traction, the boss rushes in and mucks around."

Catching herself at nodding in agreement, she put on a stilted smile. "I've come across for you, so now you can give. Which agency are you? The FBI?"

"Agency? You've got us wrong again, I'm afraid," I said.

With her wide-eyed gaze raking us, her lean face blanched. "You're not with the government?"

Mr. Kuzawa summarized our Lake Charles adventures for her, climaxing with our proposed deal with Gil and Earl.

"I've heard of crazier things in my career, but yours ranks up there." She sounded more relieved than anxious. "So, you're working for us."

"That depends. Is our deal a go or not?" said Mr. Kuzawa.

"We haven't heard anything back," I said.

"Come on inside, and we'll talk some more."

She unlocked the sheet metal building's door and toggled on the overheads. The light caromed off the dark blue Porsche I assumed was Sizemore's sporty car. Its sleek shape didn't match the boxy vehicle I'd spotted in the Chewink Motel's parking lot the night Ashleigh overdosed.

"Gil told us they followed Ashleigh and me to the Chewink Motel," I said.

"After they tracked her car there with no results, they returned to our field office," said Agent Sutwala.

"Actually their stakeout wasn't all that clever because I saw them parked in the motel lot."

"No damn kidding," said she with a slight smirk before she turned serious again. "I was hired to work here and gain Sizemore's trust, but I still haven't found his narcotics source. My leading theory is a covert greenhouse or a hydroponics operation. I observe his drug mules in their hatchbacks transporting out the dope, but how does it get here? Where does it come from? Do you see my problem?"

"As I said, we can help you with that," said Mr. Kuzawa.

She steadied her hazel eyes on us. "Where is Sizemore's pot growing?"

"We'd love to show you but . . ." I glanced at Mr. Kuzawa.

"But only if our deal has been blessed," he said.

"What if I call and see where we are on that?" She turned, left us, and closed the door to a makeshift office at the end of the building. My last glimpse saw the black phone cord snaked under a shag carpet remnant.

Mr. Kuzawa stopped in his tracks. "This is interesting." He had walked over to the rear of Sizemore's Porsche. I watched Mr. Kuzawa toe aside the leaning sheath of plywood and send it crashing to the floor. "Is this contraption what I think it is?"

My walk headed to the spot where he stood. "It's Edna's jet ski." Instant relief spread its warmth and soothed the knots in my lower back muscles. The mud flecked, banged up jet ski had been squirreled away in here all the time. She was near us, and I knew where I'd search next.

"One crotch rocket is recovered, but one girl is still missing," said Mr. Kuzawa.

"We'll tear apart Sizemore's mansion," I said.

"Rip it down, brick by brick. If she isn't there, we'll raze the rest of the buildings." Mr. Kuzawa lifted the Porsche's hood and removed its distributor cap. "That should clip Sizemore's wings from driving off."

The swinging office door fanned the air, and Agent Sutwala's chiseled face was flushed red from excitement. "Gil tells me they've green lighted your deal."

"Put our terms in writing and have it signed off." Mr. Kuzawa laughed. "The last time I trusted you Feds, I shipped out to a police action in a cold wasteland."

Her smile turned wry. "Given your small window of opportunity, Mr. Kuzawa, I'd urge you to trust us. This case is breaking. We'll soon ferret out what you know, and you'll have nothing valuable left to trade us."

His glance at me was sharp. "They've boxed us in. We better take her to where it grows."

"Great but first we rescue Edna." My head jerked to outside and down the way. "Sizemore is holding her prisoner."

"Edna is Brendan's twin sister, so this isn't just somebody," said Mr. Kuzawa.

"But Sizemore has lived alone since Ashleigh died," said Agent Sutwala.

"Did you search the mansion lately?" asked Mr. Kuzawa.

"This morning after he rode off I ran a sweep. I stay in the bungalow out back, and I have the door keys."

"I want to comb his rooms again. She's in there. I just know it." I bristled, expecting Agent Sutwala's blunt refusal, given our time crunch.

"Ten minutes is all I can afford. Then we have to get to his narcotics source."

"Fair enough," I said, warming a little to her willingness to help.

"Are Gil and Earl leading in the cavalry?" asked Mr. Kuzawa.

"Naturally. They're the regime in charge."

"Then we'll wrap this up before they get here." He spat. "Does Sizemore own any firearms?"

"None are out in plain view, no."

"Is the pony car yours?" asked Mr. Kuzawa.

"The blue Javelin is, yes."

"Carry your car keys or Sizemore might scoot off," said Mr. Kuzawa.

"No worry. My car stays locked and my keys are in my pocket."

Our hustling arrived at the mansion, and this time no gunfire strafed us. A square of plywood patched our hole bashed in the glass panes to the French doors. She unlocked them, and we filed inside. In spite of Agent Sutwala's professional help, I felt overwhelmed. We'd dozens of places to scout for Edna. Suppressing a shudder, I racked a 00-buckshot round into my 12-gauge's chamber.

My clank made Mr. Kuzawa flinch. "Brendan, don't do that again. Hearing it, I might turn and cut loose firing."

"Sorry. I'm a little tight."

The center hallway festooned with fox hunting murals funneled us to the library. Flanked only by the canyons of unread books diverted us on to the kitchen. Depressed by observing the sink of dirty silverware and plates, I pivoted to head on upstairs.

"Hold up, Brendan," said Agent Sutwala.

This time a detail had arrested her trained investigator's eye. I'd also given the yellow door behind the pie safe a second look on my last visit in the kitchen. She asked Mr. Kuzawa and me to move the pie safe away from the yellow door. We did. She pulled it out, and the expulsion of a sweet musk wreathed us. Pot smoke and Ashleigh's favorite fragrance, I recognized. The wooden stairs sloped down into a brick-lined wine cellar. By now, I was a pro at exploring such dark, foreboding places.

Before she could detain me, I crossed the threshold. Trying to avoid any squeaks, I put down my weight at the side of the first tread. After each step down, I froze and listened until I got to the landing. My next moves were even more ticklish. I picked up a chunk of loose masonry and sidearmed it to sail around the landing's corner.

The thump marked the chunk striking the concrete cellar floor. Braced for the reaction, I hunkered down, my hands covering my head for protection. Rattling automatic rifle fire sprayed out hot rounds and chiseled jagged holes in the brick wall behind me. The flying chips pelted my hands. The ricochets whined and pinged but didn't nick me after their barrage quit. Not a brilliant move, I realized, the tinnitus singing in my ears.

Nonetheless, we had a read on the drug mules' position and numbers. Three or four, I estimated. Hearing scuffles meant they came inching closer to the bottom of the stairs. Wired and numb from all the violence, I decided to try for diplomacy.

"You're cut off," I called out to them. "It's gone down the tubes. You better give it up."

Nervous coughs instead of more gunshots came. "Who's up there?"

"The full force and authority of the DEA." Agent Sutwala was at my shoulder on the landing. "There's no exit out except through us."

"Maybe we'll plow through you."

Mr. Kuzawa who'd joined us had a chilling laugh. "We're packing 12-gauges, double-ought buck. We've trapped you in close quarters. So, bring it on, asshole. Dare you. I'll take my chances on who comes out on top."

Nervous coughs sounded again. She knew the most effective way to parley with them.

"Look, we know you've got the young lady. Don't add a kidnapping charge to your rap sheet."

"Where's Sizemore?"

"He's on the run. Be smart. Don't take the weight for him. Surrender peacefully, flip on him, and plead down to a lesser charge."

"Either that or we charge in, shotguns blazing away," said Mr. Kuzawa.

They weren't up for playing heroes. "What's your idea then?"

She laid down their surrender terms. "Slide your weapons on the floor within our view. Stand by the stairway in single file, your hands reaching high."

They had a survivor's smarts. Banana-clipped automatic rifles scraped over the concrete floor. I counted three. We swept down the steps, our 12-gauges aimed, our fingers snug on the triggers. Keeping one eye on the upstairs, Mr. Kuzawa kicked away their weapons and protected our rear.

The three drug mules, their arms held up, were squat, toad-skinned, and cruel but not dim-witted even when half-stoned. They knew the drill. Serve your time, make parole, and fall back in the queue toting the contraband. I'd been a customer of theirs but not anymore.

"Brendan, snap to and round up Edna. She must be here."

Mr. Kuzawa's command spurred me to act. I left them and probed a side tunnel appearing recently excavated. It angled into the danker catacombs. Expecting to see a hydroponics operation set up to grow the reefer, I darted into a chamber. This one contained a bunk bed, its three levels rumpled. The ladder-back chairs sat yanked away from a wood table. On top of it, I saw a pile of shelled crabs, a greasy deck of playing cards, and a plastic bong smudged black from usage. But I ran into no Edna.

This far below ground, I felt too insulated to hear any noises made upstairs in the mansion. This chamber was the barracks to house Sizemore's couriers transporting his illicit wares to peddle and enrich him. The narcotics profits had financed his political ambitions. Seething rage propelled me to cut down a narrower tunnel into an even more wretched, low-lit cavern. A movement in my peripheral vision spun me in a half-turn. A scruffy captive behind the panel of steel bars had sprung up from the floor.

"Hey, Brendan . . ."

Her husky salutation fell on my ears.

"Edna—you're alive." I smiled at her. "And now safe."

CHAPTER THIRTY-ONE

An ecstatic Mr. Kuzawa frisked the drug mules' pockets to fish out the keys. I led him down to Edna's cage, and he undid the padlock to open the barred door. She shuffled from her prison, mincing a few tentative steps and wobbled on her feet. Reaching out, Mr. Kuzawa steadied her. "Easy there, girl." Smiling her thanks, she regained her balance, and we returned to Agent Sutwala holding the drug mules at gunpoint.

Edna's eyes were lusterless while abrasions and bruises marred her face. She moved her puffy lips. "I thought you'd never find me."

"Didn't you hear our gunplay break out?" asked Mr. Kuzawa.

"When?" she replied. "Down here stays quiet as a morgue, and you lose track of time. Where's Cobb?"

"He's in town with the other agents," lied Mr. Kuzawa, his leathery face unexpressive. "Agent Sutwala, please show Edna where she might get cleaned up. We'll hold things together down here."

Agent Sutwala assisted Edna up the steps and then returned while Edna scrubbed off some of the grime.

"You told us Sizemore left on horseback earlier," said Mr. Kuzawa.

"He saddles his Appaloosa and takes long trips over his bridle paths."

"Where do his bridle paths track?"

"After tracking into the hills, they peter out near some old lake."

"Sizemore is at Lake Charles," I said, remembering the horseshoe prints I'd seen there on Saturday. "He's ridden to Lang's Teahouse and the old marina. That's where his goons attacked Cobb and me, but we beat them back."

The eavesdropping drug mule snorted at me. "I should've gone back to blow your shit away, especially since you—"

"But you didn't, did you?" My glare clashed with the drug mule's hate-filled eyes. Mr. X, his partner mowed down by my bullets and now rotting on the bottom of Lake Charles, had no part in this conversation.

"I remember Lake Charles is on our topographic maps," said Agent Sutwala. "Is that where Sizemore grows the pot?"

"Beacoup of it," replied Mr. Kuzawa. "We saw it with our own eyes."

"Where is Lake Charles exactly?" asked Agent Sutwala.

"North on this side of Will Thomas Mountain, and it shouldn't be far the way the crow flies."

"Take me there," said Agent Sutwala.

She herded the drug mules down the tunnels to Edna's former cage and padlocked them inside it. The mouthy one flipped us the bird, and I laughed at him. We found Edna, and Agent Sutwala led us from the mansion. Gil and Earl's wine-colored sedan hadn't breezed up the driveway, and there was still no sign of Sizemore. Edna, Agent Sutwala, and I squeezed into my cab truck as Mr. Kuzawa clambered over the tailgate. I saw him fork a thumb over his shoulder at the mansion.

"Set a Zippo to it."

"Whose? Mine or yours?" I said, rotating the ignition key. He sure did like to burn stuff down. Just then, a flicker of recognition in me solved a riddle. "Just between us, do you set your Zippo to torch the woods for the fire crews to rush in and douse?"

"Why not? The people need work, and Uncle Sam is plenty flush."

Agent Sutwala dealt us a glance. She didn't realize after all these years and fires, I'd identified Jerry Kuzawa as our well-intentioned but misguided Robin Hood arsonist. His palm thwacked the top of my cab truck's roof.

"On to Lake Charles," he said.

CHAPTER THIRTY-TWO

My tire impressions left from our Saturday outing were still visible in the sand to the lane branching off the state road and leading to Lang's Teahouse. I feared my guess Sizemore had come this way on horseback was wrong. The dance pavilion's ruins came into sight where the lane veered to the left. The braking cab truck slew in the sand.

I keyed off the engine parked on the same spot as on Saturday, more than a quarter-century ago now it seemed. Our trailered bass boats still loitered behind the bushy hedge. My roving glance halted a few strides shy of the T-dock where I'd sank Mr. X into his watery grave. After vaulting out of the truck bed, Mr. Kuzawa made a half-circle, absorbing our drab surroundings.

"And to think the cream of the bands jammed here," he said.

"This marina turns my stomach." Edna rubbed her goose-pimpled forearms.

"We'll soon be off," said Mr. Kuzawa.

"What happened after you left us on Saturday?" I asked her.

She inflated her chest, and her breath wheezed out as a pained sigh. "Livid at Cobb, I gunned off on my jet ski. Speaking of the devil, where is he again?"

My teeth clicked as the tragic words gummed in my throat.

Mr. Kuzawa was blunt. "A grower guarding Sizemore's dope plants killed Cobb while out searching for you."

I rebuffed her imploring eyes. "Death was fast. Sorry, Edna."

"Oh, my dear Lord." Tears wrung out of her bleary eyes and leaked in hot tracks down her sore cheeks. "Cobb … he's dead … oh, my dear Lord."

"Sis, pull it together," I told her in a confidential whisper. "Give Agent Sutwala the rest of your story, so we can end this and go home. You'd headed off toward the earth dam and . . ."

Edna's knuckle trapped the salty trickles to her tears. She sniffed. "Cobb had pushed my right buttons. He always could." She sniffed again. I hope she didn't break down sobbing before she resumed her story. "I flew over Lake Charles. The rush of the air swooshing against my face was great, and it also helped to cool down my hissy fit."

"We heard your jet ski's engine," I said.

"Right. When I reached the earth dam, I buzzed along it." Throwing back her shoulders, she gulped to draw in more air. "A man carrying a crossbow schlepped out of the woods and stopped at the lake's edge."

My nod encouraged her. "Yeah, I think we met."

Her fingers tucked away a strand of the red hair blowing into her lips. "Curious, I watched him. He crouched, scooped up a handful of the lake water, and shook his head. I yelled over to him. After glancing up at me, he startled and signaled, acting as if he'd something on his mind.

"Completely clueless, I puttered over. As I pulled up on the jet ski, he lunged and walloped me over the head with something hard. I fell unconscious. Later when I came to with a monster headache and a big lump, I found myself tied up and sitting in a campsite not far from the lake. Did you happen to find my barrette I left behind?"

I dug it out of my pocket to give her.

"Thanks. The two men argued over who owned the baggie of dope. I knew they grew it there, and I'd learned their dirty, little secret. That scared me. If they wanted to shut me up, I was toast. So I pretended I was out of it. Later, the same one marched me at gunpoint out to the state road where they'd hid a jeep in the laurel. He drove me to the mansion and forced me into the hole to lock up where you freed me."

"Did the man left at the campsite keep the crossbow?" I asked her.

"Yes—and he killed Cobb, didn't he?"

I nodded, my eyes roving over Lake Charles in the direction of their campsite in the high country.

Agent Sutwala's head shifted. "Hey all, an Appaloosa just wandered up and grazes near the cattail reeds." Her nod directed our attention to the riderless horse with its hand-tooled saddle. Its scabbard held a scoped, high power rifle.

"Sizemore has scrambled off," said Mr. Kuzawa.

But Agent Sutwala who'd studied her subject's behavior since May understood the craven way he thought. "No, Sizemore is a coward. He'd never run willy-nilly into the bush. He's hunkered down here, banking on the probability we'll figure he's fled on foot and strike out after him."

"Try to call him out," I said to Mr. Kuzawa.

Agent Sutwala nodded her approval.

"Sizemore!" Mr. Kuzawa's drill sergeant voice boomed. "It's all over now. The DEA is here." He brandished his 12-gauge and racked a shell into its chamber. "You killed my boy Cobb. So the DEA is your best deal. Or your ass is mine. You don't want that, believe it."

A muffled response issued from under the T-dock. "Stand easy. I'm coming out."

"Toss all weapons." Crouching in her stance, Agent Sutwala aimed her 9 mm straight on the T-dock. "Hands behind your head and move into the clear. Do it slowly. Nothing sudden."

Like the cornered rat he was, Sizemore did as ordered and duck-walked out from under the T-dock, the bright sun hurting his eyes. The flamboyant lawyer wore tan jodhpurs and a white shirt above riding boots sleek and black as his thoroughbreds.

"You pay the piper," said Mr. Kuzawa. "No more holing up in basements or lamming off."

His overconfident smile under the Van Dyke beard ridiculed us. "Pay for what? I've done nothing unlawful."

"Then why did you crouch under the pier?" I asked.

He shrugged. "I heard a truck engine and played it safe. It was a perfectly natural reaction."

"Uh-huh. This is a strange place to ride a horse."

"Not really. I do it twice every day, morning and evening."

Using his new revelation, I cobbled together the final stray ends. "I know why you do. You pick up your pot cuttings. Too bad you wasted your time by coming today because we trampled under your gardens."

"Then where's your evidence for my alleged crimes?" He strutted over and gloated at me. Agent Sutwala covered him. "You've destroyed it all."

His blast of rancid breath repulsed me. "Those bulging saddlebags hold your harvested pot. Your growers pack it here. More than what is in your saddlebags streams out of Lake Charles. The larger gardens probably grow on the grassy balds. Your drug mules will grab a plea deal and testify about the rest of your set up."

"We've already sketched out the basics," said Agent Sutwala.

Sizemore switched his gray eyes to her. "You're really the DEA?"

"Duped you when you hired me, didn't I?" She glanced off at Will Thomas Mountain. "Finding this narcotics source is our linchpin evidence. You're shut down for keeps."

"Snatch off the saddlebags," I said. "That's what lands our dope pimp behind bars."

"I'll bury you," he said.

"Too late. You already drove my life underground." My gape parried with his gray eyes that I last saw shine with sadistic glee in my prison cell before he sapped me to recover in a hospital ward with a concussion. "What did you pay Herzog to double cross me?"

"You're confused. I never brought in Herzog. He was a buffoon."

A pang of doubt stunned me. Had we misread Herzog's treachery at the wayside? With Agent Sutwala standing there, I didn't dwell on it but asked, "Why did you kill Ashleigh?"

Sizemore was mute but his hate-blazed face just as well confessed to it.

"She deserved better than you," I said.

Sizemore muttered for my ears only. "You think so? She was a murderous, little slut."

I crafted a likely scenario of her murder. "That night when we returned from The Devil's Own concert, you heard our van pull up at your mansion. You knew Ashleigh and I went to the Chewink Motel. She'd partied there before, no doubt. You gave us plenty headstart before you cantered off after us in your Porsche."

Sizemore yawned but his droopy lower lip quivered, a telltale nervous tic I'd seen him use in my prison cell. I was driving my wooden stake into the monster's heart, so I hammered even harder. "By the time you arrived, the bored DEA boys had left the parking lot, and Mrs. Cornwell was asleep. For a price, either she or the maid had slipped you a duplicate key.

"So you stole into Room 7 and gave the toxic PCP to Ashleigh. How I don't know. A syringe probably. Then you duct taped the junk PCP under the bed table. Your less-than-perfect frame job had pinned me in the middle."

The haughty Sizemore laughed. "You've got a vivid imagination, but no direct proof."

"On Ashleigh's homicide, not yet. But on drug trafficking, big time. I'm sorry to foil your plans for a future cocaine ring. Maybe you can sell it in the yard."

"You're nothing but trailer trash," he said, an unsmiling slur.

Rage balled up my knuckles to smash in his leer of superiority. But restraint weighed in, and I slow counted. One … I couldn't stoop to his level. I was no thug. Two … but the putrid vapors breezing off Lake Charles defiled my nose. I saw the parade of dead men: Mr. X at Lang's Teahouse, Acne Scars the punk robber at the store, the archer at the growers' campsite, and Herzog at the wayside. Three … all of the dark shit—betrayal, greed, lust—had run into my life from Lake Charles. So I reached back to slug a right cross at Sizemore's chin.

"Don't, Brendan. " Her face and words tough, Agent Sutwala dodged Mr. Kuzawa's restraining hand and approached me. "Take a breath … relax … good, there … now, back away, and I'll take control. Do it, now."

Her incisive command told me the violence had to stop. As she commanded, I faded away from Sizemore. But my fists didn't go lax, and neither did Sizemore's oily smirk.

Agent Sutwala stepped between us, saying to Sizemore, "You have the right to remain silent . . ."

CHAPTER THIRTY-THREE

Mr. Kuzawa's eyes skimmed the ominous, battleship gray clouds bunching over Lang's Teahouse. "The damn hurricane will hit us if we don't hustle."

"I hope it blows up and levels the earth dam and Lake Charles dies." After I reseated the Magnum loads, I wedged the .44 into my waistband. I wasn't in the mood to take any shit off anybody.

Mr. Kuzawa, laughing, cracked the bond seal on his fifth, and we alternated tipping the Jack Daniels. It scorched all the way down. Invading the laurel hell, we set Will Thomas Mountain as our compass bearing. Pearly wisps of haze shrouded the grassy bald while Lake Charles reeked of a morgue's drain. The smell of death was fitting. Seeing the algae scum brought to mind our bass boats still racked on the trailer at Mama Jo's house. The Umpire Bank would soon repo them. I didn't care. We'd left Edna's jet ski in the sheet metal building. Evidence, said Agent Sutwala. Again, I just didn't care.

The morning packed a joint-numbing chill. I flipped up my jacket collar, and my coughs racked my lungs. Jags of pain drilled my temples. One consolation was the early frost had killed the gnats and deer flies. Coming to the ruins of the pot plants in the first glen, we redoubled our gait. Mr. Kuzawa had brought the sheaf of a rolled up sailcloth, and I lugged along the hatchet I'd sharpened earlier on a buhrstone.

"Something should be left under the rocks."

My nod was terse. "Jesus Christ couldn't tunnel out of there."

"Don't go dragging Him into this." Mr. Kuzawa kissed the upended Jack Daniels bottle, then said, "This Lake Charles mess is all of our own shameful doing."

"I heard that."

My palm swiped off the fifth's glass rim, and I nailed a hearty swallow. The booze re-fired my near comatose heart, and we slogged on until passing under the firs into the growers' old campsite. The abandoned black pot and fishing equipment were still there. The stench from Cobb's crude sepulcher needled our nose linings. My glance didn't include the dead archer, but the crossbow's shot arrow still creased a streaking coppery blur in my brain.

"Earth to Brendan." Mr. Kuzawa glared at me. "I said we'll stove that dead shitbird in Cobb's place."

"The DEA wants the dead shitbird."

"A piss-ant drug mule? Think again."

"But his mama will probably want him."

"Then let his mama hike up and get him like I am my boy."

I shrugged.

We crouched low, our fingers clawed at the sepulcher's flat stones, and within the next five minutes, we disinterred Cobb.

My hand cupped my nose and mouth. The heaves seized me to retch, but I swallowed back the rising bile.

"Just breathe through your mouth," said Mr. Kuzawa.

"I did and tasting it is worse than smelling it."

"You'll live."

I'll omit any physical description of Cobbs' earthly remains. Think maggots. Enough said. He weighed down Mr. Kuzawa's sailcloth, and I feared it'd rip and spill out Cobb. After we swapped out the two cadavers, we buttoned up the sepulcher by refitting together the same flat stones.

Swinging the hatchet, I hacked down a tote pole from an oak sapling. Mr. Kuzawa broke out a few pieces of coat hangar wire, and we lashed the corpse-laden sailcloth through its grommets to the notched out tote pole. Mr. Kuzawa balanced one end of it over his shoulder, and I hefted up the opposite end.

"Ready back there, Hoss?"

"Hit it."

Our pacing in lock step, we marched off. The cold rain driven by the rising winds slashed and flouted us. I imagined how bedraggled we had to look tramping off the mountain.

* * *

We tucked Cobb's remains knotted in the sailcloth beside the tool chest, sloshed up to sit in the cab, and my truck groaned off, hauling us away from Lake Charles. I flipped on the heater and windshield wipers. The rain cascading down mauled our progress. After shattering the empty fifth on a rock pile, the wet Mr. Kuzawa cranked up his window and produced a new fifth. We laughed and chug-a-lugged. Booze always makes life's dark times funny as shit. The wipers slapped at the sheets of rain on the glass. He pointed the fifth to behind us.

"Set a Zippo to it."

"I'd say so."

I wrenched around in my seat for a parting snapshot of the tattered dance pavilion and old marina. Then realizing how Cobb and I would never again bass fish curdled the booze heavy in my gut.

"We were damn near brothers."

Mr. Kuzawa replied, his murmur brusque. "Too bad you didn't see how much until now."

I nodded but I'd had my fill of Lake Charles.

"Do those weird dreams still leave you buggy?"

"Not so much these days."

"They'll lighten up. The battle fatigue drains away. Trust me."

"Thanks," I said, then, "Did you know my dad at all?"

"Angus? Sure, we knocked back a few when we didn't raise a little Cain. Why?"

My shrug coincided with the tires' solid hum gripping to the wet blacktop on the state road. The wind buffeted the cab truck, but I skippered us with a rock steady hand. "I never got the chance to know him."

"He did Mama Jo wrong by cutting out early like he did. I can see it was rough on you. I also grew up without a real dad."

"Did you search for him?"

"No, I always knew where to find him. He'd wiggled up inside a bottle. It was shameful for me to go and shepherd him home." Mr. Kuzawa gave the fifth of whiskey he clutched a doleful eye. "I guess I didn't learn much by doing it."

"Why did Angus leave?"

"The denizens in Umpire are schizoid. Either they love you or they hate you. Angus fell in the latter camp. It wasn't from what he'd said or did. They just tarred him as a black sheep. He always struck me as square enough. He battled a thirst for whiskey, but then only the Baby Jesus wears a shiny halo."

"I might go look up Angus."

"Why? To put a bullet in his brain?"

I forced a laugh. "What was it like joining the Army and leaving Umpire for Korea?"

"Different day, same shit. The top brass awarded me a Purple Heart for the enemy shooting me in the latrine. Truth be told, my proudest coup was staying off the V.D. report. Just don't let Uncle Sam draft you. Tell you why. I can guarantee you a rock skull president sits behind every war."

"Got it," I said.

"Say, that DEA babe is sharp."

"Who?" I flicked my eyes from the drenched roadway, and he grinned at me. A burst of wind slamming the cab truck snapped my eyes back to our front. "But Agent Sutwala is all business."

"Uh-huh. She digs your moves. I've noticed the way she watches you."

"Do you think so?" I smiled at the not-so-absurd idea and then asked, "What happens after Cobb's funeral?"

Bending forward and narrowing his squint out the cab window, Mr. Kuzawa picked up a glint shining there off in the rain. "Oh, I always keep a few irons in the coals. That's the key to life, Brendan. Having options and leaving them open."

I nodded as if I took his meaning, but I didn't.

* * *

Three days later, my grief and regrets blunted by Jack Daniels, I sleep-walked through Cobb's funeral service. It featured the usual condolences, tears, and pallbearers (I was one of eight). I wished they'd cremated him and scattered his ashes across a sunny, natural lake. Dark, dirty places, starting with graves and mineshafts, terrified me.

For the service, Mr. Kuzawa nailed shut Cobb's coffin using the hammer I brought. With a little finesse from the DEA, he fudged Cobb's death certificate to cite a fatal drowning in Lake Charles. Edna and I just played along, but few bought the cover story. She added a sprig of mountain laurel atop Cobb's coffin lid, a fitting tribute, I thought.

Afterward a pair of gravediggers revved up a backhoe and planted Cobb in his final resting place just two plots over from my Uncle Ozzie's tombstone (1892-1964). But it was Cobb's stark reminder of our mortality that ushered me pinch-lipped and pale-faced out the cemetery gate. Then my life started on its upward trend.

CHAPTER THIRTY-FOUR

Yellow Snake's roly-poly prosecutor went ahead and filed the motions of dismissal to rescind my homicide charge of Ashleigh Sizemore. I suspected the DEA spearheaded by Agent Sutwala leaned on the locals, maybe threatening to expose their political corruption. She was my hero. Over a short time, Ashleigh's homicide dropped off the cops' radar and then into the cold case bin.

Ralph Sizemore never confessed to her murder, but I stuck to my pet theory. He'd sneaked into Room 7, injected her while asleep in bed with me, and taped the baggie of tainted angel dust under the bed table to frame me. His team of legal superstars couldn't help him skate.

He and his drug-trafficking henchmen went to prison with no chance at parole until my middle age. Their federal penitentiary stood in godawful Nevada, very different from Sizemore's tony digs in Yellow Snake. How the mighty had fallen. Word came back he tried to bargain for a sentence reduction by snitching on me as the two drug mules' killer. But Joe Law just said good riddance.

Besides going cold turkey on reefer and nicotine, I also aced my booze cure. Yep, I cleaned up my whole act. It was a bitch, too. I thanked God I had an edge. The jugs of mountain branch water Edna kept stocked in my fridge accelerated the process.

"You don't have to do this, but thanks."

"Glad to help you out." Her coy glance engaged me. "That DEA lady is a hottie."

"She's a real pro, yeah."

"Have you called her yet?"

"I keep her business card handy." I couldn't blame my sudden hand sweat on the detox. Maybe I was falling in love again.

"Ring her. Today." Then Edna blinked at me. "The cops never found Cobb's killer. Is he buried at Lake Charles?"

"Why do you ask?"

"I'd feel better by knowing it."

My glance caught her shudder, and the horror mangling her face. Harrowing images of what befell her at the growers' campsite rocked me. I smelled the gamey bedrolls. I visualized her pinioned to them, writhing as the stoned growers raped her. Had the bastard Herzog stood by and leered at it? The old rage carved new vicious slices to my gut.

"What went down up there?" I asked her.

"N-n-nothing happened . . ."

The seconds crawled into hours. She didn't break off our stare down. I did. "He won't touch you again."

She nodded. "I'm relieved to hear it."

"Did you know Ashleigh Sizemore?"

"So-so. She was the friend of a friend."

"But did you party with her?"

Edna reacted with a yucky face. "No, never. Why the third degree?"

"I heard some talk," I said, brushing aside the topic.

"Didn't you have bad dreams about Ashleigh?"

"Not so much now but let's not talk about it."

"Sure, if you forget I was in that campsite."

"Deal." But I knew not a day would pass without my stewing about it.

* * *

Agent Sutwala returned my call and allayed my jitters. The white, crystalline PCP, she reassured me, tasted caustic as battery acid. PCP also warped your sense of time and left you feeling weightless. You grew delusional, and some users did a Brodie off a bridge.

"If you'd ingested any PCP, we probably wouldn't be having this conversation."

"Even if, I'll play it safe and stay off any bridges. I appreciate the information, Agent Sutwala."

The silence over our connection lengthened. My excuse to call her on the PCP use was supposed to segue into less intense topics. At last, she spoke.

"Can we drop the formality, especially since I'm a short timer. Just call me Veera."

"Sure, Veera." I didn't ask why she was bailing from the DEA. Mr. Kuzawa had had his reasons, and hers had to lie much in the same vein. The field office reports touted Gil and Earl's glowing exploits while Agent Veera Sutwala rated a slight acknowledgement buried somewhere on page three, if any mention at all. But something more basic arose.

"With the wrong plumbing, I'll never fit in there." Her voice was so downbeat, and hearing it broke my heart.

"Sorry to hear that."

"Thanks. I'm no quitter, but I'm no masochist either." She sounded wound up with some concerns to air, and I was a patient listener. "Three years ago you'd be amazed at what it took. The perp had drawn down first. Clean shoot, case closed, my boss told me. Routine investigation. I was so gullible. The investigation went on for months before they finally exonerated me. It's extra tough on the job when your own people doubt you."

"I can empathize," I said, eyeing Cobb's lethal .44 on the countertop.

"This Sizemore case was the last straw. I didn't even rate an 'attagirl.' Shit. Maybe I'll move back to Boston. I don't know. Whoa, listen to me rambling on like this to a stranger."

Me, a stranger? Hearing that smarted a little. I detected a hint of loneliness underlying her litany of professional setbacks.

She reclaimed some of her spunk. "How are you bearing up?"

"I'm staying on the beam."

"Sorry about your friend Cobb. That's a toughie."

The lump in my throat was like swallowing over a golf ball. "Thanks."

"This phone call must be costing you a mint. You'd better go."

"Stay in touch, Brendan. I'd like to hear from you. Bye."

Her sincerity lingered in my mind as a tantalizing perfume left in a candlelit café. I liked Veera. A whole lot, I'd soon come to discover.

* * *

Following Mr. Kuzawa's advice, I boycotted my local draft board. The last legitimate war, he told me with a subversive smile, was in Korea, but his doubts on that deepened. Uncle Sam had lied then, too, he decided. It wasn't long before he sold his place to a land developer, gave away his war medals, and skipped town. I called over one day, and the phone company had disconnected his line. Pete Rojos passed on the rumor Mr. Kuzawa had hitched on with Cullen and the Smoky Mountain Rangers.

Perplexed, I sorted it out as the best I could. Maybe our disenfranchised war heroes like Mr. Kuzawa only felt dignity while hanging out with the ranger elements. Maybe he felt the heat from the police investigation of the store robbery we'd pre-empted in Yellow Snake. Maybe he wanted to make sure Cullen kept his mouth shut about moving the late Herzog's Mercedes from Lake Charles and parking it at the wayside for the faked suicide. All I knew was there'd be fewer brush fires blazing up in the mountains, and I'd never lay eyes on Mr. Kuzawa again. I also went ahead and registered with my draft board. Pick your fights, I concluded.

* * *

The autumn rains deluged us and doused the ridge fires. Our mountain air sweetened, and you could breathe in deep again. After my pressman shifts, I fell into bed and slept a lot sounder. I caught up on my back rent and paid off the Yellow Snake hospital bill. By Halloween, our shop buzzed over the impending RIFs and shipping our jobs offshore for coolie wages. Options. That was the key to life, Mr. Kuzawa had told me, and I set out identifying mine.

Lake Charles' days were numbered. The all-wise TVA declared the earth dam unsafe (*it was*), dynamited a hole in it, and drained the lake dry. But even when emptied, Lake Charles hadn't finished with me. A geezer using a metal detector to find the coins left by the young couples at the dances uncovered the skeletal remains to an adult male. Mr. X's .223 rifle (his bullet had grazed my side during their night raid on Cobb and me) made the metal detector chirp. The bones rested a few paces away from the T-dock. The carp had let me down.

The discovery of Mr. X's bones raised a stink. The DEA put up a smokescreen but for how long? I went into a funk, and Mama Jo noticed it. I'd driven over for lunch followed by another bat extraction from her attic.

"You fished at Lake Charles. Any ideas on the dead man?" She sent me a frank gaze.

"It beats me. Maybe he's our own D.B. Cooper."

"Not funny." Hands went on her hips. Her hard eye contact didn't fall away from me. "You want to try again?" The pause grew awkward.

"All right, I won't lie. Some dark stuff hit us at Lake Charles."

"Leave it at that then." She acted as if she already knew the worst. "Please go pen up my goats. Axel from across the street let them out. Then we'll evict the bats. Hopefully this time will be permanent."

* * *

That same afternoon I dropped by our public library behind Mr. Rojos' shop. Huddled over a back table, I riffled through the newspaper archives and culled out some intriguing tidbits. The articles I read described fellow citizens who'd felt their lives were in danger and had killed their aggressor. In each instance, the DAs didn't file criminal charges. Justified self-defense, they ruled it. Clean shoot, case closed, as Veera had told me.

The self-defense label appealed to me. I reconciled the Lake Charles casualties—Mr. X ambushing us at Lang's Teahouse and Cobb's killer notching an arrow in the crossbow for me—in the same manner. The rationale did much to ease my guilt. A more recent article reported the three young thieves from New York we caught at the Yellow Snake store had shipped off to prison downstate. Reminded how damn close I'd come to wearing penal orange, my freedom tasted all the sweeter.

CHAPTER THIRTY-FIVE

Evenings alone in my flat I vegged out, listened to FM radio beamed out of Chicago, and hoped Cobb, like Ashleigh, would pop up in a dream. The bastard didn't. Once or twice, I broke down and cried in the shower. But for the most part, I kept my chin up, and my shit wired tight.

I put up the window and removed the dreamcatcher Salem gave me and trashed it. My bizarre dreams tapered off and then quit altogether. I assumed all the pot's THC had sweated out of my fat cells. I'd promised to give Salem a phone call when I kicked my nasty substance habit so I tracked her down to her dorm at Vanderbilt University in Nashville. I felt brash and smug.

"So, you're a big college girl now."

"Uh, yeah, I guess I am. Why did you call, Brendan?"

"You asked me. Remember?"

"But only if you had quit smoking your pot."

"Done."

"Uh-huh. Simple as that, eh?"

"It wasn't simple but I'm clean."

"I'm happy for you. Really."

"Thanks. Really."

"I was sorry to hear about Cobb."

I lost the brash and smug. "Thanks."

"Are you seeing anybody?"

"Damn, you're still blunt as ever."

"Is that a yes or no?"

"Actually I'm getting ready to leave for Valdez."

She laughed in surprise. "Better you than me. Why?"

I was cool. "Personal reasons."

"I was glad to get away from Umpire especially after Herzog …"

"Yeah, that was strange."

"I've no idea why he drove to Lake Charles. Do you?"

"A hunting trip is what he told me."

"What he did was terrible. Do you know why?"

"No. We didn't get personal."

"I liked him even if he was an oddball."

"Herzog was an A-1 asshole. Trust me."

"You shouldn't speak ill of the dead."

"Uh-huh, I'm shaking in my boots."

"Did you get your legal squabbles straightened out?"

"The kid is all right, Salem."

I heard the silly college girls laughing in the background. "Look, I gotta go," she said. "Best of luck in Valerie."

"Valdez. Right back at you."

"Be good to yourself, Brendan. Bye."

Only after I racked the phone headset did I realize I hadn't asked if she was dating a steady. Did it matter? That week I just grew antsier. What was I to make of my life? Then my old plan resurfaced. My palms itched to do rugged, honest labor. Toiling on a logger crew with my dad held its glamorous sway. My letter to him was terse and matter-of-fact. I posted it to general delivery, Valdez, Alaska. It was a long shot, and I didn't expect a reply, but one came back.

The letter I picked up from Mama Jo's house was my first contact with Angus Fishback since I'd wailed in diapers. He was no longer a ghost. My tingling fingers tore apart the envelope, and I skimmed what he'd scrawled in a loopy but legible style on chintzy motel stationary.

Hey, Brendan,

What can I say? Your mom & I were babes ourselves when we had you. We'd already married, so you can't be a love child or as that. But like I said, we were wild & green when it came to parenthood. Still, we tried to do our best, at least in those early days. Then I let itchy feet get the better of me—I split for good.

Believe it or not, it was my plan to return to Umpire, but time sneaked off. I called once but hung up on the third ring. The pipeline was my gravy train for a long ride, then our work fell off. Now a skeleton crew keeps it humming. I toil in timber. It's gut-busting work, too, even for a veteran as me. We use skidders & winches, but our rookies start out playing gopher while they pick up the ins and outs. You could swing it, I'm sure.

Oh yeah, your mom & I went to the dances at Lake Charles. Lang's Teahouse was our happening spot. In fact, you happened there, if you get my drift. I don't know about now, but in those days the lovers couldn't wait to hear the tunes. Hot bands jammed till dawn, & your mom was always the last gal to leave the party. She lived to go shake it. Ah God, Lake Charles …

Anyhow, I didn't mean to go on like this. My hand is getting cramped, so I better sign off. To field your question, sure, why the hell not drive on up? Valdez isn't the live wire it was, but we can catch up over a brew. Let me pay.

Cheers,

Angus Fishback

P.S. Say hello to your sister Eleanor & give my best to your mother, even if she curses my name on her every breath!

For Christ's sake, he'd botched getting Edna's name right, but I stowed my duffel in a ratty, old sea bag Cobb had left in my cab truck and set aside his .44 to pawn later. After some debate, I also inserted the "Song Lyrics by B. Fishback" journal, but I left my detox literature on top of the fridge.

My trip downtown put me in the gas line behind a yellow Malibu. The daughter and her infirmed mother had parked on Main Street after my last dentist visit. This time they waved first, and I returned it. Similar gas lines lay in store for me, but I couldn't let such an inconvenience run my life. I unclasped the St. John of God (the patron saint of printers) medallion, from my rearview mirror and stuffed it in the glove compartment.

While topping off my gas tank, I said a Hail Mary for my cab truck to survive all the rigors of my trek north to Valdez. I pulled the dipstick, glugged in a quart of SAE 10w30 motor oil, and knelt to inflate my tires. Quilly, the elderly station attendant, ambled up, his nod a guarded one.

"You're not behind bars."

"No sir, the cops dropped all the charges."

"Uh-huh." He crouched and screwed on the plastic cap to a pressure valve stem. "Your shyster Herzog didn't make it so well."

My pulse locked in mid-beat, but after a quick breath, my tone remained offhand. "Yeah, I heard he fell into a funk. Bummer."

"The whispers going around say he'd some help with eating that bullet."

"People say what they will." My hands waved off his concern. "But I wouldn't read too much into it."

"Uh-huh. Taking a long trip right now isn't a bad idea." He accepted the air hose from my trembling hands to coil up and rack on its hook.

"Thanks for the tip," I said. "And the air."

"Any time."

Back at the steering wheel, I winced as my lower back muscles kinked in knots. I flooded the carburetor before the engine coughed over. My pace was slow as I sweated under my shirt. Back at my flat, I settled down enough to write out my resignation letter to Longerbeam Printery. By breaking the lease, I'd forfeit my security deposit. Collateral damage, I figured. Mama Jo was up watching, she said, *The Dukes of Hazzard* when I phoned and let her in on my decision.

"Well, I blame it on that damn letter from Angus."

"No, I'd been mulling over the Valdez trip."

"Don't get suckered. He's smooth as an insurance salesman."

"He wrote me *all* about Lang's Teahouse," I said, fishing for her comment on my possible conception there.

"Yeah, we flocked to the dances." Mama Jo sighing over nostalgia let down her guard a little. "Jerry Kuzawa took me *more* than Angus ever did."

The cagey nuance to her voice left my mouth dry. That's what the bombshell she dropped did to me. All the recent times he'd called me "son" came flooding back into my mind. Did either Edna or I even resemble him by that much? "Mom, is Jerry Kuzawa our father?"

"None of your damn business." She clucked her tongue and lightened her tenor. "All I want is let the Lake Charles shit stay up there. Are you agreeable to that?"

"Done. Lake Charles is a buried memory." Nodding, I swallowed. Twice. Saying goodbye wasn't as simple as I'd thought it'd be to do. "Give my best to Edna."

"Will do. Before you go, two things. One, don't forget me."

"Done." I hesitated a little. "And ...?"

"Those goddamn roads run both ways, and you can always return." Her voice thickened with rising tight emotion. "Send me your new address, and I'll mail your Christmas gift."

"Will do. I love you, Mama Jo."

"Right back at you, baby boy."

Hanging up, I debated if the roads actually did flow both ways, and if I'd ever return to my native Tennessee. It didn't matter. I felt primed to make Valdez or bust. A scratching near the bottom of my door was the tabby cat Oscar, a refugee from Mrs. Wang's flat down the hall. So I fed him and plucked Veera's business card from under a fridge magnet. I tapped her card on my thumbnail, deliberating over whether or not to call her.

Better not. I was keen to get an early start on my journey. Richard Pryor was on TV. He laughed at life's bad shit. After laying her card on the futon, I stretched out on the sofa, my head settling into the pillow, and by the next commercial, I'd dozed off.

We holed up in Room 7 at the Chewink Motel. Ashleigh's chunky calf fell across my leg on the bed. The reefer smoke pungent as burned incense made my nose run. She passed the joint to me for the next toke. A first, I declined her offer.

A smile crooked the corners of her mouth. "I need to get some money together."

"What, big daddy's allowance isn't enough for you to squeak by on?"

"Cut the sarcasm. I plan to kill Ralph, but I need your help to do it."

"What's that?" My heart thumped in my throat.

"You heard me fine. My idea is foolproof." Her eyes, a pair of hot jet opals, twirled in their sockets. I gawked as her upswept red hair

combusted into a fiery tiara. "I thought of using his Luger to stage it as a robbery gone bad, but I've concocted a tidier way. We'll lace his mountain-grown pot with toxic PCP and poison him to death."

"You're nuts."

"Oh, quit it. They'll dry my tears and send me to grief counseling. Everybody will pity poor, little Ashleigh."

I watched the fire engulf her arms, shoulders, and throat. Sweat pocked on my brow. I felt the fire's gathering intensity and raised my forearms to use as a heat shield.

"So that's why Ralph killed you. He did you before you did him. Either way, I was a pawn caught in the middle."

Absorbed by her scheme, she ignored me. "Once he's out of the picture, meet your new teenager millionaire. We can splurge, Brendan. Join me."

"No. We're pulling in opposite directions. I'm set to find my father, not to destroy him."

"Really? After all this time, why bother?" she asked, my dreams' stalker consumed by the column of smoke and fire.

I awoke and with a clear mind dismissed my dreams as a vile brew from the crucible of emotions roiling inside me, heated by Ashleigh's murder and Lake Charles. I felt pity for her. Her overweening ambition to outshine her father had blinded her moral conscience. Or maybe she didn't know any better. Maybe that facet of her maturity had never developed as she grew up in her rarified rich girl's world, its axis greased by privilege, money, and greed. Whatever but she and I were finished.

Her salient question gave me pause. What did I expect to gain by taking off for Valdez? Did I feel too pumped over it? On one level, the father-son reunion struck me as naïve and melodramatic. Hell, I didn't even drink beer anymore. One lousy missive sent in nineteen years didn't exactly engender strong filial ties. In short, I reassessed and thought Angus was an asshole. If I erased Lake Charles from my brain, maybe Umpire wasn't a bad place to live.

Oscar, purring, leaped up into my lap. Thinking, I stroked his soft fur. Then I reached over him and took Veera's business card off the futon. My thumb pecked in her numbers, and she greeted me with surprise brightening her voice.

"Say Veera, are you into bass fishing?"

THE END

REFERENCE SOURCES

"An Overview of Sawmill Operations." Knowledge Base Article. Woodweb Woodworking Industry Information. (http://www.woodweb.com)

"The Straight Dope: DEA's New Museum Is a Monument to Self-Destruction." Peter Carlson. *The Washington Post.* May 6, 1999.

"Going Down in Valdez." Harry Crews. *Blood and Grits* (New York: Harper & Row, 1979).

"Bass Boat Evolution." Ronald F. Dodson. *Honey Hole Magazine.* 2004.

The Blue Ridge and Smoky Mountains. Jim Hargan. (Woodstock, VT: The Countrymen Press, 2002).

"Busted!" Margot Roosevelt. *Time.* July 27, 2003.

"Drug Cartel Linked to Sequoia Pot Farm." Miles Schuper. *Valley Voice Newspaper.* October 26, 2002.

"Sawmill Operations, Appalachian Hardwoods & Eastern White Pine." Griffith Lumber Company, Inc., Woolwine, VA. (http://www.griffithlumber.net). Also, thanks to Bruce Griffith for extensive notes on 1950s sawmill operations.

Steele, P.H., Philip A. Araman, and C. Boden. "Economic Choice for Hardwood Sawmill Operations (ECHO)." Forest and Wildlife Research Center, Bulletin FP 252, Mississippi State University.

Kingsport Press Strike Collection 1961-1982. East Tennessee State University, Archives of Appalachia, Johnson City, TN.

Kingsport (Tennessee) Press Strike Collection, 1961-1967. Special Collections Department, Georgia State University Library, Georgia State University, Atlanta, GA.

"The History of the DEA from 1973 to 1998." Drug Enforcement Agency, April 1999 (http://www.usdog.gove/dea/pubs/history).d